PETRIFIED

BOOK ONE OF THE KEEPER CHRONICLES

BEN MEEKS

— Ben Meeks

Notes for Clarity

Cearbhall: An Irish name. In Irish a "BH" together makes the "V" sound. So, this is pronounced Care-vall, similar to the name Carol.

Tortured Occult Motorcycle Club: In this book there are multiple ways that the club is referenced. Either as the Tortured Occult, the T.O., or Tom C. The latter being a name made out of the acronym which references the group as an individual. Regardless of which term is used, it references the entirety of the club.

Colors: A reference to gang colors, a way of identifying membership of a group. In this case, the symbol on the back of a kutte that designates someone a member of a motorcycle club is their colors.

Grimoire: A spell book, often containing dangerous or sinister spells and rituals.

Cupita: Female life partner.

Cupitus: Male life partner.

Kutte: Leather vest worn by members of a motorcycle club.

CHAPTER·1

"Where'd you get this old beater anyway? It sounds like it's about to fall apart," Holt said.

"That's called character," I said.

"Don't get me wrong, Obie, I'm sure it was a nice truck at some point but it's a little past its prime," he said.

The old Ford groaned and puttered through the curves of the mountain roads, creaking at the joints like an old man straining to get up from his rocking chair. It was true it had seen better days. The paint had faded from a vibrant blue into a more pallid shade accentuated with rusted spots and lines. It still had a kind of style with large rounded wheel wells and a triangular hood that formed an aggressive edge at the front. From the right angle it reminded me of a parrot's face.

"I bought it new in forty-one, they don't make them like this anymore." I patted the dash to let the old girl know Holt was full of it. "Don't listen to him, old girl."

"It's a good thing, too. This thing's a death trap. I mean, did it come with these lap belts or did you put them in yourself? It doesn't even have AC. The high is what, ninety-eight today? We're going to die of a heatstroke before we get there. I'm sweating bullets over here and don't get me started on the choke. You know what else has a choke? A lawnmower. You're driving around an oversized lawnmower that don't even cut grass."

"You'll get used to the heat. You've only been here a few months, it takes time, and show some respect, this truck is older than you are," I said, crossing the center line to cut the curve.

"Exactly. That's my point, and can you keep it in your own lane or does this hunk o' junk just not drive straight?"

"Everyone up here crosses the line at some point or other," I said, returning to my lane.

Holt ran a hand through his black hair, pulling it out of his face. He stared out the window, shaking his head. He must have decided it was a lost cause because when he spoke again it was all business.

"So, what's the plan? We go in and rough him up a bit?" he asked.

"I was planning on talking to him."

A confused expression crossed his face. "What do you mean?"

"You know, spoken words put together into sentences to convey ideas or emotions," I said.

"You think you're just going to show up and say, 'Hey bub, would you please tell me where the demon you've been talking to is hiding', and he's just going to tell you?"

"Why not? It's worth a shot," I said.

"It's stupid."

"What would you do?"

"I don't know." He looked out the window again at the passing trees. "Break some fingers maybe? Whatever I need to do to get what we need to know."

"You can always be mean later, Holt. If I need to break his fingers then I will, but if I can just talk to him then that's better for everyone," I said.

"I guess."

He didn't sound convinced, but he would come around. We hadn't been working together that long, after all. Still it's odd. I am sure Cedric didn't operate like that. I didn't know where this *break fingers first and ask questions later* attitude was coming from. I flipped on the blinker and pulled into the gravel parking lot of the Inclusive Assembly of Christ. The church was a plain, single-story brick building, wholly unremarkable other than the large cross on the outside wall. The parking lot had two cars parked up front. I pulled in line with them, giving me a front row seat to the cross.

"Just stay in the truck. This shouldn't take more than a couple minutes," I said, killing the engine. I gave the outside of the building a quick scan for security cameras, an occupational habit.

"Why don't you stay here, and I'll go. I bet I could have him spilling his guts in two minutes."

"That's what I'm afraid of, another mess to clean up," I said. "That reminds me, maybe you could do some dishes when we get back? Think about it."

I got out, giving the area one last look, while Holt scowled in the passenger seat.

"Hey, why don't you leave it running so I can use the AC," he mocked.

I ignored him and walked inside through a pair of plain glass doors. The entryway was more elaborate than the plain exterior suggested. It had tile floor with fake flowers, pictures, and crosses covering every available surface. I sniffed the air, specifically looking for the sulfuric smell of demons. Instead of the demon stink, it smelled like a library, full of old knowledge.

An open door to my right had a sign that read Steve Heck, Pastor. Inside, a man thumbed through papers at a large wooden desk. I knocked on the doorframe to get his attention. He was short and pudgy around the edges, sporting a button-up shirt and graying hair.

"Hey, I'm Obie. I talked to you on the phone," I said, leaning into the room.

"Sure, come on in," the man said, sparing only a glance up before returning to his papers.

I walked in, closing the door behind me. The room was a large rectangle and the desk's position on the far side left a good twenty-five feet between us and only accentuated how much wasted space there was. Bookcases, pictures, and Christian paraphernalia covered the room, with a spare pew resting against the left wall beside another door. He stayed focused on his papers as I approached.

He looked up when I arrived, eyeballing my Han Shot First shirt, and extending his hand without getting up. "Steve Heck, Pastor."

"Nice to meet you." His hand was limp and clammy, like shaking a dead squid. He smelled like spearmint gum and old cheese, with a hint of rotting garbage underneath.

This meeting was probably a waste of time, like Holt thought, but still I had to try. I sat in a chair in front of his desk, taking a moment to scratch the stubble on my face. My hair and nails grew quickly, quickly enough to make any kind of style more trouble than it was worth. My look could vary anywhere from clean shaven to full beard with a dirty blond mop on top of my head. Judging from the length of growth it was getting closer to the mop persuasion and time to cut it all off. The chair was a plain, boxy thing with lopsided padding that made me squirm to get comfortable. Not the first time that being in church had made me squirm.

"What can I do for you, Obie?"

"I've been following what you have been posting about demons," I said.

He leaned back in his chair, focusing on me instead of the paperwork. The light coming through the window to my right reflected off his head. A shadow passed in front of the window and all I could think was Holt had gotten out of the truck.

"It has been attracting a lot of attention lately," he said. "Let me guess, you are here to tell me that demons don't exist and I've lost my marbles. Well, Obie, putting the biblical support for them aside for a minute, I have seen them, and I assure you they are quite real."

"Yeah, I know."

He perked up at my validation. "So, you believe me?"

"Of course, Steve," I said, shaking my head. "I've had the pleasure of their company on multiple occasions."

"If you are familiar with them then you understand how misunderstood they are," he said.

"Yes, people have all kinds of misconceptions about them." I hoped the subtlety of my statement wasn't lost on him.

"That's great! I would love to meet some of them that you know. Do you think they would be interested in a personal relationship with Jesus Christ?"

"I don't think so," I said, shifting my weight to the other side of the chair. It wasn't any better. "From what I have been reading from your blog, it sounds like we have had very different experiences. In fact, I would suggest that you reconsider trying to convert them."

Steve tapped his fingers on the arm of his chair. "God loves all His children and as He created all of us, what people call demons included, they deserve a chance at salvation."

"I'm not here to question your conviction," I said.

"Then why are you here?"

I shifted my weight back to my left side. "You've mentioned a specific demon you refer to as P.V.T. and I was hoping you would tell me how I can find him."

"Her," he said.

"What?"

"P.V.T. is a her, not a him. She explained to me how once word got out people would come looking for her and that they would hurt or kill me to get what they want. You understand if I'm cautious."

"I'd be suspicious if you weren't," I said.

"So why do you want to find her?"

"It's my job," I said.

"Your job? Are you with the two guys that came by last week?" he asked.

"I'm not sure what you're talking about. I have another person that helps me out, but that's it," I said, wondering what trouble Holt was getting into.

"Then who do you work for?" he asked.

The clicking of high heels on the tile outside caught my attention. I started to wonder if this P.V.T. could be in the building. He did say it was a she. But I would have smelled it and demons don't generally wear heels. Probably just a secretary. Steve was oblivious to the sound of course, as the clicking would be out of earshot for a human. I wasn't your average human. Hell, I wasn't human at all, not anymore.

"An interested third party," I answered.

"What would you do if you find her?" he asked.

"I just need to make sure that she isn't a threat," I said. Telling him that I already knew she was a threat and I planned on jumping ahead to the eliminating the threat part of things wasn't going to get me what I wanted.

He thought about it for a minute before answering. "I can talk to her about it and see if she would meet with you."

"Why don't you tell me how to find her and I'll save you the trouble," I said. "You clearly have a lot of important work to do here."

"I can't do that. I am responsible for protecting my congregation so I'd have to be sure you wouldn't hurt her. You understand how people have judged them because of the way they look. I admit they can be hard to get used to but . . ."

"It's not safe for you to be playing with demons. You don't know them like I do," I said.

He paused, stunned at the abruptness of my statement, and then continued. "'Go ye therefore, and teach all nations, baptizing them in the name of the Father, and of the Son, and of the Holy Ghost.' Matthew 28:19."

Why is it whenever people start quoting scripture I feel like my face is melting into my shoes? "I understand what you're trying to do, but the path you are on will get you killed. If there's one thing I know, it's demons. There's plenty to do for your own kind, this world is sick enough. Why not spend a long meaningful life making it a better place for the people around you?"

"Are you threatening me?" he asked.

"I'm trying to save you," I said.

"And if you can't save me?"

"Then I have to stop you."

He clearly took this personally, leaning forward with a sneer. "How would you stop me? Would you kill me?"

"I'd rather not, but even if I don't, someone or something else will. Your days are numbered on the road you're on," I said. "That's not a threat, it's just a fact."

He pointed toward the ceiling. "I have to stick to my conviction and trust in Him."

This was pointless. "Listen, Steve—"

"Pastor Heck."

"Sure, Steve, if you don't want to tell me that's your business, but if you don't let me help this is going to end real bad for you. It may not seem like it but I'm the only friend you've got in all this," I said.

"I appreciate your concern, but I'm afraid I have another appointment in a few minutes that I need to prepare for," he said, picking up his pen and returning to his papers. "I trust you can find the way out on your own."

I sat there for a few seconds trying to think of what I could say to change his mind. I couldn't come up with anything and I didn't want to start breaking fingers so I stood up to leave. "Thanks for your time. I'll be in touch."

"With all due respect, I would rather you didn't come by again," he said, not looking up.

I turned and headed for the door. I had to get to the bottom of this and nothing was going to come from Steve right now. I would just have to pay him a visit at home to get some answers. We could have a more private conversation there. A sigh of frustration escaped my lips when I made it outside and found the truck empty. Tracking on gravel can be tough but Holt's scent was still strong. I picked up another familiar scent underneath his: noxious sulfur. There was a demon about. I followed the scents into the woods to the right of the church, into an overgrown graveyard. Holt stood close to the center, looking around the tombstones.

I walked cautiously to where a wooden fence had once enclosed the graveyard. It had long since fallen down, with only a hint of the decaying wood left behind. "What is it?" I whispered.

"Not sure. I didn't get a good look at it, something small and fast. What happened to these graves? I think the bodies are gone," he said moving from one grave to the next.

I stepped over the remains of the fence for a closer look. The ground in front of each headstone was an open crater, they had all been dug up. The tombstone closest to me was dated 1979. Some of them dated much farther back. The people in the older graves would have been buried in a shroud or a wooden box, nothing that would still be around. This grave was more modern with a large metal casket lying open. The skeleton had been disturbed. I could see pieces of bones, some fragments and some whole, tossed haphazardly around the grave. Whatever did this definitely removed a few choice bones.

"Over here," Holt said from the far side of the graveyard. "You've got to see this."

I walked over to find the answer to the mystery of the missing bones. They had been arranged in a central pile about three feet in diameter with three rows on each side of varying lengths pointing off in different directions. The end of each row came to a point with a bone that had been cut sharp. I knelt for a closer inspection.

"It looks like a weird compass, like you see on old maps," Holt said over my shoulder. "What do you think it is?"

"I don't know, maybe some kind of marker or cantrip? Whatever it is, it's not good," I said. The breeze shifted, blowing against my back, bringing with it a smell akin to rotten eggs. "You smell that?"

"Yep."

I stood and turned to see a small grey face peeking up over a headstone. The imp crawled up on the headstone, giving us a clear view of it. It stood almost two feet tall with four arms, grey skin, and long claws on its hands and feet. Its long arms and pallid complexion made it look like a miniature resurrected gorilla, with a Cheshire cat smile. A line of black barbed quills ran down its back. By far my least favorite thing about imps was catching them.

"What's it doing?" Holt asked.

He was right, this was strange behavior. Imps are small and not inherently powerful. They use their speed and size to evade; they never go toe-to-toe or expose themselves like this.

"Something's wrong," I said, trying to put the puzzle together.

It clicked just as pressure, followed by severe pain, shot through my calf. I looked down to see one of the sharpened bones sticking out of the front of my leg. The bone pile behind us had stabbed me with the row closest to where I was standing. Holt jumped to the side, avoiding a similar strike meant for him.

"Get the imp," I said through gritted teeth.

The five rows of bone that didn't have me impaled moved underneath the center pile, lifting it off the ground like a spider. The orientation of the bones suddenly made more sense: they were legs. I bent forward to support myself with my hands and donkey-kicked its center mass with my good leg, sending it flying back into the woods. The bone piercing my leg was ripped free, leaving a gushing wound that was quickly filling up my shoe.

Holt was busy chasing the imp around the graveyard and not having much luck catching it. I wasn't going to be much help until my leg healed. The skeleton monster came shambling out of the woods like a Model T with loose wheels. My kick didn't seem to have done any real damage. I was going to need a weapon. With nothing but tombstones and rotten sticks on the ground to choose from, I hobbled over to the closest headstone and pulled it out of the ground. I lifted it into my right hand and hurled it like a discus. It spun vertically before hitting the ground and rolling. It collided with the legs on the right side of the bone spider, severing them. They flailed on the ground like fish out of water as the monster crashed to the ground.

My sense of accomplishment was short lived. The legs that remained churned rhythmically like a tiller, pulling the body across the ground. I liked it better with all its legs attached. I pulled up another large headstone and lifted it over my head, waiting for the spider to claw itself into range. When it was a few feet away, I slammed the stone on top of it. Bones crunched from the impact of the stone. It lay still for a moment before the legs started clawing the ground again, leaving long gouges with their sharp points.

Luckily the weight of the stone held the monster in place. I took a third tombstone and slammed it down on each leg individually to sever them.

When that was done, I flipped the other stone off and the round pile shook like boney Jell-O, unable to propel itself in any direction. I drove the stone down on it repeatedly until whatever dark magic was holding it together released its grip, letting the bones fall into a loose pile.

I turned to find myself alone in the graveyard. Holt must have chased the imp into the woods. My leg had already stopped bleeding but there was still a large wound that would take a bit to heal. It would be done soon but in the meantime it still hurt like hell.

I pulled off my shoe and poured out the blood. Taking off my sock, I wrung it out before putting the bloody sock in the shoe. Opting to walk back barefoot, I started limping my way back to the truck.

"It got away," Holt said, coming out of the woods a minute later. "I almost had it."

He had a few of the barbed quills in his hand.

I waved him over. "I see that, let me help you with those."

He held up his hand for inspection as he reached me. There were three barbs but they weren't in too deep. I grabbed them and yanked them clean without any warning.

He jerked his hand back with a yelp. "You couldn't have done that a little gentler?"

"What's the fun in that? It's better to get them out sooner rather than later. Besides, you'll be healed up in a minute," I said, continuing to limp back to the truck.

"How's your leg? Want me to jab a stick in it?" he yelled from behind me.

"Let's go," I said. "We've got somewhere to be."

He jogged up beside me. "Where are we headed?"

"Steve's house. It's time for plan B."

CHAPTER · 2

There's a point where people don't come back. From what he had posted online, it sounded like Steve was close to learning how to open a portal. I have to get to him before he goes that far. It's not that practicing some minor magic, or a single summoning, is going to corrupt him, but once people get a taste for the power behind it, they can have a hard time giving it up. If he didn't fall victim to the power, he would to whatever came through the first portal he opened.

Finding Steve had been easy, I read an article in the paper about a local preacher touting salvation for otherworldly creatures. From there all it took was a quick trip to the library for some internet research and I found everything I needed. Most people thought he was crazy, but the details he wrote about told me it was for real. What worried me the most was a book he described. A grimoire of ancient knowledge and rituals. If this P.V.T. really had one I had to get it. A book like that wasn't something you want to be unaccounted for. Books have a way of spreading ideas and these ideas have to be contained.

His house was on the edge of a subdivision backed by some woods and a small creek. This was a nice setup for me because it gave me an easy way in. I parked my truck a couple miles away on the side of highway 575 and pulled my knife out of the glovebox. It was carved out of solid mahogany with an eight-inch blade and a leather-wrapped handle. Symbols carved into the blade instilled it with magical energy. While it was wood, with the enchantments it was as sharp and strong as anything forged, and it didn't set off metal detectors.

"Nice hardware. You got one of those for me?" Holt asked.

"Nope." I tucked the knife into the belt of my shorts and got out of the truck.

Holt followed me as we walked into the woods on the side of the highway. "So, Obie, I know it's our first real job together but how about you let me take point on this one? Let me show you what I can do."

"I'm sure Cedric trained you well and I appreciate the enthusiasm, but I would prefer you see how I handle things before you start doing things on your own. You guys were only together for what, thirty years at most? It may seem like a long time, but you're still new at this," I said. I didn't get the impression he liked that answer but he didn't argue, which was a pleasant change.

Steve's backyard was surrounded by a wooden fence that backed up to the tree line. It gave us plenty of cover to check things out without worrying about being seen. The grass needed a trim, it was up to knee height. A small patio had a table with a few chairs, one of which was flipped over on its side. I stood behind the fence, watching and listening. I could hear some kids playing out on the street, a random car passing, and Holt's impatient shuffling in the leaves. The neighbor's houses were quiet and there was no sign of anyone home. It was late afternoon, sometime between when kids got home from school and adults got home from work. It looked clear.

"Let's go," I said and jumped the fence. We crossed the yard to the sliding glass door on the back of the house. The lights were off, making it hard to see in. Holt stepped up to the glass, cupping his hands around his eyes to see inside.

"Nothing. Want me to bust the door in?" he asked a little too eagerly.

I pushed the handle and it slid open freely. "I think we're okay."

The smell of rotting food drifted through the open door. I held my nose as I stepped in to a small dining area, kitchen adjacent, open to the living room to my left. It looked like what you would expect for a pastor's home. The décor wasn't fancy. It largely religious themed, with a picture of Jesus on the wall in the dining area with blood dripping from open wounds on his head and hands. Not my choice of a picture to hang where you eat, but to each his own I guess. The open floor plan didn't do much to contain the mess or smell. The table in front of me was covered in empty soda bottles, fast food wrappers, and other debris that might have had a chance to make it into the garbage can, if it wasn't already overflowing onto the floor. I opened a pizza box on top of the pile, half-eaten pepperoni. A large stack of mail, most of it unopened with PAST DUE stamped on the front, sat in a pile on the kitchen counter. Shuffling though the stack I found a plain envelope with "Steve" written on it by hand at the bottom. Curious guy that I am, I had to check it out.

> *Steve,*
>
> *I don't understand what is happening to you. What you are doing isn't right. I will always love you, but I can't stay and watch you do this to yourself. I will be staying at Belleview, apartment 1703. Please get help.*
>
> *Candice*

A lump in the envelope turned out to be a wedding and engagement ring. At least I didn't have to worry about the wife coming home.

The sound of splintering wood caught my attention. I turned to see Holt ripping a large flat screen off the wall.

"What the hell are you doing?"

"I'm going to stick this in the truck. My games would look awesome on this baby," he said.

"We're not here to loot the place."

"What? You said I could take things," he said.

"Don't you think a guy walking out of the woods with a TV might draw some attention? That's the last thing we need. If you're going take things, take small things, things you need."

"I can handle a cop, I'm not worried about them," he said.

"Sure, you can take a cop," I said. "The thing about cops is they don't fight you one-on-one. If you take on that one, you'll have ten more chasing you down. Next thing you know you're getting run over by a tank or locked up in a lab getting anal probed. So, for all our sakes, just put the TV down."

He tossed it into the fireplace, cracking the screen. "Fine, what can I take then?"

"Nothing with a serial number," I said, looking around. I spotted a few crumpled up bills on the counter beside some Chinese containers that maggots were going to town on. "Here, here's four dollars." I threw the bills over the couch into the living room.

"Four dollars won't buy a TV," he mumbled as he picked up them up.

"You could just go buy one. Hell, you can afford a nicer one than that. There's plenty of money from dust coming in," I said.

He shrugged. "Maybe for you. I didn't have anything when I came here and since this is our first hunt together the money isn't exactly rolling in."

"Just be patient, you should have something to work with real soon," I said.

"Soon? It takes months to turn a demon into dust, and after that wait I'm only getting a portion of it between your cut and Hob's cut. There may not be enough left to get something nice."

"I'll buy you a TV if you shut the hell up, how about that?" Why did Cedric have to die and stick me with this guy? I could deal with him later, right now I had more important things to think about. "Come on, let's get to work."

I put the letter back in the envelope with the rings and shoved it into one of the pockets of my cargo shorts before heading upstairs. I found an office that appeared to be where Steve spent most of his time. The walls had summoning circles framed like artwork. On the desk, I found a small plastic container about half full of a light grey powder. Under it were copies from a grimoire he had scribbled notes on during his sessions with the mysterious P.V.T. It was basic stuff: demon descriptions, summoning incantations written out phonetically. I popped the top off the container and gave it a sniff, it smelled like minerals.

"What is it?" Holt asked.

"Pixie Dust." I took a tiny pinch and placed it in my palm and focused my intention. The dust burst into a clear gray flame that novaed in a few seconds. "What did that tell us?" I said turning to Holt.

"Gray is on the lower end of the demon spectrum, so the dust was made from a demon without a lot of inherent magic. The flame burned clear and at least from here the powder looks uniform in consistency so it is well refined, a passable lower grade powder," Holt said.

"Good job, here's your TV," I said putting the top on and tossing him the container.

He deposited it in the cargo pocket on his leg, leaving an obvious bulge. "Sweet."

It left no doubt that this was the real thing. Not a good sign for Steve. More concerning than the dust and demon literature—where did it come from? P.V.T. probably supplied it to him. If she had access to dust it might complicate things. Hopefully she didn't have a large supply sitting around.

"All right, let's change to krasis. Steve should be home soon," I said, kicking off the flip flops I kept in the truck for when something happens to my shoes.

"Hell yeah!" Holt closed his eyes and concentrated, starting his change.

I reached back and opened the Velcro I had sewn into the back of all my pants, loosened my belt, and started to change into my real form, one of part man, part otter. My body contorted and elongated. My feet turned to paws, claws grew from my fingers and toes, a long muscular tail grew out of my back, and my head rounded out, growing long teeth and whiskers. Light brown fur covered everything from head to claws, finishing my transformation in a matter of seconds into the half-man half-animal form known as krasis.

Holt's body, being much newer to this than mine, made the change slower. After centuries or even decades of changing between forms, a kind of muscle memory eases the transition. It took maybe thirty seconds for his body to take its new shape. He was something new in our world. Thera, the Earth Mother, had always linked her Keepers to predators. Holt was the first to be bonded with a domesticated animal, a Doberman. It was a curiosity why Thera chose to stray from her normal routine, but I guess one advantage to being the boss is that you get to do what you want. Holt groaned his way through the change, panting when it was finally done. His loose clothing now stretched tight by his muscles, with black fur sticking out from underneath.

"Still getting used to it, huh?" I asked.

"Yeah, it's a lot better than it was," he said. "The first time took a couple minutes. It was like getting run over by a steamroller, covered in salt, and scraped back into a pile with a shovel. You remember your first change?"

"I remember my first time in krasis but the pain of the change I forgot a long time ago. It doesn't last forever." I could see Holt smirking. "What?"

"Don't get me wrong, you change fast, but you look like a stuffed animal, not exactly scary. You sure you don't want me to handle Steve?" he asked.

"I'm sure. I can be plenty scary if I need to. See?" I raised a lip and put my finger on a canine. "I've got big teeth, too."

"You have a couple big ones but not like this," he said giving me a low rumbling growl and revealing a face full of pointy teeth.

"You're very scary," I said casually so as not to give away that he really was rather intimidating. "Let's bust up these circles."

He got excited about that and started smashing them with his claws, mutilating not only the pictures and frames but the wall behind them as well. They were cheap frames with a plastic cover instead of glass. The one I did I just put a claw in through the plastic and dragged it down through the circle. Not even noticeable compared to Holt's work. When I was done he smashed mine anyway, for good measure.

"So, what's with the Velcro on the pants?" Holt asked catching his breath.

"Just a little modification for my tail. It's necessary unless I want to wear a kilt everywhere."

"Is that what you did before Velcro, wore skirts? The first thing Cedric did was dock my tail. No problem with pants for me," he said, turning to show a slight bulge at the base of his back.

"For a while I had a version with buttons, but it got all droopy in the back, so it wasn't the best."

He chuckled. "Yeah, anything that makes you look like you crapped yourself is probably a bad idea."

"How were things with Cedric?" I asked to change the subject.

"It was great. He really got me. I really felt like I had a place there. Ever since he was killed it hasn't been the same."

"We all miss him. Cedric was one hell of a Keeper. Give it some time. I'm sure you will come to like it here. How long were you with him for?"

He looked up in thought. "About twenty years, not long enough."

"I was with Cearbhall, my teacher, for about a hundred as an apprentice, and we worked together for almost another fifty after that," I said. "Just focus on the work and I'm sure you'll feel right at home before you know it."

"Focus on the work? I can do this in my sleep," he said.

"You haven't been at it that long, you some kind of expert now?"

With a smug look he said, "What can I say, poopy pants, some people are more talented than others."

That remark wasn't going to fly. "Don't call me that."

"What are you going to do, otter boy, cuddle me to death?"

I squared up to him. "You're out of line."

"Cedric never got all bent out of shape over nothing. Why do you over-react to everything?"

It was clear I was going to have to teach him a lesson in manners. That was no problem, hell, it would be fun. Before class got officially under way, the front door opened. Steve was home. The lesson would have to wait.

CHAPTER · 3

The door closed and footsteps stomped their way up the stairs. I was glad too; if he had gone into the living room and seen the mess Holt had made with the TV, we may not have been able to get the jump on him. I gave a nod toward the corner of the room and Holt moved to it without argument. I ducked into the next room down the hallway and peeked around the doorframe. When Steve walked passed, carrying a briefcase in one hand and a bag of fast food in the other, I followed behind him quickly and quietly. He went in the office but didn't turn on the light. He plopped down in the office chair in the dark, put his briefcase on the desk, and fumbled with the bag of fast food.

Trying to lean against the doorframe with an air of nonchalance, I flipped the light switch. "That smells like a bacon cheeseburger. I've never had one but I have to admit sometimes I am tempted to swing through the drive-thru to pick one up. Are they everything they're cracked up to be?"

He swiveled around slowly, wide-eyed and clutching the bag to his chest like he was trying to protect it from the Hamburglar. Holt stepped into the center of the room, staring him down with bared teeth and fierce eyes. It didn't seem necessary. Steve didn't appear to have any real fight in him.

"Are you from the other world?" Steve stammered.

"Nope. I'm a red-blooded American, just like you," I said.

He looked at me with a puzzled expression, then realization dawned over his face. "It's you, from earlier today, that stupid shirt."

"There's no reason to get nasty," I said.

"You're here to kill me then," he said, more to himself than to me.

"I'm just here to talk, Steve. There doesn't have to be any killing tonight."

He motioned with his chin toward Holt. "What about him?"

Holt bent forward and snarled. "Yeah, I'll kill you. First you're going to tell me what I want to know."

So dramatic. Before I could tell him to chill out, chanting started from one of the other rooms. The voice was scratchy and deep. Holt and I swapped a look while Steve, unable to hear it, sat oblivious in his chair, clinging to his dinner.

"I got it," I said, moving into in the hallway. "Be nice."

I followed the chanting to a spare bedroom, but the source wasn't visible, it seemed to be coming from the entire room at once. The demon must be using some kind of magic to hide its location. Giving the room a quick once over turned up nothing but an open window with a few claw marks on the sill. What concerned me most is what I could smell. Even over the rotting garbage from downstairs I could smell the stink of this demon.

I sniffed around the room. The smell seemed slightly stronger from the closet and the chanting stopped abruptly when I stepped in front of the door. I drew the mahogany dagger from my belt and reached for the door handle. No sooner had I turned it than the door burst open on me. Something small and fast shot out, little more than a blur scurrying under the bed. The chanting started again where it left off. If I could find the circle and destroy it, the demon could chant for the rest of its life and it wouldn't make a difference. Peeking in the closet, I found a circle scratched roughly into the wall over a nest of torn up paper and cardboard, with bones of what looked to be dogs and cats scattered around it. No doubt missing pets from around the neighborhood. A swipe of my knife rendered the circle harmless.

Some talking in the other room caught my attention. Holt laughed and said, "Go for it." A gunshot followed by a heavy thud made my heart sink, especially since it was followed a few seconds later by Steve beginning a summoning of his own. I left the room, closing the door behind me, hopefully trapping the demon for the time being.

In the office I found Holt lying face down, bleeding into the carpet. Steve was leaning back against the desk, holding a revolver in one hand and his summoning notes in the other. Everything on the desk had been knocked off, except the monitor that was sitting face down beside the container of dust Steve had retrieved from Holt's pocket. He had a cut on the side of his face; Holt must have started the interrogation without me. Steve whipped the gun in my direction when I stepped into the doorway. He motioned toward the ground with the gun but continued his chanting.

I raised my hands, dropped my cheeks, and opened my eyes wide. In this case I wanted to prove Holt right, I'm not threatening, just a cute oversized otter. It's not always a bad thing to be adorable. If he got me with a head shot, I would be out for a while before my body could heal itself. It looked like Holt had avoided a direct hit, but it was enough to take him out of commission for a bit. I couldn't afford to lose that time, with a demon loose and potentially more on the way. I knew Steve's incantation, I had a minute, maybe more, the way he was reciting it. I would have to talk him down.

"I'll put it away," I said, moving the knife slowly down and tucking it back in my shorts. "There Steve, everything's okay but I need you to listen to me. I know it doesn't seem like it but I'm here to help you. He's not dead, by the way. He's going to wake up in a few minutes and he's going to be pissed. I don't blame you for shooting him. I've wanted to shoot him more than once. But that's not your only problem, you have a demon in the other room. They don't care about you or your beliefs. I don't know why but they are using you. I don't care about the gun, keep it, just stop the chanting and let's get you somewhere safe until we can get this figured out."

He didn't stop.

"You know you need a circle for that, right? We destroyed them all. It's not going to work," I said.

Just as he finished chanting, Steve reached over and lifted the monitor revealing a summoning circle wallpaper on his desktop.

"That's new," I said.

I wasn't even sure a digital circle would work, never heard of anyone trying it before. We stood looking at each other, waiting for something to happen. Uncertainty crept over his face and just when I decided that his incantation was a dud, a pinpoint of orange materialized in the ceiling. The air began to churn around the room as the light became a circle steadily increasing in diameter. As the circle grew, the air picked up speed, sending loose papers, dust, and debris flying around in an office-themed maelstrom. Heat began to spill out of the expanding portal.

The air pressure must be higher in the demon world because whenever a portal is opened, a giant vortex of stank comes billowing out of it. Maybe one day I will get used to it, but it's awful every time. That may be due in part to my hyper-sensitive otter nose. I think it was a combination of the smell and the heat, but when I was new at this it wasn't uncommon for me to lose my lunch when portals opened. It wasn't a problem for me anymore. Steve, on the other hand, was clearly not as acclimated, and wasted no time retching all over the wall of his office.

I broke into a sweat from the intense heat pouring into the room. Since the portal opened on the ceiling, I expected to see the demon sky, but instead it was like someone took a painting of a landscape and hung it on the ceiling. A red and barren scene stretched off in the distance. It was a rookie mistake; the worlds hadn't been aligned properly, Steve probably messed up the incantation just a bit. I moved back out into the hallway to escape the heat and stench, and if something came tumbling through the portal I didn't want it to fall on me. Holt was on his own. I say "if" but I knew something would come though, something always comes through. The question was, what?

As if on cue, the floor shook with a loud thud—we had company. It made a sound somewhere between a shriek and a squawk, and I recognized it immediately: a hellhound. The orange light and wind told me the portal was still open. Steve was so new at this he may not know how to close it, assuming he wanted to. There was enough dust in that container to keep it operational for a few minutes. There could be dozens of demons here in that time. I had to shut it down before anything else came through. I turned to go back in the room when it felt like I had been punched in the back of the head. I had forgotten all about my little friend under the bed. It stunned me at first, but the clawing on my head and neck snapped me out of it. It felt like it was trying to burrow into my skull. I reached back and grabbed whatever I could get hold of to pull it away.

I could feel the blood running down my back as I pulled an imp, glistening with my blood in the orange light, off my neck. I had it by its back, which is a very inconvenient way to hold an imp. The barbed spines common on many of the smaller demons were already working their way into my hand. We sized each other up for a second before it went full-on honey badger, hands, feet, and tail flailing wildly, its little jaws snapping wildly trying to get ahold of me. The blood made it hard to hold onto and the movement pushed the barbs deeper into my palm. It was only a matter of time before it got away, time I didn't have. I clenched my teeth and then my hand. The barbs sank in deep, sending shooting pain up my arm. The resistance suddenly gave way as the demon's bones shifted with a loud pop. It howled and writhed in pain. I reared back and pitched it into the wall, sending it straight through the sheetrock, disappearing into a newly minted imp-sized hole.

My hand was thoroughly pin-cushioned by more barbs than I could count, with more running up my arm from the imp's thrashing tail. Another shot boomed from Steve's office. It was probably too soon for Holt to be awake, so Steve was most likely coming to the difficult realization that he was going to need my help. Instinctively, I reached for my dagger with my right hand, but I couldn't really grab anything with all the barbs in my palm, so my left would have to do. From the doorway, I saw the hound. It looked like a six-legged hairless dog the size of a Saint Bernard, with big red Chihuahua eyes bugging out of its head. It was standing over Holt's still lifeless body and had Steve backed into a corner. The shot had gone into its shoulder, pissing it off more than anything.

Before I could intervene, it lunged for Steve, sinking its shark-like rows of teeth into his abdomen. He screamed as it lifted him off the ground and shook violently side to side. Steve's body wasn't up to the strain and the part of him in demon's mouth ripped free, sending the rest skidding across the floor, leaving a red streak behind him. He came to a rest close to where I was standing. His intestines, still attached to both pieces, unraveled across the room like a Slinky stretched to its limits. The scene gave me pause for one reason. The portal was still open, swirling papers and gushing stink into the room. I guess it's possible that someone could maintain a portal while having a large piece of themselves ripped off, but I have never seen it. It would take someone accomplished, well beyond Steve's ability, or anyone else I have known for that matter. He was still conscious, screaming, crying, and pulling the loose pieces of himself back like a rope.

Movement on the ceiling caught my attention. Another hound was investigating the portal. When it saw what a tasty treat Steve was, it would no doubt come through. This was getting out of hand quickly. The demon scarfed down the chunk of Steve, thrusting its head forward repeatedly to catch the dangling pieces. It turned to get another morsel and spotted me in the doorway. Charging the room, I slashed my knife across its face, sending it reeling back, and spun, whipping the monitor with my tail, then turned to face the hound. The monitor exploded and the portal on the ceiling slammed shut with a loud crack. The wind abruptly stopped. Papers in the office drifted gently to the floor. Without the orange light coming through the portal, the room returned to the more earthly glow of the overhead light. A hard thud shook the floor behind me. Something else must have made it through before the portal closed.

The hound screeched through its bloody teeth and charged. I jumped back and slammed the heel of my right hand down on it, sending its head into the floor. My hand exploded in pain from the barbs still stuck in it. Throwing myself on top of the hound, I wrapped my right arm around its neck, pushing my weight down to keep it pinned to the floor, being careful to keep my legs away from the snapping jaws. This left my other hand free to drive my knife repeatedly into the beast's underbelly. I held on until its strength drained away enough to let it go. As soon as it was safe, I pushed off the floor and spun to face the room, ready for another hound. Instead I found half a hound lying dead on top of Holt. It had gotten caught halfway through when the portal closed. Fine with me. Without the portal pushing rotten air into the room, thick smoke began coming in from the hallway. I could hear fire crackling downstairs.

A whimpering from the doorway caught my attention. Steve was still with me, barely. Tears ran down his cheeks and he was looking at me quiet and unmoving. I could have tried to heal him but he was scattered all over the room, and probably wouldn't have survived anyway.

"I'm sorry I couldn't help you," I said. I wasn't going to let him spend his last minutes on earth burning alive, assuming he lived that long. One strategic stab later and he was pain-free. I wiped the knife off on his shirt and tucked it back into my belt.

Moving to the stairs to check out the fire, I found the entire bottom floor engulfed, and fire was already crawling its way up the stairs. The imp stood in the flames on the bottom step, leaning against the wall with a grin and one leg hanging limp. The flames were moving fast and while they circled the imp, it didn't seem to mind. This was pretty much its natural environment after all.

"Burn," it said in a deep burping voice.

I wasn't expecting it to know any English. That told me it had either been here for a long time or had been working with something that has. Demons don't hop out of the portal reciting Shakespeare. There's no way I was going to tangle with a demon, even a small one, in the middle of a house fire. This one got a pass tonight.

"Rain check," I said.

Back in the office Holt was just pulling himself out from under the partial hound. "What happened?"

"Grab that half a hound and head out the window. The house is coming down," I said.

"What?"

I didn't wait to explain. I grabbed the whole hellhound and heaved it through the window. The glass exploded as its body tumbled onto the roof and off into the yard. I hopped out the window and jumped down to the grass. The backyard was lit up like Christmas from the fire and was too warm for my liking. I dragged the hound to the back fence and tossed it over before jumping myself. There I waited, watching the upstairs window for Holt. I thought I saw a dark figure perched on the edge of the roof. I blinked and it was gone, I wasn't sure it was there at all. I stood still, watching and listening when he finally came out, lugging the other hell hound on his back.

"What is it?" he asked when he finally made it over the fence and saw how on guard I was.

"Nothing, what took you so long?" I asked.

"The dust was spilled everywhere. I couldn't save any of it. I did get my shoes though," he said.

It wasn't until then I remembered my flip flops burning up in the house. I lose a lot of good shoes that way. We changed back to human form before making our way through the woods back to the truck. We were battered and bloody, so even though we looked human again, we weren't in any shape to be seen in public. We waited on the side of the road for a break in the cars before moving out and tossing the hounds in the back. I grabbed a tarp and some bungees from behind the seat to cover things up. In a few minutes we were pulling out. Firetrucks screamed down the interstate in the opposite direction.

"I have to admit, Obie, I was wrong about you. I thought you were kind of a pussy. One of those guys that talks a good game but is afraid to get their hands dirty. What you did back there, though. Killing two hounds, ripping that asshole's guts out, and burning his house down—damn, that's cold blooded. Oh, and you have to tell me what you did to the other half of that hound," he said.

"Maybe, one day." I wasn't about to correct him. If his conclusions bought me a little peace, then that's all right by me.

"Where to now?" he asked.

"I'm going to get rid of these hounds, drop you off at the house, and then I have to do something about this," I said, showing the barbs in my hand.

"Wait, those are imp barbs. You killed another demon . . . That's what I'm talking about!"

CHAPTER • 4

"What are we doing here?" Holt asked, looking down rows of corn as we drove by.

"This is Hob's farm," I said.

"Wait, Hob, that's the duster," he said, excitement in his voice.

"Sure is. I don't know if you will meet him this trip though, we're just dropping off today. We will be coming here a lot. If you don't meet him today I'm sure you will soon." We drove past the farmhouse toward the back of the property where Hob conducted his other business. "Actually, there he is now," I said, pointing to an overall-clad figure sitting in a swing on the porch. He wore a baseball cap that kept his hair mostly contained, which did nothing to hide his pointy ears.

"Kinda bold to have his ears out like that," Holt observed.

"He's a bold fella, but no one comes back here, and if they did he has people for that," I said giving him a wave as we passed.

He gave us a wave back, not breaking the rhythmic swaying of his leisure.

"Should we stop and say hi?" Holt asked.

"We'd be here all day. I just want to drop these demons off and get out of here. Trust me, you will do more than enough chatting with Hob," I said. "He's a talker."

Most dusters are magical experts and Hob was no exception. Some people think the amount of dust he has access to at any given time makes him a threat, and they might be right. He left his elvin kin in Germany, coming here for a quiet life of farming. He made a good living from it until we approached him about supplementing his income with some knowledge from the Old World. He was reluctant but saw the good in establishing a steady dust trade. His condition was that his involvement remained secret. The secret probably wasn't as well kept as it should have been—Holt makes one more—what could it hurt?

Past a few more fields, we pulled up to a two-story red barn tucked away by the tree line. I backed the truck up to the doors and we got out.

"Give the door three good knocks," I said as I started untying the tarp.

Holt walked up to the large double doors and tapped on it with his knuckles three times.

"They aren't going to hear that, really go for it," I said.

He looked a little uncertain but delivered three strikes to the door in slow succession. Nothing happened. I went around the truck to untie the other side.

Holt turned to me, placing his hands on his hips. "Well?"

"Give them a minute, they don't move so quick," I said.

After another thirty seconds, I had the tarp off the hounds in the back of the truck when a speakeasy style viewing slit slid open ten feet up the wall. A large gray face looked down on us.

"Come back here and let them get a look at you," I said to Holt who had remained close to the door.

He moved back and after a short inspection the opening slid shut. *Ka-Chunk*, a heavy lock was opened. *Ka-Chunk, ka-chunk*, two more followed suit before the large doors were swung open, revealing an ogre, roughly twelve feet tall with stone gray skin and a blank expression lumbering over us. He came outside, grabbed a demon in each hand and took them into the barn. Hob hired ogres because they are huge, loyal, and they lack the imagination to use dust, intentionally or accidentally, but most importantly, they don't mind the smell. The perfect worker for a duster.

"Hey, buddy, wait up," Holt said.

"His name's Eric."

"Eric? Really?" he questioned. "Hey, Eric, hold up a second."

Eric ignored him, disappearing inside. Holt followed in protest. The inside of the building looked more like the industrial processing facility that it was. All the equipment was steel, the floors were a dark red tile, and everything was spotless. The machines were custom builds Hob made to refine Pixie Dust. Eric put the demons on a massive scale to the left of the door.

Holt walked up in front of him. "How long is it going to take to get the dust from these?"

Eric gave him a blank stare and said nothing, continuing with his work.

"Earth to Eric, anybody home?" Holt said waving a hand as close to Eric's face as he could reach.

"You really shouldn't antagonize ogres," I said.

Holt spun to face me. "He's antagonizing me. I'm just trying to get a couple questions answered."

While all this was going on, Tailypo Wilix, the foreman of the facility, had made his way behind Holt. A rather pudgy goblin with dark green skin and long pointy ears, bald on top with grey hair on the sides, he wore black plastic-framed glasses and barely came up to Holt's knees. He held a clipboard in one hand and a pencil in the other that he promptly stabbed into the back of Holt's calf and withdrew. Holt yelped and stepped forward, running into Eric, who didn't seem to notice.

"What's the big idea?" Holt shouted when he put together what had happened.

"You're in the way and you're bothering Eric," Wilix said. "Obie, you do know what a secret is, don't you? As in this is supposed to be a secret facility, hmm?"

"Actually, this is Holt, my new apprentice. I expect he will be making plenty of drop-offs in the future so I'm just showing him the ropes," I said.

"Mm hmm, let's see then, 387 pounds," he said, cocking his head back to peer at the scale's readout through the glasses resting on the end of his nose.

He climbed a ladder to get a closer look at the demons. "One-and-a-half hell-hounds." He shot me a look of disapproval.

I smiled and shrugged. He went to make some notes on his clipboard when he noticed the end of his pencil had Holt's blood all over it. He stuck it in his mouth, swirling his tongue around until it was clean, and made his notations.

"So how long will it take to get dust?" Holt asked.

Wilix tapped his pencil against the clipboard in thought before climbing down and replying. "About three months. Eric, go ahead and move them to the freezer, please."

"Three months? Can I get an advance or something?"

"Come on, let's get out of here," I said, before Holt could embarrass us further. "Thanks, Wilix and Eric, appreciate ya." Eric gave me a nod as I directed Holt outside. "Get in the truck, let's get out of here."

"We didn't talk percentages or anything," Holt said when we were back in the truck.

I cranked the engine. "Percentages of what?"

"You know, the dust, how everything is getting split up."

I put the truck in reverse and started backing out. "What were you thinking?"

"I figure you've been doing this long enough where you have a nice bit saved up. Since I'm just getting started I should probably get a little more. Maybe a seventy-thirty split? That should get me up to speed pretty quickly," he said.

"It's not a cash operation. You have to have an account set up before you can do anything, remember? Did you get your account set up?" I asked, already knowing the answer.

"Nah, I haven't had time. I'll get around to it," he said.

"Let's wait till you do before we start talking business," I said.

Hob wasn't on the porch anymore when we drove by the farm house. Maybe if he was I could have dropped Holt off and subjected him to hours of Southern hospitality as punishment. I never thought having an apprentice would be this hard. I could really use a vacation.

"I'm going to drop you off at the house and get some help with these quills. I'll swing by the church on the way back and see if Steve left us any clues there. Just take tomorrow off. If you feel like it you can go get your account set up and we'll figure out how we're going to split everything," I said.

We were going to split everything fifty-fifty, he just didn't know it yet, and I wasn't in the mood for another argument. That was actually generous for how much of his slack I had to pick up.

CHAPTER · 5

Naylet lived deep in the mountains close to Suches, Georgia, the modern equivalent of a one-horse town. The house was small, one room and a loft; I had helped her build it decades ago. In typical nymph fashion, she loved plants and she had a perfectly maintained lawn and garden. It was after dark when I pulled into my normal parking space, gravel hissing a protest under the tires. The light shining through the front window told me she was still awake and I couldn't help but smile. I shut off the truck, got out, and headed for the front door.

A nymph's garden is distilled life, concentrated like Thera's essence. Being one of her servants, I was particularly sensitive to it. The area felt more alive than the surrounding woods, the sound of running water coming from behind the house increased that perception. Lightning bugs danced in the yard, crickets chirped in the woods. The katydids' rhythmic chanting always seemed like the heartbeat of the forest to me. The night was hot and muggy, as only a Georgia night in the heart of summer could be. This place was special and I loved it here. I gave the door a courtesy knock as I let myself in.

"Anybody home?" I said, dropping my keys on the table.

The house had a studio layout, with the kitchen and bathroom on the far side, and a combined dining and living area we called the lounge by the front door. The walls were covered with storage and shelving. There wasn't much open wall space and what little there was had been covered by pictures of people and places, many of them Naylet drew herself. I was featured in a couple of them, which is quite a compliment considering the amount of real estate and the long history competing for it. A ladder led up to a small loft sleeping area. Naylet popped her head over the edge, cascading her golden curls down, concealing her face.

"You're late," she said. "I was starting to think you weren't coming."

"Sorry. I had a little trouble at work today."

"Nothing too serious?"

I held up my hand with the barbs protruding and wiggled my fingers, making the barbs wave. "I lost another pair of shoes and this."

"That's gross," she said.

"Can you help me out?"

She tumbled off the loft, landing gracefully on her feet, and held out her palm. I put my hand on hers and she looked closely at my injuries.

"Yep, you healed up nicely. We're going to have to cut them out," she said, sounding a little too happy about it.

"I think there's a few more in my back," I said, giving her a sheepish grin.

She pulled out a spare blanket and pillow and laid it out on the floor. "Take your shirt off and lay down."

I tried to remove my shirt but it was caught on the barbs imbedded in my back. She stopped rummaging in the kitchen for a minute and returned to help.

"I think this shirt's had it. It's full of holes back here. We're going to have to cut it."

"I am going to kill the hell out of that imp when I get my hands on him. This is one of my favorite shirts," I said.

"It's ratty. You should have thrown it out already," she said.

I lay down while she went back to the kitchen. She returned a minute later with a scalpel, scissors, a plate, and a newspaper.

She handed me the paper. "Remember when we didn't spend our nights doing minor surgery?"

"I remember when I did my best without you," I said. "This is a lot better."

"Mm hmm. Stay still."

I spread the paper on the floor as she cut the shirt revealing the barbs. It had become our routine that I read something to her while she patched me up. It started as a way to distract me from the pain but turned into something nice that I did, even if I wasn't being cut on. Reading to her had become one of my favorite pastimes.

"So, what's going on in the world today?" she asked. That was code for *This is going to hurt*. Before I could answer I felt the pinch of the scalpel.

I looked at the front page and read the headline: "Baby Stephanie missing ten days. Police say no new leads. Deborah Olson says her newborn daughter was taken from a second story window around 10:30 P.M. while she was downstairs. Police investigate all possibilities. Continued on page— Ow! Damn Naylet."

"Don't be such a wimp," she said with the distant tone that comes with focus. "I hate that kind of news."

"Yeah, I would think you would be used to the terrible things humans do to each other by now."

"Unless it wasn't human. The baby was taken from a second-story window and the police have no leads? From what I have read there aren't any witnesses or any evidence at all. Nothing they are sharing anyway. That's why the baby's picture has been plastered everywhere. They are hoping to get lucky with a sighting."

"So what, a ghost decides it's lonely so it floats into a random house and takes a baby? Hate to break it to you but a ghost wouldn't need to open a window," I said.

"It would to get the baby out, genius, but I never said it was a ghost."

She had me there. "I don't think so, this has 'inside job' written all over it. The mother did it. Had to be," I said. "She probably tossed the kid into a dumpster or off a bridge. Humans are crazy like that. I heard a story about a guy in Atlanta that threw a baby out of a car on the interstate."

"That's horrible," she exclaimed, giving me a poke with the scalpel that I am pretty sure had nothing to do with getting barbs out of my back.

"Hey, I didn't do it. Just calling it like I see it," I said.

"Well, when I saw her pleading on the TV to have her baby returned I could tell she didn't do it. A woman can tell these kind of things," she replied.

"A nymph can tell those kinds of things maybe," I said. "And when did you see her on the TV? You don't even have one."

"When I was out with the girls last week. Don't think my life revolves around you, Obie."

"I wouldn't dream of it."

"So . . ." she said.

"So, what?"

"Are you going to look into it?" she inquired.

"Look, if you don't want me around so much you can just say so. You don't have to make more work for me," I replied, turning to look at her.

"You know that's not what I'm doing. That baby needs help, and if you can help her then I would like you to do whatever you can to make sure she gets home to her mother safely."

"I tell ya what. I'll stop by first thing in the morning before I follow up on my other lead," I said.

"You promise?"

"I give you my word as a gentleman."

She pushed my head back to the paper with the dull side of the scalpel. "If that's the best you can do I guess I'll take it. Now find me something happy in there. This stuff is depressing."

"You know this is a newspaper, right?"

"Ok, that's all of them from your back," she said. "Let's move to the table for your hand. Don't bleed on the couch."

I got up off the floor, taking the plate of bloody quills and moving it to the table. There had been six in my back but my hand had that beat easily, not to mention my arm.

"What would you think about taking a trip? Maybe to the beach?"

She stopped working on my hand and looked me right in the eyes. "What's the matter?"

"Nothing. I just thought it would be nice to get away, that's all." I looked down at the paper.

"What are you trying to get away from?"

"Nothing . . . Everything . . . I don't know. Things with Holt haven't gotten any better. He got himself shot tonight and I had to handle everything by myself. Then he tells me he should get a bigger cut of the dust than me. It's like he's living in some fantasy world where he is actually contributing something."

"What would you think about having kids?" she asked out of left field.

"I think that's the opposite of a vacation. Where did that come from?"

"Just something I've been thinking about," she said. "We've been together a long time and we would be good parents."

"I'm not disputing that. I'm just not sure Georgia is ready for a bunch of little wereotters running around. You know that's what they would be right?"

"I think the world could use more of them actually," she said.

"We don't live together, what about that?"

She turned my hand over in hers deciding where to start. "We can fix that."

"And Holt?" I asked.

"We can figure all that out later. I'm just asking if it's something you would be interested in."

"Yeah, I'm interested," I said. "How about this: we get away for a week and when we get back we'll figure all that out."

"When did you want to go?" she asked.

"As soon as I take care of this P.V.T. situation. I should have a little free time after that."

"I need a couple days to take care of the Japanese beetles eating the peach trees, so that will be perfect. Don't worry about a thing. I'm going to plan the whole trip," she said.

We chatted for most of the hour it took to remove all the quills, about places to go and things to do. Seeing a sea turtle was on the top of her list. I didn't really care as long as I got away. When she was finished, I tied up the quills into a bundle. I would drop them off at Hob's next time I was over there.

"I'm going to get a shower. I still have a change of clothes here, right?"

"Yeah, go ahead. I'll get them for you," she said.

The water felt great and it was nice to wash off the dried blood and grime. The only sign of my injuries was a little discoloration in the skin. By morning there would be no trace.

"Let me get your back," Naylet said, sliding into the shower with me.

I had no objection, of course, it felt great. I turned around to face her and she kissed me.

"What's that for," I asked.

"Be careful, okay?"

"Hey, there's nothing to worry about. This time next week we are going to have the sand in our toes and drinks in our hands."

I tossed my clothes off the loft onto the floor and kissed her on the cheek before climbing out of bed as quietly as I could. I had been laying there staring at the ceiling and listening to Naylet's gentle breathing for hours. Having a personal connection to Thera was good in a lot of ways, the rapid healing was a plus, and learning to channel her energy to heal others came in handy. Being hooked into a power that great also meant that Keepers didn't sleep; we never get tired since we live in a state of constant regeneration. It also means we don't have to eat. We *can* eat, but most choose not to. When you don't sleep, nights can be tough. If you don't stay busy they drag on for what seems like forever, even with the best of company next to you. You find ways to pass the time, get some reading done, learn a language or three, maybe pick up a ukulele every now and again. I became a Keeper when I was just into double digits, it's been so long now I don't remember what sleep is like, probably like being knocked unconscious but without the headache when you wake up.

I got dressed, filled the coffee pot, and set the delay for an hour, she should be getting up around then. Leaning against the counter, I thought about what Naylet had said about having kids. I imagined taking them down to the creek to teach them how to catch crawfish or watching them play in the yard. Having kids wasn't something I had thought would ever happen but now that it was a possibility, I was starting to look forward to it. First things first, I had to find P.V.T. and get the grimoire. If I could arrange a little revenge on that imp for messing up my shirt, all the better. I let myself out and crossed the yard to my truck. The sun would be up in a few minutes and I had a lot to do.

CHAPTER · 6

About an hour south in Alpharetta, I pulled up to what was more of a mansion than a house. It seemed like another world compared to the modest means I was used to. A massive white building with Roman-style pillars and an immaculately kept yard made me feel out of place in my cargo shorts and tee shirt. Being around expensive things has always made me uncomfortable. Through no fault of my own, things tend to get smashed up when I'm around and it's a lot of liability, if it can be traced back to you. The sun was just coming up when I parked in the driveway. I wondered if anyone was up yet. I got out and walked up the stone steps to the front door. I hesitated, feeling a little self-conscious about my casual attire.

"Too late now," I said, ringing the doorbell.

There were no sounds from inside the house. I couldn't see a car in the driveway, maybe no one was home? If so I could break in and have a look around. A place like this was bound to have a security system. Even better, if no one answered I could just tell Naylet I tried but no one was home. She would probably bring it up again, but it would get me off the hook for now. Just when I had given up and turned to leave, I heard footsteps inside. A woman opened the door. It was evident she was fresh out of bed, sporting a bathrobe, messy hair, and puffy red eyes.

"Hello, Ms. Olson? My name is Obie. I was asked to look into the disappearance of your daughter Stephanie," I said. "I'm sorry to show up unannounced but I was hoping you could spare a few minutes to talk to me."

She rubbed her eyes. "You don't look like a detective."

"No, ma'am, I'm not."

"Do the police know you are here?"

"No, I work independently of the police, kind of like a private investigator."

"Do you have any credentials, like a badge or something?" she asked.

I shrugged. "No, ma'am, I'm afraid not."

"Are you some kind of scam artist? Oh I know, you work for a tabloid, right? Trying to get some pictures or some front page quote to make me look like I did something to my little girl. Why don't you crawl back to whatever sewer you came out of and leave me alone."

"I'd be happy to. I just made a promise I would see if I could help you. Sorry to bother you." I turned around, happy to have gotten out of this so easily.

"Hey, what could you do that the police can't?" she called after me.

Crap, I must have been too eager to leave. I should have pushed a little more until she slammed the door in my face. "I handle . . . special cases. I may not even be able to help you. To be honest, my girlfriend has been following your story. She heard the police didn't have any leads and asked me to check it out. I would just need a few minutes to look around, if you're interested. Ten minutes and I can tell you. If you don't want my help, I will be happy to tell her I tried and you weren't interested. I have a lot of other things going on today."

She paused for a moment, looking from me, to the stairs behind her, and finally rested her gaze on the ground. "What would you need?"

"I need to see where Stephanie was taken from, and answers to any questions that come up."

"Give me your driver's license. Anything fishy and I'm calling the cops."

I took out my license and placed it in her hand. She pulled her phone out of a pocket of the bathrobe and took a picture before she handed it back.

"Top of the stairs, first door on the left," she said, stepping aside and opening the door wide.

The room was painted light pink and had all the expected trappings of a newborn girl's room. A crib sat in the corner beside a changing table. Two windows were juxtaposed on the wall to the right of the crib. I stepped into the center of the room, taking stock of everything.

"Tell me what happened," I said.

"I had put the baby to bed and was downstairs cleaning up. I heard the alarm beep from a door or window being opened. We were here alone, her father was working late again, so I started looking around. I couldn't find anything open downstairs. Stephanie had started crying upstairs and I was about to go up and check on her when I heard a voice whisper on the monitor and it sounded like someone whipped a sheet, like when you make the bed and hold one end and shake it up and down. I ran up here as fast as I could, but by the time I got here Stephanie was gone."

I stepped over to inspect the window. "And you found the window open?"

"Yes. The first thing I did was look out but I didn't see anything. I couldn't have been more than a few seconds behind whoever took her. It's like they just disappeared."

"Tell me about the voice. What did it say? Male or female?"

"It was a woman's voice but I couldn't make it out," she said. "It was just a whisper."

"Where's her father now?"

"I don't know. He accused me of doing something to her. He left and hasn't been back since." She folded her arms across her chest like she was giving herself a hug. "The police took me in and questioned me for hours. They should have been out looking for her."

I looked out the pair of windows into the back yard. The tree line was about thirty feet behind the house. "Which window was open?"

"The right one," she said.

Unlocking the window, I opened it to look out. While the baby's room was located on the second story of the house, the back yard was dug out for basement access making it more of a three-story drop. Definitely not something that a ladder could be taken down from quickly or that a normal human could jump without sustaining injuries.

"Were the windows locked?" I asked.

"Yes . . . No . . . I'm not sure," she replied. "I think they were, but I have gone over it in my head and second guessed myself so many times, I just can't be sure anymore. If they were unlocked, they shouldn't have been."

I noticed a notch on the window sill. It looked like a knife had been stuck in the wood. I put my finger on the mark and had an idea. In my other forms I have non-retractable claws. Sometimes they leave marks on things. If I grabbed this window sill I could leave a claw mark from my thumb on top like this and . . . Sure enough, under the sill there were four similar marks. I lined my fingers up to the marks. The hand that left these marks was smaller than mine but whatever had come here had claws and had grabbed the sill, leaving indentations in the wood.

I grunted an acknowledgement and closed the window. Ms. Olson was leaning against the door with her arms still holding herself. I walked over to the crib but it wasn't much to look at, just a bare mattress.

"The police took the bedding," she offered from the doorway.

"Is there anything here that Stephanie had with her that night?"

"No, the police took everything. Wait, there is one thing. I had forgotten all about it. Her bunny. She wouldn't sleep without her bunny. Hang on." She disappeared from the room and returned a moment later with a stuffed animal. "It was in the middle of the floor. I picked it up that night before I looked out the window and carried it into the bedroom when I called the police. It has been there ever since."

I took it and turned the small stuffed animal over in my hands. I saw a spot on the side where the fur was matted and greasy. It had a faint smell of rose and spices, but there was something else there I couldn't recognize.

I held it out for her to inspect. "There's a spot on the rabbit here, do you know what it is?"

She looked it over with a confused expression, "No idea. I hadn't noticed it."

"Do you recognize the scent?"

She gave it a sniff. "Not sure, some kind of perfume maybe? I haven't smelled anything like that before. What does it mean?"

It meant that she was never going to see her kid again. I wasn't sure if it was a good thing the child wasn't devoured on the spot, at least then she would have some closure, even if she would have been blamed for it. The flapping of the sheet she described had to be wings. Something came in, took the baby, and flew away, leaving marks on the windowsill on the way out. The baby wouldn't have been taken unless there was a plan for it, and a demon with a plan is a terrible thing.

"Well?" she asked, snapping me out of thought.

"I'm going to do my best to help you. From what I have seen, I believe this case falls under my area of expertise. I will do my best to find Stephanie," I said. "I want to stress that we are already ten days past the time she was taken and the chances of a positive outcome at this point are pretty slim."

"So you believe me?" she asked.

"Mrs. Olson, I am one hundred percent certain you are telling the truth."

She touched her mouth as her eyes began to tear up, and she hugged me.

"I said I would only take ten minutes and I'm already a couple over. May I borrow the bunny? It could help me locate her."

"Yes, thank you."

"Thanks, I will let myself out," I said, moving toward the door.

"Wait, how do I get in touch with you?" she asked.

"If you need me or have any kind of trouble, there's a motorcycle club in Dawsonville beside Rock Creek Park. They are called the Tortured Occult, they know how to find me. Tell them that Obie sent you and they will keep you safe and get in touch with me. They look rough but they're just a bunch of teddy bears. I'll let you know if I find anything."

She followed me out into the hallway. "Okay, please let me know as soon as you find anything."

"I will, I promise."

She showed me out. Naylet would be happy to hear she was right. The bad news is the trip to the beach would have to wait. It's always something.

CHAPTER·7

I parked the truck by the graveyard where we had the run in with the imp. I hadn't noticed it the day before, but an old road, overgrown with weeds and trees, led up to it from the front of the parking lot. From the growth I guessed it probably hadn't been used in ten years or more, a perfect place to keep the truck out of sight while I worked. I never liked to park out in the open. Maybe it's a habit that comes from having a vehicle that stands out, or maybe I am just paranoid.

After getting ambushed by the imp yesterday, I was going to be good and sure it didn't happen a second time. A quick pass around the grave-yard checking for fresh scents reassured me that I didn't have any surprises in store. Nothing stood out, the bones were still sitting crushed under the tombstone. They fell further out of spider shape when I nudged them with my foot. I walked over to get a look at the church. The parking lot was emp-ty, as expected. I shouldn't have any company considering that Steve would be tied up in the morgue, and with the boss gone the secretary didn't have a reason to come in. When word got out, the church would become a center of activity. I had a day or two tops before memorial services and arrange-ments for new leadership would make it impossible to find any clues. I need-ed to get in and out now while things were still quiet.

The church was right beside a road, anyone could drive by and see me poking around. The fact that I didn't see any cameras yesterday probably meant there weren't any; a small town church like this wouldn't have much of a security budget. Worse than cameras, though, were nosy locals, word might already be out about Steve burning up last night. Anyone driving by that knew about it might find a stranger at the church suspicious. I found some bushes to stash my clothes in and took the form of an otter. That would be the best way to get in under the radar. I circled the building first and found two entrances, the glass double doors in the front I had used yesterday and a metal door in the back. There were a few windows, most with the blinds drawn. I would have to go in the front. A key would be nice, but I hadn't thought to get one off Steve when I had the chance, so a rock would have to do. I looked around until I found the right rock for the job. It was the size of a tennis ball and would definitely break the glass. I picked it up and walked on my hind legs to the door. A couple good whacks cracked the glass. Holt can make fun of me if he wants, but having thumbs in all three of my forms is a real advantage. Let's see him smash a window when he's taken the form of a Doberman. Maybe if he used his thick head.

One more solid hit and the glass broke, a little more than I wanted. It shattered into large sharp pieces, raining down jagged shards that could seriously hurt me if I didn't move. I scurried away just in time to avoid the glass that shattered on impact with the concrete. My first thought was how I would have been remembered. Cedric was ambushed and ripped apart. He killed many of his attackers and bought enough time for his apprentice to get away. A noble death. Oh, and then there was Obie who was beheaded by a plate glass window, just shameful. My second thought was that it was a much bigger hole than I intended. I was going for something smaller than a human could get through. Too late now, better get to work. I put the rock on the inside of the door to make it look like it was thrown through and jumped in, being careful not to hit the door and risk dislodging more glass.

I did another sweep for unearthly scents. Two hallways lead off in opposite directions. I took the left hallway, passing activity and classrooms. A set of double wood doors at the end of the hall were labeled as the sanctuary.

I went back to the other hallway, following it around in a large circle to a second sanctuary entrance. Nothing looked or smelled out of place. I went back to the entryway and Steve's office.

I had no choice but to change back into human form. Having otter thumbs is great, but they don't do any good if you can't reach the door handle. It wouldn't have mattered anyway; after the change was complete, I found the door locked. A small matter really. I slammed my bare foot into it, splintering the frame and throwing the door wide open. Starting with the desk, I sat down, rubbing my naked bum in the soft leather. After visiting his home, I thought the garbage I smelled on him yesterday had been from his house. Sitting behind his desk I had a different vantage point. The garbage can under the desk was overflowing onto the floor. The mess was concealed, so unless you were sitting behind the desk or had heightened senses, you wouldn't know it was there. I wondered if anyone knew that his wife had left him. He was probably keeping up appearances, hiding the stinky stuff out of sight to keep his image intact. Another reason why going public about demons didn't make sense. There had to be something here to shed some light on his strange behavior.

Rifling through the drawers turned up nothing but office supplies. The large desk calendar had a couple notes on it but nothing that looked important. I found the page of the calendar for last month in the garbage with some ketchup stains on it. I unfolded it on the desk, noticing right away that Steve's schedule had freed up a lot since last month. The first two weeks of this calendar had something on almost every day then tapering off for weeks three and four. That's when I saw it:

P.V.T.

MOCA GA

3 PM

The handwriting looked like the note I'd found at Steve's house. If his wife made the appointment she might have some insight to who P.V.T. is.

The other mystery was Moca, GA. I had never heard of that town before. Maybe it was in south Georgia somewhere. I didn't get down there often.

My thoughts were interrupted by the familiar sound of tires on gravel, someone was coming. Looking out the window I saw a patrol car rolling up to the church. There may have been more clues here but I was out of time. I ripped the note out of the calendar and shoved the rest back in the garbage can, being careful to cover it back up with some of what was on the floor. Didn't want to leave any clues as to what I was looking for. Time for a strategic exit out the back. I tried the side door, hoping it wasn't a closet. I was in luck, it opened into a classroom. From there I made it back to the hallway, out of sight of the lobby. The metal door I had seen outside had to be in the sanctuary. It was my best chance to get away unseen.

There were no windows, not even the fancy stained glass ones, so the room was dark except for an emergency light mounted on the left wall. Rows of pews stretched out in front of me, facing a pulpit with a pew on each side and a large cross on the back wall. I found the door I had seen from the outside hidden behind a curtain. I moved the curtain and pressed the handle stepping out into the bright summer sun. I squinted as my eyes struggled to adjust to the light.

"Police, don't move," a voice shouted.

Without hesitation, I grabbed the handle and retreated back into the building. The door slammed behind me and locked. Why did I do that? I should have run for it. I could have easily outpaced him in the woods and changed forms, effectively disappearing. While they were out chasing me it would have been no problem to circle around to the truck and roll it out quietly before more cops showed up. Now they would be calling for backup and have their guns out. Making a run for it now could get me shot. I needed another plan.

The best way to get past cops that are looking for you is to be someone else, in this case something else. I moved back through the hallway toward the front door, stopping just out of sight of it. I crumpled up my clue and shoved it in my mouth, tasting the paper and stale ketchup, and changed back into an otter. Moving down the hallway I didn't see anyone outside but I knew someone was there—they wouldn't leave the front unguarded. Being careful around the broken glass on the floor, I hopped through the hole in the door and walked into the sunlight. A police cruiser sat caddy-corner to the building.

"Police, let me see . . . What the hell," a voice said from the direction of the car to my right.

I turned to see an officer with something between surprise and confusion plastered on his face, pointing a pistol in my direction. He must have reacted to my movement before putting the pieces together of exactly what was happening. I stopped and stood on my back paws, raising my front paws in the air, I couldn't resist. I could make out the scents of two people. I am sure his partner had already told him he had spotted someone inside which explained why his attention was split between me and the door. He kept looking over like someone was going to jump out of the door at any second. I couldn't help but laugh, which sounded like a lot like a human laughing after breathing helium with a few squeaks thrown in for good measure. Lowering myself down on all fours I headed off toward the hill and the safety of the brush. I spotted the other officer at the side of the building with his gun trained on the door I had tried to come out of a minute before.

I made my way up the embankment, disappearing from sight into the bushes. I found a hidden spot where I could see the parking lot. I couldn't risk driving away with cops around; it would attract too much attention. I would have to wait them out. A few more patrol cars showed up, followed by a black Explorer. A man sporting a righteous mustache and wearing a polo shirt and khakis got out of the Explorer. He adjusted his pants around his portly belly and draped a badge on a lanyard around his neck. They all took strategic positions around the building but didn't go in. Shortly after, a woman in a sedan drove up and parked in the back. She didn't get out of the car but the mustached man went over, chatted for a few minutes, and took a key from her. Must be the secretary. That's when things got exciting. A few stayed in the front but most went to the side door where I had been spotted.

They unlocked it and poured in, shouting commands at the empty church. It was kind of funny, really. Part of me wanted to be there to see their faces when they figured out no one was there.

The shouting died down and a few officers trickled out here and there. They would no doubt do an extensive search to find me. The man that showed up in the Explorer was talking to the first two on the scene. I could tell from his hand motions and body language that he was talking about the otter that came out and went up the hill. He gave the hill a questioning glance before walking over and appeared to be looking for tracks though I doubted he was an expert tracker. It's not hard to follow tracks in eroded dirt. When he found them, he stood looking at the hill in thought. After a minute, he walked off in the opposite direction toward the road. When he got to the entrance to the parking lot he stopped and examined the ground again. I wasn't worried about that. After so many cars coming in there was no way he could pick my truck tires out.

I hadn't thought about the tracks my truck had left in the grass. He turned around, examining the parking lot, and must have noticed the grass pushed down from where I had driven up to the graveyard. Before I knew it, he was walking up the trail and on the way to discovering my truck. That I didn't expect—well played, mustached man. The wind shifted and I got a scent of him: Old Spice and dog, terrier maybe. I could try to distract him, but I couldn't keep him away forever, and couldn't move the truck while they were around. Talking to him wouldn't help because I couldn't give him any real answers. He would probably try to arrest me and I couldn't let that happen. I could always kill him. Sooner or later someone would figure out he was missing and come looking. By the end of it I would have to kill them all. I could see the headlines: Police force murdered, otter taken into custody for questioning. Pass. The thing that made the most sense was to do nothing and wait.

He walked into the clearing and spotted the truck. He drew his gun and moved forward, checking the cab first before moving on to the bed. Finding it empty, he holstered his gun and walked around to the back of the truck, pulled out a notepad, and jotted down my tag before going back to the cab to peer in through the window. I knew he wasn't going to see anything; I keep my truck clean. He looked around, making sure the coast was clear, and pulled some latex gloves out of his back pocket. He put them on and tried the passenger door—I guess Mister Mustache sees a little leeway with the law. I wasn't in the habit of locking my doors but there wasn't anything for him to find except my license, the wooden knife in the glovebox, and my gear bag behind the seat. None of it was illegal. Strange, absolutely, but not illegal.

He rummaged around for a minute before getting into the glovebox. He paused before holding up my wooden knife between two fingers, eyeballing it. That was a problem. If he held it by the handle, I could have a dead cop on my hands. If I changed to human form it would just lead to more questions, why I was in the area and naked to boot. It's possible the guy that got a glimpse of me at the door could identify me. If so, they would try to arrest me. *Just put it back asshole.* I scraped the ground with my back legs, sending leaves flying and making some noise to get his attention. He whipped his head up, looking in my direction. I sank down into the leaves. Sitting still, I'm sure he couldn't see me. After a few seconds without finding the cause of the sound, he put the knife back and closed the door. He put the gloves back in his pocket and stood, facing my direction, watching and listening for what had made the noise. When he was satisfied he wasn't going to find anything, he gave up and headed back down the trail.

I was stuck there for most of the day before they had finished processing the scene and cleared out. I was itching to get out of there but I waited another thirty minutes after the last car left just to make sure I wouldn't be followed. I had a new lead and needed to get back to Naylet to report in. I would never have admitted it to her but I was looking forward to seeing her reaction to the news. I would get a thorough round of *I told you so's* and she would be a little too smug about it but she would be happy. When I was satisfied the coast was clear, I changed back into human form, got dressed, and headed back to Naylet's house.

CHAPTER · 8

There weren't any lights on when I pulled up to the house. That seemed a little strange, it wasn't Naylet's night out with the girls, she didn't say she was going anywhere, and it was much too early for her to be in bed. Maybe she went out; she does love to point out how much of a life she has outside of me. That might not be a bad thing, between this missing baby and the recent demon issues. A couple days to focus on work might be good, it would get us on that vacation a lot quicker. Still, I had to check in, just to make sure everything was okay.

Leaving the truck running, I got out and headed for the front door. As soon as my foot hit the grass I knew something was wrong. I couldn't tell what it was. I stood frozen in my tracks looking for something out of place. The lightning bugs were flashing, the katydids chirped, a bobwhite sang in the woods off to my right. I could smell the leaves and earth of the woods. Everything looked the same but it felt differently, it felt empty. The vitality Naylet had cultivated in the area seemed to have drained away. Covering the yard and steps leading to the front door in a few strides I turned the knob and let myself in.

"Naylet, are you here?" I asked the empty room.

I had to question if my nose was playing tricks on me. A faint scent of spices lingered in the house, the same scent that was on the bunny in the truck. A half-finished cup of coffee sat on the counter beside a few sweet potatoes, peeled but not chopped, as well as a few other ingredients, hinting at the dish that was being made. Pecans, brown sugar, banana, chia seed—I knew this. It was a casserole Naylet makes for breakfast sometimes. It was closer to dinnertime now. That wasn't the only strange thing. Pictures that normally hung on the walls were in a pile on the table beside the newspaper I had read the night before. Turning the light on, I checked the loft to find it empty. Flipping through the pictures I noticed a couple had been taken out of the frames. One was from about forty years ago, the last time we took a trip to the beach. It was the only physical evidence that I had ever worn bell bottoms, and one of the happiest times of my life.

Maybe whatever had taken Baby Stephanie had come after Naylet; that would explain the smell, but it didn't explain the pictures. Still, none of this made any sense. Sitting down at the table, I pondered my next move. Nymphs weren't known for being fighters but if she got away she could disappear in the woods. She probably had some trouble, ran out, and was staying hidden until she knew it's safe. If she was laying low, she would come out when she heard me. I had to check the woods.

Heading back to the truck, I grabbed a flashlight out of the bag I kept behind the seat and turned to start my search. Stopping dead in my tracks I paused for a second before going into the glovebox to get my knife. I tucked it in my shorts, better safe than sorry, and headed for the storage shed. I didn't think she would be there, but it was close and I might as well check. It was neat and tidy; she likes to keep things in order like that. Some people might call her O.C.D.; I don't. Gardening tools hung on the walls, and bags of soil were stacked neatly beside a wheelbarrow in the corner. I made my way around the house. It all looked normal but I found a set of tracks heading off into the woods behind the house. Naylet had made a reading garden by a stream that flowed at the bottom of the hill. The tracks led off in that direction, and from the small tufts of dirt thrown behind the track it looked like she was running. The path wove its way through the woods and down a hill for about two hundred feet, which I covered at full speed. It opened into a mossy area beside the creek, with flower beds scattered around the edges. A bench sat off on the right side. She was nowhere to be found.

"Naylet," I called. There was no answer.

I held the flashlight low, sending the beam across the ground and discovered a pair of tracks in the grass. It looked like Naylet's and another set I didn't recognize. The new set looked humanoid with distinct claw marks around the toes. I didn't recognize them. Being that they appeared on the ground out of nowhere, whatever it was could probably fly.

There was a chase. I followed Naylet's tracks, telling the story of how she evaded her pursuer around the entire clearing in large circles. The clawed set took a much more direct approach. Wherever Naylet had gone, this creature followed her, leaving straight lines of tracks with scrapes in the ground from its claws. Keeping up with Naylet was tough, even for me; whatever this thing was, it was quick.

Naylet's tracks escaped into the creek. It was four feet wide and barely a foot deep. The clawed tracks skidded to a stop, avoiding the water. That was a hint—demons hated water. The stranger's tracks disappeared, the demon must have taken flight again. That left me with nothing to go on. I was a good tracker, but no one was good enough to track in moving water or through the air. I stepped into the stream, the cold water biting at my feet, and shone the light downstream looking for clues. Coming up with nothing, I turned upstream, revealing a figure hunched low in the water, almost completely submerged. I stepped forward, cautiously moving to the side to get a better look. It was Naylet. Only her head and one arm was raised out of the water, shielding her face.

"Naylet, are you alright?" I asked, taking a cautious step forward.

There was no response, not so much as a flinch. She had a stillness with the absoluteness of death. I moved forward a few more steps and could see she was wearing shorts and a red tee shirt, no shoes. Her skin looked to be a light grey color. I was hoping it was a trick of the light, but the closer I got the more I was sure it wasn't. I didn't know if it was just in my head, but the whole area took on a feeling of heaviness, like the woods before a hard rain.

When I was close enough, I reached out and touched her hand. It was solid and cool to the touch, not living, but as if she had been carved from a piece of stone.

I moved around and knelt beside her, my breath catching in my throat. It was definitely Naylet but I had no explanation for what had happened to her. Although I had only seen it a couple times in all the years we had been together, I recognized the expression on her face: fear. That was it for me, the tears started to pool in my eyes. I wiped them away and took a breath. There's no time for that.

"Hang on, Naylet, I'll get you to Livy. She can fix this," I said, trying to convince myself as much as her.

I've been around a while and thought I had seen just about everything, but this one was new. Naylet may not look that tough, but she was mean as a snake in a pinch, it was one of her many endearing qualities. The tracks told me she couldn't get away from her pursuer but there was no evidence that she put up a fight either. I only knew one thing about whatever did this to her: it was dangerous. A breeze drifted through the woods from behind me and I was sure I could smell the perfume I had found at the Olson house. It was faint but it was there. I was about to shift into krasis and track down where it was coming from when I was distracted by the sound of a car pulling up to the house. New lights, combined with my truck's lights, shone over the crest of the hill and through the trees, making it look like a scene from the *X-Files*.

"Were you expecting company?" I asked Naylet's lifeless form.

I couldn't very well go up the hill in krasis without knowing who was up there, but I didn't want to stay in human form if I had to face whatever was lurking out of sight in the woods. Deciding to keep my human form, at least until I knew who had come knocking, I lifted Naylet out of the water. With one arm under her legs and the other across her back, I carried her out of the stream. In the past I have never had trouble picking her up, she couldn't have been more than a buck twenty-five, tops. This transformation, however, added the weight of stone and not just the look. It actually took some effort to lift her. Walking toward the hill, I thought of the wheelbarrow I had seen in the shed. I didn't want to leave her alone in the dark with whatever was out there. It didn't feel right. I could make it, I just might have Jell-O legs by the time I got there.

Halfway up the hill I heard the slow and deliberate crunching of leaves in the woods behind me, footsteps. I dropped Naylet's legs, spinning quickly with my light. The beam found something that leapt straight up and disappeared into the night sky with only the flapping of wings and rustled leaves to give away that it had been there at all. I had only caught a glimpse of something, a shadowy figure in the darkness, but not enough to tell what it was. I was right, though, there was something out here.

"Which one of us do you think it's after?" I asked. Naylet didn't answer.

Whatever it was, it was gone for the moment. It would be back, though, they always come back. Retrieving Naylet's legs, I continued up toward the headlights. Maybe that would deter it—I doubt it, but here's to hoping. Coming over the crest of the hill and into the headlights, I couldn't see anything but the house illuminated to my left and two sets of headlights shining in my direction. I had to get Naylet into my truck, that was a given, I just needed to figure out who was there and how in the way they were going to get. With no time to beat around the bush, I started walking straight across the yard. Halfway there I caught a whiff of Old Spice and dog, now with a hint of B.O. I knew who it was before I stepped past the beams to find the mustached officer from the church.

He must have had me followed, something I should have noticed, another slipup I guess. It's not like he couldn't look up who I was and my home address from my tag if he wanted to. Regardless, I wasn't in the mood to deal with this. He got out of his Explorer with the kind of smirk on his face I instinctively wanted to wipe off with light violence. He had to have seen me as soon as I came over the crest of the hill. I could have easily gotten away from him but that meant leaving Naylet behind. I would play along for a bit, disposing of a cop and his car is one more thing that I really didn't want to deal with. I'd get Naylet in the truck and see how far this encounter would go.

"Evening. Detective Farwell," he said when I stepped past the headlights. He tapped a badge hanging from a lanyard around his neck as he spoke. "Does the owner of this place know you are hauling off their statue?"

"Yes, officer, I assure you she would be pleased to know that I am taking care of it," I said.

"She would be, you say? So she doesn't know you are taking it?" Right then I knew this guy wanted to bust me for something, par for the course. Unfortunately for him that's not going to happen tonight.

"Yeah, I'm afraid she's not here at the moment. I hope she will be back soon. She had mentioned that she wanted it taken care of and I wasn't busy so I thought I would do a favor for a friend. You know how it goes," I replied.

"Oh sure," he agreed. "It's awful Christian of you. Do you attend church regular? I go to Inclusive Assembly of Christ, over by Canton. Have you ever been there before?"

I set Naylet down by the truck and opened the tailgate. "I might have been by there once or twice."

"I was hoping to talk to you about something that happened there today," he said, squinting at me.

"Of course, officer, I would be happy to come down to the station and talk to you. Does tomorrow afternoon work for you?" I knew it wasn't going to be this easy.

"I'm a 'rip the bandage off' kind of guy. We could straighten it out right now," he said.

I had just finished heaving Naylet into the back of the truck and closed the gate when, for the second time, I heard shuffling in the woods. Again they came from behind me. I turned and put my arms up on the tailgate with a foot up on the bumper. I was going for a casual look but really, I was preparing to launch myself at whatever would come out of the woods.

"Sir, can you step over here, please," Farwell said.

I didn't have time for this. I could tell from the look on his face that he was about to stop beating around the bush and get down to business. Something was out there and if I didn't get him out of here he could be killed—or worse, he could live, and that would be a real mess. Maybe Thera would consider an exception to the "protect life" rule if she knew how inconvenient it was for me. On second thought, probably not. I walked away from the truck, to get between him and the footsteps. Standing with my back to him I looked into the woods for a few seconds and smelled the air. It was out there.

"Sir . . ." Farwell said, trying to redirect my attention from the trees.

I was about to turn around to tell him that I didn't have anything to discuss tonight when I was interrupted.

"Is there a problem, officer?" a woman's voice said from the trees.

I didn't recognize it or the young woman it was attached to. She was in skinny jeans and a form-fitting black tank top. Her dark clothing, combined with her dark complexion, made her seem to appear out of nowhere as she stepped out of the trees. She had long thick dreadlocks reaching almost to her waist and wasn't wearing shoes. I already figured she was up to no good, but the lack of shoes sealed the deal. You have to be careful around people that don't wear shoes. They are either going to be the salt of the earth or some monster that will try to eat your face; there's not a lot of in between. I moved back to my truck to put myself between Naylet and the new visitor.

Farwell's hand had instinctively gone to his gun. It lingered there as he spoke: "And you are?"

"I'm Naylet Kirtane. I live here. I overheard your conversation and I can clear up this little misunderstanding. You see, I did ask him to move the statue for me. I'm afraid I have been thinking some more about it and have decided to keep it. I'm sorry to put you through all this trouble, Obie. Be a dear and set it over by the shed please. I will find the perfect place for it tomorrow morning. I promise you I won't bother you with it again."

My lip curled, I couldn't help it. "Not going to happen."

I had squared up with her, put a hand on the tailgate to emphasize my point.

"Obie," she exclaimed. "What has gotten into you? I assure you, officer, he's not normally like this. What's the matter, hun?"

"Don't call me that."

Farwell had moved away during this process. He was speaking softly and trying to be discreet while we were distracting each other. It almost worked. "Hey, it's Ryan. I'm okay but need a couple marked units at my location," he said and started walking back in our direction. "Ma'am, this is getting a little heated. Could you go inside and let's take a few minutes to calm down, then we can get this figured out."

"Marked units . . . he is referring to police cars?" she asked.

It might have been a rhetorical question but I answered it anyway. "Yep, he's got backup on the way. Guess you better scurry back to whatever shithole you crawled out of."

"Don't be crass, Obie, it's beneath you. Officer Farwell, I wish you hadn't done that," she said stepping backward into the woods the way she came and disappeared into the shadows, her eyes locked on me as she went.

CHAPTER • 9

"Detective, you should call off that backup, leave, and forget you ever saw me," I said without turning around.

"We aren't done with our conversation," he said.

He's going to get himself killed. "Like I said, I will happily come speak to you tomorrow. There's business here that doesn't concern you. For your own safety, you need to leave."

He put his hands on his hips. "That doesn't work for me."

"Suit yourself."

I circled around the cars trying to locate where the imposter had gone. Neither the crunching of leaves nor the flapping of wings gave away her location in the woods. Either she was staying perfectly still or she had vanished. If she wasn't here she couldn't stop me. Farwell would, he would try at least, but I wasn't going to be arrested today. I could kill him but that just didn't seem very gentlemanly. Instead, I turned to face him and realized he was speaking, I hadn't been paying attention. Looking him directly in the eyes, I made the change into krasis. That shut him up. The blood drained from his face and he pulled his pistol from its holster but didn't start shooting, yet.

"I am going to get in my truck and I'm going to leave," I said. "We can meet so you can make sense of all this later but now isn't the time. If you try to stop me, I will have to hurt you. I don't want to hurt you, but I will, and that pea shooter isn't going to protect you."

With that, I moved to the driver side of my truck, keeping an eye on him to make sure he didn't get any funny ideas. I didn't get the impression he was going to try to take me down to the station. Placing a hand on the door handle, I was just starting to think this was going to turn out all right when something hit me like a sledgehammer. I didn't hear a gunshot so it wasn't Farwell, but before I knew what happened I was airborne. The only distraction from sharp pain in my shoulder was the beating of large wings right above me. I couldn't orient myself fast enough to make sense of what was happening. I found myself tumbling through the air into the yard. I landed hard on my back and was left gasping for breath. I raised up on my elbows to get my bearings. I had been thrown about thirty feet into the yard away from the truck. The beast touched down in front of Farwell's Explorer. The headlights concealed any distinct features and cast a long shadow across the ground in my direction. I raised a hand for a better look. The webbing between my fingers kept the light from my eyes, but the figure advancing was still a mystery.

It was unmistakably female, with large bat-like wings. Her skin looked a little shiny around the edges as if it was reflecting the light or wet, not unlike the silver lining of a cloud, but nothing good was going to come from this. There was something moving around her head and shoulders that I couldn't make out. It might be some kind of magic at work. I was recovering quickly, the injury to my shoulder almost closed. In a couple minutes it should be back to normal. Already the bleeding had stopped and nothing seemed broken. I reached back with my good arm to get my knife but it wasn't there. It must have fallen out while I was airborne. I spotted where it had dropped about fifteen feet in front of me. I couldn't get to it at the moment, it was too close to this demon. Luckily, I have claws and teeth, and they have never let me down in the past. It's a lot more work that way, but as they say, if you like what you do you never work a day in your immortal life.

"You don't know who you're fucking with, lady," I said, getting to my feet.

She laughed. "Oh, Obie, I know all about you, how your parents died, your experiences at the orphanage, when you became a Keeper, the problems with Cearbhall, when you fell in love—I know exactly who I'm fucking with, and I have to admit I have been looking forward to it for quite a while."

There's no way she could know all that. No one knows that much about me, except maybe Cearbhall and Naylet, so how did this thing? She took a couple steps forward, only a few feet from my knife now. It didn't look like she realized it was there. I started circling slowly to the left. With any luck she would play along.

"So what, you did a little research? You get all that from Naylet before you . . ." I trailed off not knowing exactly what she had done or wanting to vocalize it.

She circled to my right into the light and letting me get a good look at her for the first time. That's when I realized what the mass on her head was. Snakes, big black ones. *Why did it have to be snakes?* There was a noise behind her, it must have been Farwell but I couldn't see what he was doing with the lights in my eyes. She heard it as well and turned her back to me to face him, bad move. I didn't waste the opportunity to run for my knife. She didn't seem interested in stopping me. I grabbed it off the ground and dashed a few paces away in anticipation of an attack that never came.

Moving around the back of Farwell's Explorer, I found her standing in front of him. He was standing perfectly still by the open car door. The snakes had spread out on her head and I could see all their eyes, as well as hers, glowing yellow. She was working some kind of magic. He had her distracted and I had no intention of missing an opportunity to finish her off. That's when I saw his hands, they were turning grey, grey like Naylet. He was being turned to stone. She was not going to have another victim tonight, not on my watch. Coming up behind Farwell, I stepped between them, blocking her sight. The hair all over my body immediately stood on end and my skin tingled like I had electricity running all over me. I wasn't worried about it affecting me. Thera shields her Keepers from magical attacks, the tingling told me it was working. At least something was going my way. I lunged forward, delivering three quick jabs with my knife. One hit her jaw and the other two landed solidly on her neck, too solidly in fact. It hadn't penetrated, there was no blood or visible sign of damage. The snakes, along with her gaze, redirected their focus to me. The tingling increased to an almost painful level.

I needed to put an end to this before it got any more out of hand, and before she realized her spell wasn't working. I reared back and landed a solid punch right in her nose. Her head whipped back with a satisfying crack. The snakes flailed uncontrollably and for a second their glowing yellow eyes went out like I had flipped a light switch. She stumbled back a step, clearly stunned. I wasn't sure how much of it was from the blow and how much was from the shock that her magic wasn't working. Farwell moaned behind me and fell to the ground; better than being stone, buddy. I glanced back to see the grayness in his hands slowly receding. Picking him up, I tried to put him in his car, but the demon had recovered enough to come after me, black blood running out of her nose and hatred pouring out of her eyes.

Throwing Farwell over my shoulder I retreated around the back of the Explorer and dumped him in the back of my truck with Naylet as I passed it. She closed on me fast, screeching as she came. As soon as my arms were free from tossing Farwell in the truck I spun with the dagger, delivering a slash across the chest that would have killed her if she were any kind of decent creature. She stumbled back, grabbing her chest, and hunched forward. The snakes moved around to protect her and blocked my view of the gore that was undoubtedly starting to spill out. It would kill the grass but it's a small price to pay, if you've seen one pile of demon guts you've seen them all. The snakes moved back revealing a fanged grin. There was no visible sign of the cut except that the shirt had a large slash mark through it showing scaled breasts underneath. It hung loosely from her shoulders now, being mostly open in the front and not so form fitting. She ripped it away and tossed it to the ground.

She smirked. "Are you really so desperate to get me undressed?"

"I'll have you skinned by the time this is done."

If my blade wouldn't penetrate her scales then I would have to hit her somewhere it would penetrate, her eyes looked like prime candidates. We circled, sizing each other up for a second before moving in simultaneously. She slashed with clawed fingers, while snakes struck from all directions. I countered with quick footwork and aggressive parries, hitting away the snakes that couldn't be avoided. It was not a winning strategy, and she knew it. Between the snakes and her claws, I couldn't get through to land an attack. It became clear to me that I didn't have any real options; it was only a matter of time before I was overcome. If I wanted to take her out I was going to have to take the hits and count on my ability to heal to get me through it. I waited for as clear an opening as I was going to get, and thrust my blade hard at her face. The knife made contact but my attacking arm was struck repeatedly as snakes buried their teeth into my flesh. I dropped the knife and grabbed a snake. I gave it a sharp pull and simultaneously sent a foot into her belly with everything I had. The snake tore free in my hand as she sprawled out on the ground from the impact. Point Obie. The snake writhed for a few seconds and then went still.

She didn't appear to be in any hurry to get up so I took advantage and walked backward toward my truck, as not to turn my back on her. My happiness at the success was short lived. I could feel numbness starting to creep into my arm. She rose, leisurely and grinning like she knew something I didn't, not the best feeling. Blood ran down from her head over her shoulder from where the snake had been. She looked too happy for someone who had just had a piece of themselves ripped off.

"I have to say I'm surprised, Obie. You have always been so gentle in the past. It will all be over soon now though," she said. "The venom will make quick work of you."

"You might be getting a little ahead of yourself. I'm not dead yet."

"Yes, not dead yet. I'll give you that. You are quite resilient. I'm surprised that you've lasted this long if I'm being honest. You know you have a reputation for being a little soft? Naylet thinks so too, but she actually likes it. Look at you now, you even managed to kill one of my serpents, the part of me that is her is impressed I think. No one has given me this much trouble in a very long time."

I was getting really tired of the talking in riddles and speaking to me like she actually knew something about my relationship. "I'll celebrate later."

The numbness continued to spread. Slow enough, at first, for me to question if it was spreading at all. The fact that I had to question it told me it was spreading faster than my body could recover from it. I had a resistance to her magic; the venom on the other hand, wasn't magic. It was just everyday venom, but being from a demon and from another place meant my normal protections against everything from Thera didn't apply. Without a natural resistance, only relying on my healing ability, there was no telling how bad it would be. I needed to get Naylet and Farwell out of here now. The best place I could take them was Livy's house. It was well hidden and I had a feeling I was going to need her help soon. The longer this fight took the less likely it would turn out in my favor.

My dagger was on the ground a couple feet away from her although my fists seemed to do a better job on her than the blade. Naylet had a sledge-hammer in the shed. I pondered for a moment. If I could get to it that might do the trick. Still the blade might be able to help me if I could get her to pick it up.

"You got a name?" I asked.

"I already told you, Naylet," she said.

"I'm not going to call you that. Quit fucking around, tell me your name."

She smiled again, revealing fangs. "I have many names. Petra, Laelius, Vibiana, Colleen, Afia . . . I have more if one of those doesn't suit you."

"Why so many? You have a collection or something?" I asked.

"I collect lives, not names."

"What does that mean, collect lives?" I knew I wasn't going to like the answer as soon as I asked the question.

"It means that sometimes I require an infusion to sustain myself. I assure you, it's a painless process. The subject is absorbed, becoming part of me, leaving behind an empty shell. I gain their experiences and potential in the process. Many people are hesitant at first, but they come around. Take Naylet," she raised a hand to the statue in my truck. "She fought hard at first before I wore her down, but look at her now! She's stunning, a work of art, she will be beautiful forever and no doubt she is thrilled with the arrangement. I can almost hear her, 'thank you Petra' and 'you've saved me' she says, and I will tell you, Obie, I am honored to be able to help her. We do have one little problem though."

"What's that," I asked.

"I'm afraid I just can't let you take her from me. She's part of my family now," she said, her tone changing from joy to menace.

"That is a problem, because I'm not going to leave without her." I shifted my eyes to the blade on the ground and made sure to move my head a little to accentuate my intention.

"Sweetie, you're not leaving either way," she said following my eyes to the knife. "It is a remarkable blade, useless against me of course but the craftsmanship is very nice. Did you want it? Here, take it." She bent over and picked it up.

She held it out to me, opening her mouth to speak again, when the enchantment triggered. The air charged, building quickly, and then burst, sending electricity coursing through Petra's body. She convulsed under its effect before collapsing to the ground, steam rising from her body. The smell of charred flesh filled the air. I moved forward and nudged her with my foot to see if that had finished her off. She let out a moan, but neither she nor the snakes moved. She was tough, I'll give her that. The dagger had been destroyed in the explosion. The pieces that remained were on fire, scattered across the ground.

Having a second to breathe, the first thing I noticed was the numbness moving into my right leg. I needed to get help soon. If anyone was going to be able to counteract the venom it would be Livy. Farwell had come to and climbed out of the back of the truck. He leaned against the truck bed with his gun out but not pointed at anything, a confused look on his face.

"Get in," I said, limping toward the truck. He obliged without an argument.

It was hard to ignore how weak my grip had become when I shifted the truck into first. My hand was swollen and its sensations felt foreign. Driving straight out into the yard, the truck lurched to the right as the front tire rolled over Petra. Putting it in reverse and cranking the wheel, I backed out, running over her a second time. The dirt road leading to my rescue stretched out in front of me but I stopped. Putting it into reverse again, I backed up over Petra a third time and rolled forward until the tires came to rest against her body. Pressing the gas, the engine rattled and then burst to life in a roar. I popped the clutch, sending the tires spinning with centrifugal fury.

There was a loud thud as the tires grabbed her limp body, slamming it against the underside of the truck before she ricocheted off into the yard. I hit the brakes and looked in the rearview, the engine retuning to a steady rumble. Naylet's once impeccable yard, now gouged by my tires, with Petra's twisted and broken body littering the grounds, and small flaming pieces of my knife looked right out of a nightmare when bathed in the red glow of the tail lights.

Focusing my attention ahead instead of behind, I roared down the driveway, sending gravel flying into the woods in waves as I spun around the curves. It occurred to me it might have been better to take Farwell's car, the lights might have come in handy, but it was too late now. Livy lived deep in the mountains. The good news is that she and Naylet were practically neighbors, by country standards. Livy only lived twenty minutes away, give or take. The bad news is that the venom was working its way through my system and I wasn't sure if I had that long.

"You need to call off the backup," I said once we made it back on the pavement.

Farwell seemed not entirely aware of what was going on.

I waved my hand in front of his face. "Hey . . . Snap out of it." I tried snapping a few times to get his attention but my thumb wouldn't cooperate. "If she's still alive she's going to kill your backup, call them off."

"Ok, I'll call," he said.

He took out the phone and stared at it but didn't hit any buttons. That's when the dizziness set in. I concentrated on the road, putting my entire force of will into staying awake and delivering us in one piece. I heard a voice that sounded distant and fuzzy, it was Farwell. I didn't know what he was saying but I hoped no cops showed up. They would find a demon body and a missing detective. As the minutes passed, my right arm became completely useless, preventing me from shifting gears. I would have to finish the drive in whatever gear I was in. My vision started to blur and it was getting harder to keep the truck in one lane. There wasn't any traffic on these roads at this hour but there were steep drop-offs on the right side of the road. Since I couldn't change gears, the only logical thing to do was to keep my speed up as much as I could.

There weren't any traffic lights and only a couple stop signs that I ignored. I turned onto the forest service road Livy's house was off of and followed the well-manicured gravel road before whipping the truck off the road onto what most people wouldn't even consider a deer trail. The truck skidded down the path, gaining speed from the hill. Farwell's hand reached over and grabbed the wheel. I passed through the camouflage barrier concealing the house from outsiders. We were closing on the house much too quickly. I let go of the wheel, reached down, pulled the parking brake, and passed out.

CHAPTER • 10

I felt the warm sun and a gentle steady breeze on my fur that I have only felt at high altitude. Opening my eyes, I found a clear blue sky with a single turkey vulture gliding in lazy circles overhead. The ground was hard, it felt like a solid stone; not entirely uncomfortable to lay on, at least there weren't rocks to make things lumpy. I heard some children playing and a train whistle in the distance. Putting all of this together I knew where I was before I sat up. I had never been anywhere else like this.

"You shouldn't lie there all day. The vultures will make a meal out of you if you don't get up soon," Thera said. I turned my head to my right to see dark brown feet. The feet were attached to bountiful legs that disappeared into a thick mixture off summer grass and wildflowers that grew from her head and cascaded around her body.

She never appeared with clothes, and her appearance changed with the seasons and areas where she appeared. While she appeared like this in summer, in winter she would have almost snow white skin with deep evergreen boughs. Regardless of how she looked, if you were in the presence of the Earth Mother you knew it. She brought with her an essence of power and vitality unmatched by anything else. In any case, now it made sense how I could be close to death, with my truck careening out of control one second, and basking in the sun on the top of Stone Mountain the next.

Stone Mountain is a solid rock that reaches twenty-three hundred feet

above a relatively flat landscape. I always thought it seemed out of place—the
locals had turned it into a park complete with Confederate generals carved
on the front of it. Pain shot through my right side as I sat up; my arm and leg
were stiff and not responding. I sat on a slope a few feet away from the edge.
A landscape of green stretched out in front of me with the Atlanta skyline
off in the distance. Thera sat down beside me, her elbows on her knees, barely able to touch around her large fertile belly. She stared off into the distance.
The wind pushed the grasses back from her face.

I doubted any of this was real, of course. When she appears to me in
the real world, wind and rain can't touch her because she isn't actually there.
Her appearance is just a visual representation of her spirit. So that meant I
wasn't actually there; it felt real enough just the same. I wondered if I had
died and this was what the afterlife was like: a tourist trap. I think I would
prefer nothingness, but looking into Thera's scowling face, I decided being
left alone would be enough. It was quite possible I was bleeding out in the
cab of my truck right now. The least she could do is let me bleed in peace.

"Something has happened," she said, not looking away from the horizon.

"You could say that," I replied. I relayed the story of finding Naylet
and the encounter with the demon calling herself Petra, complete with the
snakes, poison, and running her over with the truck.

"So you let her escape," she said.

"I ran her over four times," I said. "And that's after she took a lightning
strike from my knife. I really don't think . . ."

"That's right, you don't think. You should have made sure. What if she's
not dead? She was incapacitated, helpless, and you did nothing."

"Now just hold on. I was trying to save Naylet, not to mention that pain
in the ass detective. Plus, I am seriously injured. I almost died. I barely made
it to Livy's . . ." I paused realizing I still didn't know what had happened.
"Did I make it to Livy's?"

She stared off into the distance like I wasn't there.

"Hey, talk to me. What's going on?"

"Holt is in trouble," she said.

"Isn't he always?"

She looked me in the eyes. "This isn't a joke, he's in pain."

"Do you know where he is?" I asked, not feeling quite as jovial as I did a moment before.

"He was attacked and taken somewhere. Not long after, he was in pain. Now I have lost sight of him completely and I feel my connections to others stretching thin," she said. "Whatever this is, it is affecting me directly. That can't stand."

"Do you know what's doing it?"

"It could be some demon or magic maybe. I have never experienced this before. I think whatever it is, it's centered around Holt."

"Did you get a look at what attacked him?" I asked.

Thera didn't respond. Worry swept across her face, an unfamiliar look for her to say the least. I had never seen that expression on her before and I didn't like it. Nothing shakes Thera, she is solid as the earth. She stood up and looked around.

"What is it?" I asked.

She looked around. "Obie?"

That's when I realized, she couldn't see me. I reached out to touch her leg, my hand passed through like she was an illusion. I wasn't sure if that would be normal or not since we weren't physically here. There was nothing for me to do so I sat and watched. She closed her eyes and concentrated, vanishing to leave me sitting alone. I wondered exactly how I was going to get out of the dream, or whatever it was. Maybe I would wake up whenever my body recovered. What if I didn't? Physical contact maybe? Livy was seventy miles or so north, I didn't feel good about my chances as a spirit hitchhiker.

"There you are, right where I left you," Thera said from behind me.

I twisted around to see her standing over me. I reached out and touched her leg; it was solid.

"I lost you. You need to find what is doing this and put an end to it," she said.

"It has to be Petra," I said, standing to face her. "She has a grimoire and

I think she was following me. She seems to have some kind of sick obsession with me. I just need some time to heal and I'll take care of it."

"You already let her escape once. If you can't handle this I will take care of it myself. She will not get away again," she said.

I wasn't sure about what she meant by "take care of it herself." In the two hundred plus years I have been a Keeper she has never handled a demon personally. She's never even mentioned it. "If you can handle it yourself then why did you tell me to look into it? I am doing my best to handle this up to your standard, preserving life and all that."

Her tone softened slightly at this. "Obie, do you think I am powerful?"

This caught me off guard. I was suspicious of why she would ask that question. She could create life, she created the Keepers and we are pretty powerful, as things go.

"Terrifyingly so," I conceded.

"Before the Keepers I had to handle these kinds of things myself. I could bring in a storm strong enough to level this entire landscape. I bet this Petra can't swim, maybe a flood is in order. I could submerge everything as far as the eye can see—it wouldn't be the first time. Just to be sure, I could do both of them together. Maybe a few volcanoes to make the air unbreathable. Nothing would survive but I would be rid of one demon. I can handle it myself but attrition has to be considered. I made the Keepers to be surgical instruments. I don't want to have to decimate entire populations to handle a relatively small threat. Normally these demons kill and eat. It's inconvenient but little more than a nuisance. This is different, this is affecting me directly, and it can't continue, no matter the cost. For me to handle it means destruction on a massive scale. I need you to take care of it and I need to know right now if you are incapable for any reason."

I looked out at the Atlanta skyline ahead of me and imagined what it would look like underwater. "I see. I will handle it, I just need a little time. You really used to fight demons?"

"You should see what I have tucked away in here," she said patting the mountain with her foot. Again her face dropped. "I've lost you again. If you can hear me I'll give you three days and then I'll handle it myself."

Clouds formed in the sky out of nowhere, white at first but quickly turning dark and heavy. The wind picked up, bending the trees and throwing leaves. Lightning streaked across the sky as rain started to fall. I could see and hear it all but none of it touched me. The rain and wind passed through me. I stood and hobbled over to Thera. I reached out a hand but didn't see the unevenness in the rock before I stepped on it. My already weakened ankle twisted, sending me off balance. Since the leg I needed to take a step with wasn't working at the moment. I fell backward onto the slope and started sliding. I clawed at the rock but it was smooth and slick, I couldn't get a grip. I looked up and reached out for Thera just as I slid over the edge. She probably couldn't see me, but if she could she didn't put any effort into helping me. I flipped, falling face first, wind rushing over me with the ground coming up fast. A large boulder barreled towards me, or I at it as the case may be, at an alarming rate with no way to stop. Panic set in and I scrambled for any way out. I flapped my arms and tried to grab a tree growing out of the cliff face but nothing came except the boulder. I had never fallen from this height before; I wasn't sure I could live through it. I closed my eyes tight and waited for the impact.

CHAPTER • 11

The wind stopped. I didn't feel any impact, no bone crushing injuries. I opened my eyes to find a boulder a few feet from my face. Without thinking, I brought my hands up to shield myself from the impact. Pain coursed through my body. Not a "pancaking into a boulder" kind of pain, but pain like soreness after a workout where the trainer's trying to make you cry. I lowered my arms back onto the cot I was lying on and looked again at the rock above me. I knew this rock, it was part of the ceiling in Livy's house. I had spent many nights staring up at it. She had built her home into a hillside using some protruding rock as walls and ceiling. The gaps were filled in with logs and sealed with a mud mixture, the same way it was done in the old days. To be fair it was still the old days when she built it. I still felt like death warmed up and I couldn't help but wonder if this boulder would fall free any second and finish the job. It wouldn't be entirely unwelcome.

What Thera said came back to me: something was affecting her directly and she was ready to incite mass destruction to stop it. "Why are all the women in my life lunatics?" I said, trying to stretch some of the soreness out of my neck. I was still in krasis, which didn't surprise me. The change takes a force of will. It's hard to do that and be unconscious at the same time.

"We choose who we spend time with, Obie. Maybe you just need to pick better company," Livy said from somewhere off to my left.

I turned my head and saw her sitting in a rocking chair, knitting. "I've got you, so I must be doing something right."

She smiled, put the knitting in her lap, and laid her hands, misshapen from years of use, on top of it. She wasn't much younger than me, definitely one of the oldest humans living. It's probably one reason we got along so well. While she was weathered with age in the winter of her years, I hadn't changed. I felt bad about it, watching her grow old and her body fail a little at a time.

"How are you feeling?" she asked.

I had to ponder the question. So much had happened it took me a minute to figure out exactly how I was feeling. I moved a little and discovered I was sore all over, especially my right side. My body was stiff and I felt cold. Definitely not like a badass Keeper. My right arm and leg were clearly swollen and I could feel some bruising under my fur. And that was just physically. There was a whole emotional cesspool I wasn't even going to touch at the moment.

"Like roadkill," I said, grunting my way into an upright position.

The house was one large room with a natural stone ceiling. Being mostly underground, the inside stayed comfortable, if not a little cool, year round. The mud-sand mixture used to fill in the spaces between the logs did a good job insulating. A wood burning stove that Livy did all her cooking on sat opposite the door. She burned wood or coal depending on what she could get her hands on. I had spent many days splitting wood to fuel that stove and I hoped to spend many more.

To the left of the stove was a small kitchen area that wasn't more than a prep station with some storage and an old-timey ice box. The Coolerator didn't actually take ice anymore; she had worked some magic that kept it nice and chilly. Who needs electricity when you've got magic? A small stream that ran just outside had some of its water diverted into the house through one wall, down a trough, and out another wall back to the stream. Her bed sat against the right wall, with a chest of drawers and armoire placed beside it. It was a nice set I helped her move in about a hundred and twenty years ago, and it had held up well all that time. She had a divider she could put up for some privacy if she needed it but it was in its normal spot folded up against the wall, covered with a thick layer of dust. Farwell was lying in her bed and looked to be asleep.

"How is he?" I asked.

"Not too well. He wasn't wearing a seatbelt and got all tore up in the crash. I did what I could for him but he needs more help than I can give him. We need to talk about your parking skills, Obie. You came barreling down that hill and plowed right into my house. It's a good thing it's mostly stone or you might have run me down. You did knock loose a couple of the logs on that side." She extended a crooked finger to the wall by where Farwell was lying.

"I'm sorry, Livy, I'll fix it. Where's Naylet?" I said, giving the house another look. "Were you able to help her?"

"I'm sorry, hun. I tried a few things but I think it's beyond me. You came barreling in half dead yourself, between you and him I haven't had a lot of spare time. I just about threw my back out getting the two of you in here," she said. "And lord, that snake head. What have you gotten yourself into? If I hadn't found it in the truck I might not have been able to save you. I tried everything I knew and talked to the spirits but they weren't able to help any."

I wanted to tell her that wasn't good enough, that she should journey in the spirit world until she got the answer, but I knew she was doing her best. She loved Naylet as much as I did. "Please keep trying," I said.

"I will, hun, I promise. Besides looking for answers I also was looking for her spirit. Obie, I couldn't find it. We may be able to fix this, and I hope we can, but you should be open to the possibility that she might be gone."

"I'm going to fix this," I said.

"Well, I will do anything I can to help," she said. "In the meantime, I was just about to take my medicine. Can I get you some tea, maybe a little something to eat?"

"No thanks. I just need to stretch a little," I said, pushing through the pain to raise my arms over my head.

"Are you still not eating?" she asked. "Let me make you something. You're nothing but skin and hair."

"I'm not eating because I don't need to eat, you know this."

"Just because you don't need to doesn't mean you shouldn't. Life's short, Obie, enjoy yourself a little. How about a sandwich?"

"Okay, you win. I'll have some tea," I said.

I wasn't going to argue with her about it. She would keep badgering me until I had something, so a concession was good for both of us. She eased out of her chair and walked to the stove where she put in a couple pieces of wood. She took an old coffee tin from above the stove and opened it, taking a pinch of Pixie Dust between her fingers.

Opening the stove, she threw the dust in and whispered, "Fire."

The wood burst into flames. It was an expensive way to start fires but a lot easier than matches. Closing the stove, she put some water into a kettle from the trough and placed it on top. She walked back to her chair and took a seat. Sticking her finger through the loop on top of a jug beside her chair she spun and lifted it so it rested in the top of her arm and took a long swig. What she called "medicine" was a blend of plants she collected from the forest steeped in alcohol with a touch of magic. She took three shots a day religiously to keep her young, as she would say.

A few minutes later, the tea was ready. Livy was kind enough to let me sit for a few minutes with my tea to process. I didn't drink it but the warmth coming through the cup felt oddly reassuring. It was the first time I had to think since I found Naylet. What if I couldn't get her back? What would that even be like? We had been together so long just the idea of her not being around left a big question mark over my entire future. Now wasn't the time to get caught up in my head; I still had a job to do. Besides, just because Livy couldn't do anything for Naylet doesn't mean she was beyond help, only that we didn't have the answer yet. It was out there somewhere, I just had to find it.

"How long have I been here?" I asked.

"You came in last night. What did this to you anyway?"

I relayed the story for the second time, in full detail. Livy listened patiently for me to finish and when I did, I asked her if she had ever heard of anything like Petra before.

"It sounds like a demon from the Old World, but I've never run across anything like that," she said.

"I think I'm going to get Cearbhall to help out with this one."

She paused at this. "Cearbhall? Are you sure you want to do that? You made a pretty big deal about getting out on your own. Is it that bad?"

"I don't feel like I have much of a choice. There's a lot going on here and I'm going to need some help. Thera's not playing around and the stakes are too high not to," I said. "Besides, this is bigger than me."

"How long has it been since you have seen him?" she asked.

I had to stop and think about it. "We were hunting a Siren who was working her way through free love hippies like they were going out of style. Mid-sixties sometime." I said.

"That's been a while, a lot could've changed since then."

"And a lot can stay the same. I guess I better take a look at Farwell here," I said to change the subject.

I set my tea on the floor and stood up, ignoring my body's protest. Moving hurt, but it's exactly what I needed to do to get the soreness out. Farwell wasn't tucked in, more like tossed on the bed. He was lying face up with a dried, greenish crust on his forehead that covered a bloody gash—a salve Livy uses for injuries. I looked over his body to make sure everything was in place. His limbs seemed to be on straight, that was a good sign. There was some bruising on his face and no doubt more I couldn't see.

"Let's get this show on the road," I said.

I held my hands out over him and concentrated. I could feel the energy moving, slowly at first, funneling through my body, down my arms, out through my hands, and into Farwell. This essence of life, the same power that nourishes my body and lets me get away without eating and sleeping, poured into Farwell, repairing his body. At the same time, the defects and contaminants in his system flowed into mine. A person's hurt doesn't just disappear, it has to be dealt with. In healing him, I took responsibility for it. It wasn't a big deal, my system can recover from it much more efficiently than his can. What's another hour of aching joints when I'm already beat to hell? As the energy grew a light, blue like the sky, began to emanate from my hands and eyes. Farwell groaned and began to stir. As the healing took hold, his eyes opened slowly. Confusion turned into realization, followed by horror. He jumped away from me across the bed and almost made it before the injuries that hadn't been healed yet got the best of him, sending him tumbling onto the floor. I walked around the bed to where he was lying in a battered lump on his back, holding his chest, his legs propped up against the bed.

"I think my ribs are broken," he said.

"It wouldn't surprise me. You weren't wearing a seatbelt when we crashed."

"What are you?" he said giving me a sideways glance.

"Me?" I questioned. "I'm just a guy trying to get by like everybody else."

He didn't look reassured, it was probably the whiskers. I took my human form. Watching the transformation didn't appear to give him any comfort. "If you will hold still for a second, I can fix you right up."

He didn't say anything but gave a quick nod. He didn't really have a choice. I knelt beside him and continued. Again the energy flowed with the blue light.

"It's warm," he said.

I nodded. "That means it's working."

After a minute the bruising and all outward signs of damage had vanished. The energy that had flowed into him now poured over him like a stream flowing around a stone telling me the process was complete.

"How do you feel?" I asked.

"I feel . . ." He took a minute to assess his situation, look of surprise spreading across his face. "Great! Like a teenager. Nothing hurts, not even my elbow and that's bothered me for years." He moved his arm back and forth to test it out.

"I'm sure you have a lot of questions and I'll be happy to answer them but first, it's morning. I don't know what your schedule is, but if you're supposed to be working today maybe you could call in sick while we get this worked out? I don't want them to think you're missing," I said.

He gave me a sideways glance, sizing me up. "All right, and then I get some answers."

"All the answers you want," I agreed.

"Just need my phone. Do you have it?"

I looked at Livy and she shook her head no.

"It's probably still in the truck. I'll help you look," I said.

We made it outside and my heart sank when I saw the truck smashed against the side of Livy's house. I could tell it was done for. The entire front end was pancaked into the stone, the glass busted out. It didn't even sit straight anymore but lurched off to the right, maybe a broken axle. Farwell wasted no time looking in the cab, not thinking twice about the truck, as I surveyed the damage.

My inspection led me to the back of the truck where I found Naylet, still frozen in stone but tipped over, lying face down from the impact. I hopped into the bed and pulled her back into an upright position. She was cold and lifeless as the stone she had become, more so even, because I knew exactly how much life was missing. Even the rocks are infused with Thera's essence, but not Naylet, not now. There was no energy at all coming from her, she was like a void, the same way demons feel.

"I'm going to fix this," I whispered.

The impact from hopping back onto solid ground sent a shock of pain through my muscles, reminding me that I still had a good bit of healing to do. Farwell had found the phone and was doing his best to sound sick to whoever was on the other end.

After a few fake coughs he hung up and turned toward me. "How about those answers?"

"Sure, just let me borrow your phone for a sec, I need to get us a ride."

He held it out without protest. I took it and dialed my home number. From what Thera said, Holt had been taken so he wouldn't answer but it's worth trying. It didn't ring but gave me a busy signal. Probably knocked off the hook from whatever had happened. I dialed the only other number I knew by heart. A voice grunted on the other end.

"Hey, Tico, it's Obie. Is Hank around?"

"Hang on," he said.

The gentle hum of conversation and the clanking of glasses drifted through the phone. It sounded like a busy day at the clubhouse.

After a minute Hank picked up the phone. "Obie, are you okay? We've been looking for you."

"I've been better. Ran into some trouble yesterday. Everything okay?"

"We need you, Hob got hit. You weren't answering your phone so I drove over to your place. It's trashed and there are a couple dead demons laying around," he said. "We've been looking for you all night."

"I'm at Livy's. I need a ride. The truck's broke."

"All right, don't go anywhere. I'm on my way," he said.

I hung up and turned around to Farwell. "Our ride's coming. Let's talk inside."

Farwell sat down in Livy's rocking chair while I went back to the cot. He stared at me intently with a neutral expression, his eyes following my every movement. If I didn't know better, I would think my human form freaked him out more than krasis.

"You alright there, Detective?"

"Fine," he said, continuing to stare.

"You know you're safe here, right? Relax a little."

"I know, if you wanted to hurt me you could have. I'm just coming to terms with things," he said.

"Is there something on my face?"

"Sorry, no, I am looking for a tell. Something to give away that you aren't human. I want to be able to spot your kind."

"And? What do you think? Have you figured out how the secrets to spotting ultra-naturals?" I asked.

He looked down at the tea Livy had made him. "No."

"It's going to be tough, my kind don't survive by sticking out," I said.

He relaxed back into the seat and took a sip of the tea. "What's an ultra-natural?"

"An assortment of people that keep their existence hidden from humans," I said. "You've heard of my kind referred to as 'supernatural' in the movies, but we haven't removed ourselves from the earth the way humans have so that label didn't doesn't fit."

"Why stay hidden? What do you think would happen?"

"I think we would be pursued and treated in ways that would make Nazi Germany look tame in comparison," I said.

"I don't think you understand humans too well," he said with a dismissive chuckle.

"Actually, I used to be human and after a few hundred years of personal experience I think I have a better understanding than you think."

He leaned forward in his chair. "So what happened?"

"I was just a kid. My parents had died of consumption, and I—"

"Wait, what's consumption?" Farwell asked.

"Tuberculosis," Livy said from the kitchen.

"Right, so after they passed I was sent to Bethesda. It's an orphanage down close to Savannah. Mr. Whitefield ran it and, well, we never quite saw eye to eye. I liked to run and swim and he liked the Bible and making sure all of us kids knew it and stuck to it. Whatever means it took, that's what he would do. One night I had snuck out, I did that a lot, and heard some screaming in the woods. I followed the sound and found some people torn to pieces by what I thought was the devil. It looked like a man with grey skin, wings, and these hands with extremely long clawed fingers, a real knuckle dragger. I watched as it started eating the bodies and before I knew it, it spotted me. I must have made some noise or something and got its attention. I wasn't going to wait and see what it wanted so I took off running, but it caught me. I pulled my pocket knife, all the boys had knives back then. I guess I just decided, if that was going to be it for me, I was going to go down fighting. Next thing I know this wolf man comes out of the bushes and jumps on the demon. It only took him maybe fifteen seconds to kill the thing. I'd never seen anything like either one of them. He turns to me and in this deep voice says, 'run home, little boy.' I didn't run though, maybe because the orphanage never really felt like home to me, or maybe I was just afraid to move. I couldn't really tell you. He didn't seem like he was going to hurt me, and I've always been more curious than reasonable. When he started cleaning everything up, the bodies and the demon, I helped. The only thing I had waiting at the orphanage was another punishment anyway. After we were done, he changed into man right before me. I found a new family that night. Eventually I became like him, I was given abilities, and a mission, and I've been doing it ever since."

"But you're not a wolf," he said. "You some kind of weasel or something?"

"My kind are connected to predators. He was joined to the wolf, I'm bound to the otter."

"What mission?" he asked.

"I keep the earth and everything living on it safe, mostly from outside threats. We aren't that different," I said. "I'm kind of like a cop, in my own way."

"But you have been breaking the law," he said.

"Human law, yes, on occasion. I answer to a higher purpose than what your politicians decide should be against the rules. I will tell you I only break them if I need to. It's not something I do for fun."

He considered this but didn't argue, deciding to change the subject instead. "There are multiple cases of otters being spotted at crime scenes. Every few years it happens. Is that you? Are you putting otters in these places for some reason?"

I couldn't help but laugh. "No, those are all one otter, and it's me. Just like I can take the form you saw, that we call krasis, I can take the form of an otter. Cops don't shoot otters."

He nodded. "Okay, what happens to me now?"

"Well, when our ride shows up we'll drop you off at your car."

He looked skeptical. "That's it?"

"That's it. The only thing I ask is that now, and in the future, if you think I might be involved with something you're working on, just steer clear, unless you want to get involved in all this," I said.

"Look, Obie, I don't want you to think I'm not grateful for saving me back there, I am. If I'm being honest, this is all a little too much for me. I just want to go back to things the way they were, the sooner the better," he said.

"I understand. Our ride will be here soon. We will drop you off at your car and you can go back to your normal life if that's what you want to do," I replied.

I was glad to hear him saying this. I really don't want him to be involved, or to try to become some kind of hunter like they show on TV. That's a good way to get killed. If he wanted to pretend this all never happened and bury his head back in the sand, then I would be right there with a shovel to help him dig.

"I need to talk to Livy. Would you mind giving us a minute?"

"Sure, I'll be outside," he said, standing up.

Livy came and sat in the rocking chair. "That's an interesting story, why didn't you tell him the truth?" she said once he had left.

"It was true, mostly. I just left a couple things out," I said.

She crossed her arms with disapproval. "Like that you were the one that summoned that demon and Cearbhall almost killed you for it? Don't you think that's a big thing to leave out?"

"It doesn't really matter to Farwell, besides that as a long time ago and I'm not that person anymore. We can't hold onto the past and we're all entitled to our secrets. What kind of world would we have if we knew everything about each other?"

"Still, sometimes secrets can come back to bite you," she said.

"Speaking of biting, the snake venom—Do you have any ideas about how we can get around that one?" I asked.

"Sure, hun, it's not a problem at all. All I need is some more venom and I can make you a little immunity potion. You don't think Petra would mind giving us a sample, do you?" she asked.

"I'll have to find her and ask," I said with a grin. "How long do you think it would take to make the potion?"

"Less than a day," she said. "Making it's the easy part, the materials are the challenge. I used all the venom in the head I found. You're going to have to get another, more than one would be better."

"So all I have to do is find Petra, get a sample of the venom without getting bitten or killed, and figure out some way to kill her. Maybe instead of a truck I can find a tank to run her over with. That might do it. You know anyone that has a tank?"

"Nobody that would let you borrow it," she said.

"Then I'll just have to do this one step at a time," I said.

CHAPTER • 12

The sound of an engine rumbling up to the house caught my attention. A slamming car door confirmed it was time to go.

"Sounds like my ride is here. Thanks, Livy, you never let me down."

I gave her a hug, grabbed the remains of the snake from the fridge, and went outside. A large pickup was parked beside my truck. It had Morrison Salvage and Repair in cursive on the side. Farwell shot me a glance as soon as I had both feet out the door. He pulled me to the side for a private word.

"What's going on here?"

I had a feeling I knew what the issue was before I asked. "That's our ride, what's the problem?"

"I'm not going anywhere with *him*," he said, giving a disdainful nod in the direction of the truck.

"Is it because he's black?" I knew it wasn't, but it can be fun to watch middle-aged white men squirm when accused of racism.

"What? No, he's a gang member," he said in a hushed tone.

"Not all black folks are in gangs?"

"Will you shut the hell up, it's not like that" he snapped. "He's in a biker gang, the Tortured Occult. That one percent patch he's wearing means something."

I held my hands up, palms out to him in the international symbol of non-aggression. "I'm just messing with you. I know all about the T.O."

"Not an hour ago you told me you didn't break the law if you can help it, and now you're telling me you have gang affiliations? What's the truth?"

"The truth is that the T.O. is a motorcycle club whose main focus is community outreach," I said.

"Bullshit, there are active investigations for drug trafficking, murder, kidnapping, you name it. If they are such a charitable group, how come no one knows about it?" He crossed his arms, defying me to give him an explanation.

"Because they don't serve your community," I said.

"What do you mean 'my community'? They live in my community, and believe me, they aren't providing any services that are legal," he said.

"Farwell, not an hour ago you told me that you didn't want to know these kinds of things and now you're Johnny-on-the-spot with the questions. Have you changed your mind? Are you ready to hear about all the nice things the local werebear motorcycle club does to help other ultra-naturals in the area?"

His face dropped. "Werebear?"

"Well, not all of them, to be fair. They do take outsiders as members sometimes, but the bears formed the group and lead it," I said.

"Let's just get this over with," he said and stomped over to the truck.

Hank, my mechanic and friend, had left the wrecker idling to inspect the damage to my truck. He had done all of the work on it since I bought it and I am sure it hurt him as much as me to see it smashed up. He was down on all fours looking underneath it when I walked up behind him. The back of his kutte displayed Tom C's colors; a pentacle with oak leaves and acorns in its center that formed a snarling bear face. The words Tortured Occult lined the top, with North Georgia underneath in bold lettering.

He stood up and brushed off some dirt that had collected on his vice-president patch. "What happened here?" he asked pointing to Naylet.

I shrugged. "Demon attack. It's not like anything I've seen before. It has these snakes for hair, some nasty poison, and it used some kind of magic to turn her to stone."

"Sounds like Medusa," he said.

"Yeah, if you believe in that kind of thing," I said, running a hand through my hair. "I've never known anyone who has run into anything like that. I thought it was just a story."

He reached out and touched her extended hand. "That mythology had to come from somewhere. Humans aren't that creative," he said. "Are you able to turn her back?"

"I don't know. I am going to try everything I can," I said. "I hope so."

"I hope you get your lady back. That being said, you've done a real number on my lady here," he said, patting the bed of the truck.

"Think you can fix her?"

He paused, thinking it over before nodding. "You can do anything if you throw enough money at it. It's just a question of how much it's going to cost and how long it's going to take."

I didn't like the sound of that. I had a good bit stashed away for a rainy day. I was able to keep that stash by avoiding the rain as much as possible. Most of it had come from what I collected during the gold rush. There were quite a few prospectors that tried to evoke dark magic to strike it rich. It worked well for them until they caught my attention, then it worked well for me. "Maybe it's time to retire the old girl," I said. "Put her out to pasture."

"That would be a shame. It's a great truck," he replied.

"Be sure to tell that to Holt next time you see him. Let me know what it would take to fix and we'll go from there. In the meantime, I'm going to need a ride to the house, and Officer Farwell left his car at Naylet's, if you don't mind." I pointed to Farwell standing by the wrecker, looking like a sourpuss.

"I went by Naylet's earlier looking for you. The yard's all tore up but there's no cars," he said. "Hey, where is Holt anyway? Is he all right?"

"He's missing. I was hoping he was at the house but if you didn't find him then I have no idea. You said something happened with Hob?"

"The factory was attacked, some of his workers were killed. Whoever did it made off with almost all the dust he had. We're calling a council meeting to figure out what we're going to do," he said.

"Give me a couple days. I am going to get Cearbhall to help out. Something is really wrong with all this," I said. "First, we need to get Farwell back to his normal life before he goes into conniptions."

"Whatever you need, Obie. Just do me a favor and get back as soon as you can. A lot of people are worried," he said. "The world's going to shit and we need a plan."

We loaded Naylet onto the back of the wrecker and secured her with some straps and a tarp. Farwell sat between us in the cab, looking more than a little uncomfortable as we left. I was trying to decide to tell him that his cruiser had been stolen, but since it was a short trip I opted to let him discover it organically. The ride was already awkward enough.

Hank pulled the wrecker into the gravel driveway leading to Naylet's house. I didn't want to say it with Farwell there, but exchanging a glance with Hank, I could tell we were thinking the same thing: Petra could still be around. Getting Farwell back to his life in one piece was the first priority, one less person to babysit. When we rounded the corner to the house, the most noticeable thing was the absence of Farwell's Explorer. Hank parked where it should have been and we piled out of the truck. The signs of last night's fight with Petra were clearly visible. Large lines of torn up earth, looking like a bad plow job, ran the length of the yard where I had run over Petra. They stood in stark contrast to the beauty of the rest of the grounds. The brown lines on the lush green lawn were reminiscent of open wounds. Cuts not yet healed into scars.

"No, *NO*," Farwell said in disbelief. "Where the hell is my cruiser?"

"The demon must have taken it," I said. "I think we broke at least one of its wings last night. It must have used your car to get away."

Farwell stood staring where his car should be. "I have to report it. I'm responsible for the car," he said reaching for his phone.

I put my hand on his arm to stop him. "Just hold on a minute. We can find it before anyone misses it."

"I already miss it. Besides, there's a shotgun in it. What if someone gets hurt with it? That's on me," he said.

"That demon doesn't care about your shotgun, trust me. She only took the car to get away. She's running. We will find it and get it back to you," I said. "Give me a day."

He looked uncertain at my request but reluctantly agreed. "One day," he said holding up an index finger.

"Thanks," I said. "Just hang out here for a minute and we'll get you home. I need to take a quick look around."

Hank and I walked out into the yard where I could immediately see the brown spot where Petra's body had come to rest. The large oval of dead grass was easy to pick out against the lush green. Demon blood is toxic, like an oil spill but worse. The ground was effectively dead where she had bled into it, nothing would grow there now. I could fix it, of course, when things calmed down, or it would eventually return to normal on a long enough timeframe. I would add it to the to-do list.

The spot of brown grass stank of rotten eggs and death, but I found it encouraging. If Petra bleeds then I can kill her, even if I had to do it with heavy machinery. I was debating the merits of getting a chainsaw to go *Army of Darkness* on her when Hank pointed out some smaller patches of dead grass leading off toward the shed. I found corresponding claw marks, making it clear she had dragged herself away.

"Looks like she crawled to the shed," I said.

"Krasis?" Hank asked.

I nodded, kicked off my shoes, and pulled the Velcro on my pants before making the change. Hank completed his change a few seconds after me. We were about six feet tall in human form, but in krasis the black bear biker had a good six inches on me. Where I retained my slender physique, Hank's already stocky build widened even further to accommodate the extra bulk. I would be lying if I said I wasn't glad to have some backup.

"Jesus Christ," Farwell said from behind us.

I turned around to see him walking to the back of the wrecker, shaking his head.

"I don't think he likes us," Hank said, watching him go.

"He doesn't know us, how could he not like us," I countered. "Let's get this over with."

Following the claw marks and spots of dead grass up to the shed, we found the door cracked. I took the left door while Hank took the right. I gestured a count and on three we pulled them open, ready to pounce on whatever we found.

Inside we didn't find a demon, but the shed wasn't in the same condition as the last time I saw it. A couple of the tools were scattered on the floor and the bags of soil that had been neatly stacked in the corner had been torn apart. The dirt from them formed into a mound with a depression in the center with what looked like crumpled paper piled up in the bottom of it. It reminded me of how Livy made biscuits, by using a mound of flour as a bowl and mixing directly in it. This wasn't an attempt at the world's largest mud pie, though; gun to my head, it looked like a nest. The dirt in the center had been compacted where Petra had been lying. I could smell the traces of her blood fouling the dirt. The question was, what was all the white stuff?

"Have you seen anything like this before?" I said, taking a step into the shed.

Hank looked in without setting foot inside. "It's new to me."

I took a rake off the wall and dug at the white stuff at the bottom of the mound. I hooked what turned out to be a leg on the rake and raised it to reveal a Petra-shaped skin suit, wings and all. She was injured in our fight, crawled here, and shed her skin. It must be part of her healing process. Regardless, I didn't think she would still be in the area. That's when I noticed the black mass in the bottom of the nest. I dragged the skins away for a better look. Snakes, a whole pile of them, big and black and still. I changed my grip on the rake to drive it down on the snake pile. The impact sent a shockwave through the snakes, but they appeared lifeless. Tossing the skin off the rake, I prodded the snake pile. Still nothing moved, confirming my suspicion.

"What's all that?" Hank asked, keeping a comfortable distance by the door.

"Looks like the snakes from her head. They must have been killed between the lightning and getting run over," I said.

After hearing they were dead, Hank came in for a closer look. "Big sons of bitches."

I scooped one up with the rake for a closer inspection. It was about four feet long and wasn't a whole snake, just a head and body. It was missing the tail, looking like it had been cut in half. That must have been where it had been attached to her head.

"Maybe Livy can make some more antivenom now," I said. "I am going to have to take them."

"As long as they ride in the back," Hank said. "I'd rather not have them in the cab."

Rifling through the soil bags, I found the most intact one and held it out to Hank. "Can you hold this for me?"

He didn't take it. "Why do I got to hold the bag?"

"Come on," I said giving the bag a little shake. "You're not afraid of a few snakes are you, Hank?"

"Not afraid, but I don't want to get bit either," he said.

"Ok, I'll hold the bag and you scoop," I said holding out the rake.

He took it, and once I had the bag open, carefully lifted and deposited the snakes into it, one by one. None of them were alive but I can't blame him for being cautious. Spinning the bag to seal it I walked outside and looked for tracks, footprints specifically. A set led off toward the house.

"What do you think?" Hank asked.

"Looks like she went to the house," I said. "I don't think she's still here. Let me check it out and we'll get out of here."

"Should I come too?" he asked.

"No. If you don't mind keeping an eye on Farwell I would appreciate it," I said. "He's not taking this well."

Hank changed back to human form and went back to the truck while I crossed the yard to the house with the snake bag. Inside it looked the same as before except the food that had been on the counter had been cleaned up and the pictures that were on the table had been put back on the walls. After Petra was healed did she come inside and clean up the mess? That didn't make sense. Some of the pictures were missing and empty frames hung in their place. The bed in the loft looked like it had been slept in since last time I saw it. I climbed up and smelled the sheets. I could make out the stench of demon blood and that same perfume but the bed was neatly made, the way Naylet kept it. I guess after Petra shed, she made herself at home.

CHAPTER · 13

The truck lurched onto a dirt path that didn't deserve to be called a road. It was the back entrance to Morrison Salvage and the Tortured Occult's clubhouse. The clubhouse, garage adjacent, stood in the middle of a large field. Old and wrecked cars surrounded the buildings like a metal horde laying siege to the garage. I thought of my Ford joining the ranks of this ramshackle legion and it just didn't seem right. It had been with me through too much for it to become just another anonymous occupant in this mechanical graveyard. The truth was, it would never make it out here. These vehicles were slowly and surly being parted out, the auto equivalent of decomposing. Once everything of worth was taken, they were crushed and sold for scrap. That would be the fate of my truck. It didn't make sense to repair it and keep driving it. While I would never admit it to him, Holt was right, the truck was outdated.

Hank parked in front of the garage. We got out and he went up to one of the mechanics working under a car on the lift before coming back to talk to us, notepad and pen in hand.

"He's going to take you home. Write down your number and we will give you a call when we find your car," he said, holding out the pad to Farwell.

He took it and jotted down a number. A couple minutes later he was on his way home, finally leaving Hank and I alone so we could speak freely.

"If it's all right I'd like to leave Naylet here, until I can figure out this

Petra situation. She seems to know a lot about me and if she knows where I live, taking Naylet back there wouldn't be safe," I said, not looking away from the junkyard. "I think she took Holt and may be responsible for the attack on Hob as well."

"We'll have to call a vote, but after seeing what I have seen, you have my support," Hank said. "But how could that demon do all that if you almost killed her just yesterday?"

"I don't know, but I am going to find out."

We walked over to the clubhouse, a two-story building that doubled as the premier social destination for all non-humans in North Georgia, and made our way inside through a heavy wood door with a dog door installed on the bottom. This was a safe haven for ultra-naturals and inside there was no need for disguises—in fact they were discouraged. Wearing a false face was unnecessary, unless you had something to hide. We walked through the front door into the changing room. The walls of the rectangular room were lined with coat racks and cubbies. Assorted items of clothing hung on the hooks or lay in piles around the room; shoes of all kinds filled the cubbies.

A pile of dirt in the corner caught my attention. I walked over to see a hole in the floor. Peering inside I saw a pair of yellow, glowing eyes attached to a small shadowy figure that scurried farther down when it spotted me.

"What was that?" I said taking a knee to get a better angle to look down the hole.

"A hunter chased some tommy knockers out of a mine. They are holed up at the clubhouse and refusing to leave until they have a 'safe' place to go. They're burrowing all over the clubhouse, coming up though the floor in random places. They're making a huge mess of things. I need to figure out how to get them out of here before they bring the whole building down," he said.

Knockers were a kind of fairy that lived underground and in mines. They were nice enough but not ideal houseguests. Hank and I added our shoes to an empty spot and shifted to krasis. A door on each end of the room exited to the bar. Hank and I walked out separate doors into the bar. A large room taking up most of the first story that opened to a loft on the second floor with additional tables. The bar ran across the wall underneath the loft, almost the length of the room, with a pool table and dart board on the right with the rest of the room dedicated to tables. Adan, the wererat emissary, was losing a game of billiards to a forest troll. While it wasn't as busy as it would have been at night, there was still an assortment of regulars scattered around the room that would have sent Farwell into a coma. Cotton, an artic werewolf and Torch, one of Hank's sons, both club members, leaned against the balcony, staring down at the festivities. The white of Cotton's fur next the black of Torch's reminded me of a shifter Yin Yang.

"Give me a minute to get everyone together," Hank said.

He walked over and whispered something to Hornet, a grey fox shifter sitting at one of the tables. She wore a kutte with PROSPECT across the back, showing she was applying for membership in the club. She got up and went outside, while Hank stuck his index finger up in the air, waved it around in a circle, and disappeared into the rooms behind the bar reserved for club business. Everyone wearing the T.O.'s colors started migrating into the back rooms. It would have almost been discreet if I didn't know a meeting had been called.

Now I would just have to wait. It shouldn't take more than ten or fifteen minutes; the T.O. was a lot of things but indecisive wasn't one of them. I took a seat at the bar in front of the phone kept behind the counter. Leaning forward, I reached behind the counter feeling around for it. When I located it I picked it up and placed it front of me. Holding the receiver to my ear, I dialed Hob. It rang a few times with no answer. The bartender, a wereraccoon everyone called Tico, gave me a nod from the opposite end of the bar.

"Come on, pick up," I said, listening to the metered ringing.

Tico crossed the bar to greet me. "What'll ya have?"

"The usual," I said, not paying him much attention.

He placed a napkin with an empty cup on top of it on the bar in front of me.

"You don't have to be a smartass," I said, as he moved to help another patron.

After a couple more rings a man with a heavy German accent answered. "*Guten Tag.*"

"Hey, Hob, it's Obie. I heard you had some trouble. Everyone okay?"

"Oh, *nein*, Eric was killed. The attack was late at night. He was working alone and was taken by surprise," he said.

"I'm sorry to hear that," I said. "I'm coming over in a couple days. We're going to make this right."

"Obie, the dust was taken," he said not bothering to hide the concern in his voice. "We will have serious trouble stopping anyone with that much power."

"I'm not worried about the dust. I'm just glad you're okay. Stay safe and I'll be over soon," I said.

"Mind if I join you?" a yapping voice said from my left.

I turned to see the eyes and ears of a coyote peering over the edge of the chair next to me.

"Listen I got to go," I said into the phone.

"Thanks, Obie. Come see me soon," Hob said.

"I promise I will."

"Hambone, what a surprise," I said, hanging up the phone, not feeling even the slightest bit of astonishment. I gestured toward an empty chair beside me for him to have a seat.

He slid the chair back from the bar a little and a moment later the very overweight kobold was doing his best to heave himself into the seat. After a short struggle, that I wasn't sure he was going to win, he sat beside me, panting with his tongue hanging out of the side of his mouth. He was about three feet tall and looked like a mix between a very short fat man and a coyote. American kobolds all resembled coyotes, but where other shifters could turn into humans, kobolds only had two forms: coyote and krasis. As a result, they kept their distance from humans, and since they don't blend in very well, that was probably for the best.

After a couple minutes to catch his breath he said, "Just mingling with my constituents. There's an election coming up you know. Competition looks to be tough this year. The fairies got some looker showboating around like she's already won. They just want to get one of their own elected, and I tell you, I don't know why. I've always done right by them, the ungrateful flower bugs. That's beside the point, I'm glad I caught you."

Here it comes . . . "What do you want, Hambone?"

"Your support, of course. If I had the backing of a Keeper, I don't see how I could lose," he said, giving me a hopeful look.

"I don't really get involved in politics," I said.

"Oh, I know, I know. I'm not asking for much, just your permission to let people know you support me, and if anyone asks you, just tell them that you think I'm the best candidate. Oh, I almost forgot, if you could wear this button while you're at the clubhouse it would be really helpful." He slid a neon yellow button across the bar that said HAMBONE FOR THE PEOPLE in big black letters.

I put the button into my pocket. "I'll think about it."

"Please do, Obie. We all have to work together, you know. There was one other thing I wanted to talk to you about. I couldn't help but overhear you say you weren't worried about the dust."

I knew there had to be more to it. "So?"

"Well, surely you understand how important it is to keep the dust flowing," he said, making a swooshing motion with his hands. "We would be thrust into chaos without it, hunted like dogs. It's in everyone's best interest that we find it and find it fast."

"Is it in everyone's interest or is it in your interest?" I asked.

"Obie, I am a servant of the people, that's all. I am just trying to keep everyone safe. I'm just asking you to keep the greater good in mind. You're one of our top producers, but even at your best you can't replace all that dust quickly enough. There's a lot of families in need, not just of food and shelter but peace of mind most of all."

I turned to look at him directly. "You don't think I know what's at stake here?"

"Of course you do. I'm just voicing my concern about how nonchalant you are about the dust being stolen," he said. "It hasn't even been announced yet. If we move quickly we might be able to recover it before it's missed, that's all. We need to avoid a panic."

Otis, Hank's father and president of the Tortured Occult, came out of the back room and waved me over. He was as large and imposing as Hank in krasis. They looked almost identical, except Otis was a little squarer around the shoulders and had grey on his chin. He had been around a long time and was starting to show his age.

"Maybe we shouldn't be talking about it at the bar, if it's such a big deal," I said. "Listen, I'm working on it. That's all I can tell you right now."

I didn't wait for him to excuse me or even to see his reaction. Hambone seems to forget sometimes that I don't work for him; I only answer to Thera. I crossed the room to where Otis was waiting.

"Well?" I asked.

He raised his hands, palms facing me, like he was already telling me to calm down. I knew it wasn't good news. "The vote passed but you can't keep Naylet in the clubhouse. You will have to hide her outside in the junkyard. There are a few vans out there that you can put her in. We will keep an eye on her for a few days until you can make other arrangements."

"Outside? Why can't I put her in one of the rooms in the back? Petra isn't going to bust into the clubhouse to get her." I looked around the room to see many other people absorbed in their own lives, unaware and unconcerned with my situation. "A van isn't going to offer any protection."

"It was discussed and that's what was agreed to. This is the best I can do, take it or leave it," he said.

"Sure, sorry, Otis. It's been a rough couple days. I appreciate the help."

"No problem. I'll have Hank help you find a safe hideaway," he said.

Hank came out a few minutes later. We went back into the changing room and made the shift to human form before going to look around the junkyard. Hank pointed out a couple potential hiding places and I picked an old Ford Econoline van on blocks close to the clubhouse. All its glass was intact and the doors still closed and locked although the key was long gone. That didn't bother me. If it was a pain for me to get her out, it would be a pain for Petra as well. I found a wrecked hood and bent it so it would fit in the van in front of Naylet to prevent anyone from seeing her from the windows. Once she was in place we locked the doors and closed it up.

"I need one more favor," I said. "I need some transportation until I can arrange something. You still have that loaner?"

"Yeah, no problem. I'll grab the keys while you get those snakes out of my truck. They give me the heebie jeebies."

CHAPTER • 14

The loaner wasn't a nice truck. Anything that identified it as a specific brand had rusted or been knocked off years ago. It was brown, but I couldn't tell how much of it was rust and how much was paint. Despite its appearance it ran like new. Hank was a master of his craft and I knew any vehicle he got his hands on would be mechanically solid. It took a little over five hours to get to Jekyll, including stopping for gas.

I had been to the island a few times over the years, so I did a lap around the island to get my bearings. I hadn't been here in a long time and it had changed a lot. At the same time, it seemed like the same old place. No longer in the prime of the hunting club days, when the rich Yankees migrated for the winter, now it resembled a quaint seaside community. A small shopping mall on the east side of the island was new. What was left of the original buildings, some looking the worse for wear, took up most of the developed area on the south side of the island. A golf course, some hotels, and a few rows of ranch style houses made up the difference. That's not to say that the island was crowded, far from it. Large portions of the island were left undeveloped on principle. It's my kind of place.

A part of me hoped to see Cearbhall walking down the street but I wasn't that lucky. It would take some work to find him, but I knew where to start. I parked in the historical district and after a few minutes of walking found a booklet with a map of the island that helped refresh my memory. I found what I was looking for just north of Crane Cottage. An oak tree somewhere around 375 years old. The branches stretched out, reaching all the way into the ground and back up again with limbs large enough to be trees in their own right if they hadn't been attached. Resurrection fern sat atop the uppermost branches, brown and shriveled waiting for rain to be restored to its lush green, accompanied by Spanish moss wafting lazily in the sea breeze.

I couldn't help but smile when I saw it. The tree had grown noticeably since the last time I was here but I recognized it immediately. I ran my fingers over the branches, appreciating the twists and bumps of the limbs. It's the imperfections that make it beautiful. Many of the lower branches stretched out around chest height and one in particular was flat enough on top to make a seat. I hopped up, leaving my legs dangling, and was sent back to my childhood in the orphanage. Every so often I would run off into the woods to explore on my own. I would get the speech of how it wasn't safe, receive a personalized sermon on the danger my everlasting soul was in, and then be beaten with a belt, or a paddle, or whatever was handy, for my transgressions. It had been worth it. My time among the trees is one of my oldest and most treasured memories.

"It's good to see you again, my friend. It's been too long," I said.

There was no response. That didn't bother me. In life you can't expect everyone to operate at your pace. Sometimes you have to sit and wait for them to catch up and, if you're lucky, those ahead of you will help you along.

"How have you been? It looks like you are doing well. You have gotten a lot wider since I saw you last. Your branches are really sturdy. It's really beautiful," I said.

"You always were a sweet talker," said a voice that seemed to manifest from inside the trunk.

The tree spirit manifested as a curvy woman with light brown skin with grey stripes reminiscent of a tiger or zebra, but less structured. Her hair was green and brown reaching almost to her knees, like the fern and moss on her branches.

"Let me have a look at you," she said, walking over to me.

I couldn't help but grin at seeing her. She looked more mature since I had seen her last. I hopped down off the limb and held out my hands, putting myself on display.

"No, Obie, I want to see the real you," she said.

"I thought what's inside is what matters," I replied.

She tilted her head with an expression suggesting she didn't approve. "What's the point of having something beautiful inside if you don't let it out?"

It wasn't the kind of place I was comfortable shifting. A public area in the middle of the day. I was only about forty feet off the sidewalk, with some bushes and branches between me and one of the largest buildings on the island. Anyone that happened by or looked out the window would get an eyeful of something that could make the front page of a tabloid. I gave the area a once over. There were a few people around but no one was too close or looking in my direction. I stepped closer to the trunk and shifted to krasis.

"Wonderful, you haven't changed a bit," she said, eyeballing me up and down.

I didn't want to give the impression I was uncomfortable by changing back right away. The truth is I enjoyed being in krasis; I would do it all the time if I could. Maybe that's why I liked hanging out at the clubhouse, no need for pretense. In the middle of the day, out in the open, is a different story. Secrets must be kept and cameras are everywhere now. The risk of being recorded is just too great for this kind of thing. I held this form for a couple minutes, without feeling particularly comfortable, before making the change back to human.

"I see you updated your pants," she said as I fastened the Velcro. "These are much better. The buttons weren't flattering."

"I wish I had stuck to the kilt," I said, my heart sinking into my feet. There were so many things I could have been known for in the past three hundred years, but the only thing anyone seems to remember are some ugly pants.

"We all do, Obie," she replied, not bothering to hide her smirk.

"So listen, I was hoping you could help me out. I need to find Cearbhall. Last I heard he was on the island, but we haven't kept in touch. Any idea where he is running these days?" I asked, glad to be changing the subject.

"He's still around, but he hasn't come by to visit in a while. I heard through the rustle and the roots that he fishes a lot on the pier. You might find him there. He made friends with some dogs he runs with from time to time, nothing serious, mind you, just some local pets longing for pack life. The last I heard he was spending a lot of nights by the old cemetery. There's been some shady characters sneaking around up there, at least that's what they say," she said. "Maybe he is keeping an eye on them."

"Sounds like he is staying busy," I replied, not thinking much about the "shady characters" comment. "Shady" to a plant could mean a vegetarian pulling carrots from the garden or the grounds keepers trimming the trees. "Thanks for your help. I'll come see you again soon, okay?"

"Sure, Obie, please do, and tell Cearbhall to come see me too," she said.

I promised that I would, and made my way back to the truck. I sat in the truck, pondering my next move. My best chance to run into him would be on the pier, assuming he didn't have a more private spot he liked to fish at. I could have a stakeout at the pier and move over to the cemetery tonight if he didn't show up.

I drove over and parked in a largely vacant lot by the Jekyll Fishing Center. The pier, in the shape of an anchor, was cast out into the water as if its sole purpose was to keep the island from floating away. I walked out onto the pier under the pretense of a casual stroll. People were fishing from all over it, but Cearbhall wasn't among them. It was only a few hours before sundown and there were worse places to wait. At least here I'd have a nice ocean breeze and would get to see the sunset over the water. I went back to the truck and moved it to a position to give me a good view of the pier and the sunset, and waited. I didn't have a book and the fishing center was really only good for one visit. That left me with almost three hours with nothing to do but think. I thought about Holt and wondered what Petra could be doing to him. The sooner I could find him, the better, but I needed help. He would have to hold on until Cearbhall and I could make it back.

I thought about Cearbhall, and what I would say to him when I found him. We hadn't parted on the best terms the last time I saw him. I was more principled back then, hung up on right and wrong. Cearbhall operates in a grey area that I understand much better now. We'd been bound to have it out at some point, but I never thought it would result in us going our separate ways. I decided it would be best not to bring up the past, unless I had to. We needed to focus on the future, and nothing positive would come from reincarnating old arguments.

When I had run out of everything else, my thoughts turned to Naylet. Before I let myself get too far into it I decided it was a perfect time to check out the fishing center. I got out of the truck and walked inside. Despite having a grandiose name, the fishing center was just a small building that rented rods and sold bait, food, and tourist stuff. The distraction didn't last long and by the time I had done two laps around the small store it wasn't nearly as late as I had hoped. Going back to the truck, I gave the pier one more look before climbing in and cranking the engine. The graveyard wasn't far away, but I decided to drive the long way around the island and soak up the scenery.

The sun had just gone down when I parked in front of Horton House, or what was left of it. The building had been a large rectangle, like an enormous Lego block long before Lego was a thing. Now, it was little more than a shell of a building. The walls were made of tabby, a mixture of sand, lime, oyster shell, and water used in costal construction in days past. They were partially degraded from time and weather, not to mention assholes scratching their initials or attempts at witticisms into them. Each side of the building had nine windows and a door in the center. The balcony was gone, hell: everything was gone. It used to be a real nice place. I crossed the road, walking to a tiny graveyard with a knee-high brick wall marking its boundaries. I stood in the entry looking at the graves and sniffed the air—nothing. The gravel path in front ran beside the road through the trees. I decided to take a stroll and see if I could pick up Cearbhall's scent. After walking for about ten minutes and coming up with nothing, I turned around and headed back.

A faint yellow light coming from Horton House caught my attention. It was probably just someone on their phone having a look around. From outside, it looked like someone waving around a weak flashlight. I crossed the road for a closer look. It was probably nothing, but I had nothing else going on. This whole trip was turning into a giant waste of time. I rounded the corner of the empty doorway into the main room to find a normal looking guy in jeans and a black tee shirt. A backpack was slung over one shoulder. He had his back to me and was looking up at the walls. When he turned to the side I saw he didn't have a phone, it was a pendant on a necklace he wore emitting the yellow light. I couldn't tell what the design was, but it formed a circle. He held it up to one eye and looked through it, scanning the walls meticulously. He must have heard me come in. He turned in my direction and when he saw me his head jerked back like he had been hit in the face. He jerked the pendant away and rubbed his eye with the heel of his hand.

That was a little strange, I'll admit, but by itself wasn't something I needed to get involved with. Some people use magic; it's what they do with it that's important. Magic alone wasn't a problem. "Sorry to give you a start there, thought you were someone else."

"Hey, no problem," he said. When I turned to leave he followed up with, "Who were you looking for? Maybe I could help you look?"

I heard the scuff of a shoe from behind the wall to my right. Someone else was in the house with him.

"No thanks," I said.

Halfway to the truck I was hit in the back so hard I almost didn't register the gunshot. I collapsed to the ground as the pain surged through my back and out into my limbs. It took a second for my mind to get up to speed on the fact I had been shot. My back was burning intensely and a warm wet feeling started running down my back and legs. This was bad and I knew I had to get out of here. I ran for cover behind the truck, at least I tried to; I couldn't stand up. I looked back to see my shorts were saturated with blood and clinging to my legs. I tried to move them but they weren't responding, being dragged lifelessly behind me as I crawled. The man with the looking glass, followed by a punk looking chick with piercings and pink hair, were advancing on me, guns drawn. He was again looking through the monocle and that must be how he saw me. There's no way he could make a shot like that without some kind of night vision helping him out.

"The rumors are true," he said walking up to me.

"What is it?" the woman asked, keeping her gun on me. She had a silver dagger drawn in the hand supporting the gun.

I had unwittingly stumbled on a pair of hunters. People who supply the black market with dust by tracking down and killing ultra-naturals. There was no way I was going to get away. The bleeding had stopped, the healing was underway with a tingling already returning to my toes, but all this guy had to do was keep popping rounds into me, assuming they didn't try to kill me outright. I only had one chance to make a move before they figured it out.

"Let me see," the woman said.

Her companion held the monocle to her eye so she didn't have to free a hand from her weaponry. "We hit the jackpot, look how he glows. Hey, he looks like he's healing up pretty fast, we should get him secured quick."

"Let's do a couple more, just to be safe," the man said before firing three more rounds into my chest.

The impact slammed into me as the bullets tore through my body. I fell back, not even able to scream, only gasping as my lungs filled with blood. They actually laughed at seeing my body fail. That's when I saw it behind him, a single eye glowing yellow, bounding up and down in a charge. The world disappeared into a tunnel as distant gun fire and screaming echoed in my ears. Then all was quiet.

CHAPTER • 15

I woke up face down in a bathtub, the cold porcelain chilling my cheeks. It felt good, but took a second for my mind to come around to what had happened. Getting shot once wasn't one of my favorite things, let alone four times. I was glad to have been unconscious for the healing process—you miss a lot of pain when you're unconscious, small blessings. I wasn't sure where I was in the healing process. I didn't have any pain but I hadn't moved yet either. I took a minute to move every piece of my body, just a little wiggle, starting with my fingers and toes, moving through my arms and into my back. Nothing hurt, so I pulled myself into a seated position in the tub. I was still wearing my clothes and they, along with the white porcelain of the tub, were covered with blood, some pooled and dried into a rusty brown around the edges. A few pieces of mushroomed metal, the bullets expelled by my body during the healing process, rested in the blood.

Through the open door of the bathroom I could see a small studio apartment. A kitchen was directly beside the bathroom, with a bed and a couple of chairs facing a TV against the far wall. A playground and palms illuminated by streetlights were visible through the sliding glass door. Some folded clothes had been placed on top of a towel on the toilet. A note covered the pile that read: *Out, clean up the blood*. It was a familiar scribble; I could recognize Cearbhall's handwriting anywhere.

My skin had a crusty feeling as I climbed out of the tub for a quick look around. I was alone, as I expected. I wish Cearbhall had waited around for me to wake up, but at least now I had found him, even if I had to wait for him to get back. I returned to the bathroom for a shower and got in with my clothes on. I stuck my fingers through the holes in my shirt where the bullets penetrated. I'm going to have to go shopping. I pulled the shirt off and rinsed as much of the blood out of it as I could. I was throwing it out but like so many things in my life, bloody bullet-ridden clothes tended to attract attention, even in the garbage. After rinsing my clothes, I started on my body, working on the tub last. When I had finished, and was double-checking the tub to make sure I didn't miss anything, I heard the door open.

"Hurry up in there. I need to get cleaned up," Cearbhall shouted from the other room. "We've got work to do."

"Good to see you, Obie, glad you're okay, Obie, it's been too long, Obie, we should catch up," I mumbled to myself as I turned off the water. I pulled open the curtain, grabbed my soggy clothes out of the tub, and stepped out. "All yours."

He stepped around the corner in human form wearing a red shirt and a black leather kilt. The shirt looked wet in places, and it wasn't until I smelled the iron that I realized it was blood. He wasn't wearing his eye patch, not something I was used to seeing. The skin healed over the eye socket gave his face a hollow look, like a painting with a blank spot in the canvas.

"Lose your eye patch?" I asked, grabbing the towel from under the clothes.

"Quit wearing it actually," he said, stepping past me into the shower. "It got hard to keep up with and I just asked myself one day who I was covering up for. I don't care who sees it, and I don't care what anyone thinks about it, so why bother?"

"Sure. I'm just not used to it, that's all," I said. I dropped my wet clothes in the sink and began wringing the water out of them. "Have you heard from Thera lately?"

"Not in a while. She doesn't talk to me much anymore. I kinda just do my own thing now," he said.

"What is your thing exactly? Does it have something to do with the couple I met at Horton House?" I asked.

"Yeah," he chuckled, stepping inside the shower. "I sent all the ultras off the island and started a rumor that Bigfoot is wandering around. Hunters come and I make them see the error of their ways. The gators are fat and happy, even if the hunters aren't."

Having wrung out all the water I could, I put my clothes in the trash and put on what Cearbhall had left out for me. They were loose but got the job done. "What do you do with all their stuff?"

He swished the curtain open and stepped out of the shower naked. "There's a little chop shop on the mainland that takes the cars," he said, grabbing a towel and drying off. "I know a guy that will buy all the guns he can get. Not sure if he collects them or sells them. Whatever he does with them, having the serial numbers scratched off doesn't bother him. Everything else gets cleaned up and donated to Goodwill. You wouldn't believe the tax deductions I'm getting." He dropped the towel and went into the kitchen. "Things like this on the other hand," he held up the pendant recovered from the man who shot me in the back. "Haven't decided what to do with them yet, just keep them in the junk drawer for now." He slid open a drawer and added the item to a pile of trinkets.

"Quite a collection," I said.

He contemplated the pile before slamming the drawer shut. "Yeah, I've been doing this a while. Let me get dressed and we'll go."

"Where are we going?"

"A little side project," he said grabbing some clothes out of the closet. "Last week I was out for a run with a few strays in the area. It was the middle of the night and we had come out of the woods beside the road, just jogging, minding our own business. Out of nowhere this big car swerved off the road to hit us. It wasn't an accident, he wasn't drunk, just some guy wanting to hurt something."

"Did he hit anyone?"

"Just me. It took me a few days to track him down but I found him," he said.

"So, what, you want to kill this guy or something?"

Revenge killings by Keepers aren't by the book, but they have been known to happen. It would be a little naïve to think a people whose existence centers around violence don't have the tools within easy reach at all times.

"I'm not going to kill him. He's not going to get off that easy, and besides, he shouldn't even be home right now. This douche likes his toys but if he can't be responsible with them then I will take them away in the most painful way possible," he said. "I hired some gremlins to make sure he has car problems for the rest of his life. Of course, I want to get the first shot in myself. Sugar in the gas tank, drain the oil, you get the idea."

"You take up your free time with vandalism now? This is what retirement looks like," I said, crossing my arms.

"Who said I was retired?" he said.

"What do you call this then?" I asked.

"Justice," he replied. "This guy deserves it."

"No doubt, but it's going to have to wait." I looked him in the eye. "I came here for something more important."

"The guy ran me over, tried to kill me and others just for the joy of it. Making him pay is a top priority," he said.

"Something's wrong with Thera. Holt was taken and I think he is being used to get to her. She came to me yesterday and said she was being cut off from us. I don't know how exactly. Hob's place was attacked, a bunch of dust was stolen. I'm not sure what's going on."

"Who's Holt?" he asked.

"My apprentice. He was working with Cedric before, well, you know."

"Your first apprentice. Well aren't you something?"

I couldn't tell if he was mocking me or not, but I had a feeling he was.

"Can you not? There are more important things going on right now." I was afraid my visit would bring up some old hurts on both sides, looked like I was right.

"Fine. So what did she say exactly?" he asked.

I relayed the encounter on Stone Mountain. "I think I know what's doing it," I said when I had finished. "Is the truck outside? I want to show you something."

"It's out front."

He led me outside to where my truck had been parked. We were surrounded by what looked like single story seaside condominiums. The area was well maintained, with palm trees planted in strategic locations around the property. My truck was parked across the street beside the dumpster.

"Take a look at that," I said, pointing to the bag in the back.

He looked a little puzzled but reached over and started opening it. "What is it?"

I didn't answer, figuring it would explain itself once he got it open. When the knot was undone he recoiled a bit at the stench coming out of the bag. I could smell it from the other side of the truck as well. He rolled the bag so as not to get his hands dirty as he explored to find out what the source was.

"That's what I wanted to talk to you about. I think that's what's doing this," I replied.

When the snake head met the light his face fell into a blank expression. He stood still, not saying anything for a moment. Then, not worrying about touching the rotting head anymore, he grabbed it. He starred at it for a few seconds before squeezing it. Gasses bubbled from its nostrils and juices ran from the stump where it had previously been attached. The skull cracked and collapsed under the pressure. His face had changed from blankness to hate, lips curled in a snarl and eye burning into the carrion. When it was as crushed as he could make it, he threw it into the dumpster. It ricocheted off the wall with a splat, and he spit on the ground after it disappeared inside.

"I've fought these demons before. They're bad for sure, but they aren't strong enough to mess with Thera," he said, not looking away from the dumpster. "What makes you think this is the demon causing problems?"

"She had a grimoire, and Hob was attacked. Someone stole all the dust he had, Holt was taken, and now Thera is being attacked directly. I suppose the timing could be a coincidence, but I doubt it."

He thought this over for a few seconds. "The question is how did this 'Petra' know how to find Hob? These demons can turn people to stone, like in the old myths, but they kind of take the memories the people they've turned. They know what those people knew. We need to find who she turned. Then we will know what kind of trouble we can expect. She shouldn't have been able to turn Holt. She got her hands on someone that knows you, when we find out who we will know how much trouble we are in."

I looked at the ground and shuffled my feet. "Actually, it was Naylet."

He stood frozen, seeming to process the news before responding. "Well that's unfortunate."

"My cupita was turned to stone and all you can say is 'that's unfortunate'?"

"We have bigger problems than your love life," he said. "We've got to get back now. You check with Hob to see what he can tell us and I'll check on Livy. We'll meet back at your place."

CHAPTER • 16

The sun was just coming up when I pulled the truck onto the dirt road that ran between the fields to the main house. I drove slowly, not because of the condition of the road but because they didn't know this truck, and I wasn't expected. I came looking to prevent trouble, not start it. I didn't really like showing up unannounced but, everything considered, it would be okay. Stopping short of the house, I rolled down the window, looked out into the cornfield, and waited. After a minute, I was pretty sure someone was there. No scent or sound hinted at a presence in the corn but I had a prickly feeling at the base of my neck like I was being watched.

"I need to see Hob, it's important. Where can I find him?" I asked the stalks.

A figure seemed to materialize out of the corn, taking a couple steps out of the field. It looked to be more plant than man: skin that looked dry, the tan color of old husks, with yellow hair fading into brown like corn silk. The face was smooth and looked like a tree that has had the bark scraped off, with two slits where eyes should be but lacking a nose or mouth. A large hound with similar characteristics walked out beside him. These were known as corn demons, although they weren't demons like Petra. They came from another place that I am told is completely plant, but I'd never seen it. A strange but pleasant race, they don't talk much, not having a mouth, but more importantly, they don't cause problems. Hob brought them from Germany to help with the farm. The plant man raised a finger pointing to the barn opposite the house. I gave him a wave and drove over. The two disappeared back into the field in the rearview.

The barn door was open, light spilling out into a picturesque scene of country nightlife. I parked in the light, no doubt spoiling the scene but making my presence known at the same time. Inside Hob was elbows deep in a tractor. He stood up and walked toward the truck when he saw me, wiping the oil off his hands with a rag.

"Who is this stranger that shows up at my door? It can't be my old friend Obie, ja," he said when I got out of the truck.

"Sorry, Hob, I would have stopped by sooner but I've had a lot of trouble over the past couple days," I said. "I'm glad I didn't wake you."

"I am out of bed at four-thirty every morning, working by five. You have missed all the excitement," he said, rubbing the grease from his fingers.

"So, what happened?" I asked.

"As I have said on the phone, Eric was killed. He was finishing up the processing for the day when we were attacked by many demons. It was over only a few seconds after it started. Some of the corn demons responded but they were overwhelmed." He smiled, putting an arm around my shoulder. "What is it the children do, showing and telling? Come, I will show you the damage and you can then tell me about your trouble."

We hopped into the truck and headed to the barn on the back of the property behind the fields, the processing center for his operation.

I didn't feel like going into all the details, so I kept it short and sweet, "There's a demon that . . . well . . . it's new to me. Closest as I can tell it is like the old Gorgon myth. Snakes on its head, wings, some nasty poison."

"It turns people to the stone with the glowing yellow eyes and black snakes on the head?" he asked, placing his hands on his head and waving his fingers in a decent Petra impression.

I nodded as I parked in front of the barn. "Yeah, pretty much exactly. Cearbhall said they take people's memories?"

"Not exactly," he said. "They don't take the memories, they take the people, the entire life, past and future."

"What does that mean, how do they take a future?"

"As far as I can tell, this demon is a kind of parasite. It takes in the memories, ja, but it also prolongs its own life from the life force of the victim. Do you know of children going missing? The little babies?" he asked.

"Actually, for the past year, human infants have been disappearing. Naylet had me look into the most recent case a couple days ago."

"Come, let me show you something," he said, getting out of the truck.

I got out as Hob slid the door of the barn open. It looked the same as it did a few days ago except the back door had been busted in. It was boarded up as a temporary fix. There was broken wood on the ground and claw marks on some of the posts. In the center of the floor a dried grey pool of ogre blood marked the spot where Eric had fallen, surrounded by darker pools of demon blood. Hopefully, he took a few with him.

"They came in through the back," he said, holding a hand out toward the smashed up door. "It seems at least six demons attacked together but the gorgon wasn't with them. Eric never stood a chance. They carried off the dust that was ready to go out, ten crates in all. I am told they were mainly hounds and athols. They were led by an imp with a bad leg. Once they secured the dust the athol flew off with the imp, leaving the hounds to keep us busy."

He led me to an industrial style freezer and opened the door. I was hit with a blast of cold much stronger than I expected. Walking inside was like stepping into a blizzard. Multiple fans moved the frigid air so forcefully it seemed to cut straight to my bones. Demons hung upside down, including the hound and a half I had brought him a few days before. They were covered with ice and frost.

"These are the demons we were able to kill from the attack," Hob said, pointing to a row of three hounds and one athol. The athol looked a lot like an imp but was man sized with wings instead of a second set of arms. People called them flying monkeys because they looked so much like winged gorillas with crazy eyes and big teeth. "This demon isn't working alone. It is organized and with that much pixie dust it will be very dangerous."

He was right about that. Ten crates were enough to do just about anything. Petra had to have a plan for it, and that plan seemed to involve Holt.

"They knew where to find you because of Naylet? Because Petra knows everything she knows," I asked.

"This Petra doesn't know what Naylet knew, she is Naylet. At least a part of her is," he said.

"So Naylet is still alive then?"

"No, Obie, she was sucked up," he said. "She may still exist, but only as part of Petra."

"Right, but they could be separated? You're the one that says magic can do anything. I would just have to restore Naylet's body and put her mind back into it. What would I have to do to do that?"

"The body you can do. If you kill the demon and put its blood on one who was turned, they will be restored, but they will not be the same person. I've seen it before," he said. "You should find another way."

"When you say not the same person?" I questioned.

"It's like they have amnesia, there is nothing in them," he said. "I would help you with anything, except for this. I will have no part of it."

That seemed easy enough. I just had to kill Petra, which I had to do anyway. "That shouldn't be a problem."

"Oh no, but the problem will come later. The blood brings the darkness. The few that have been restored all became murderers and such," he said. "You should not use the blood. Good things do not come from it."

That wasn't reassuring. It's possible that if the body was restored without the mind that was what happened. If the person's mind was restored they couldn't be corrupted like that. They would know who they were and have the same values as before. That was the key for successfully restoring Naylet.

"Ok, what about getting her mind back. Is there a trick to that?" I asked.

"As far as I know it can't be done."

A corn demon appeared in the door to the barn. It raised a hand to its head, its long leafy fingers positioned from its ear to where its mouth would be if it had one. Then it pointed in my direction.

"You have a call," Hob said.

We drove to the main house where I found a rotary phone with a fifteen foot cord off the hook. "This is Obie," I said, pressing the phone to my ear.

"Glad I found you," Hank said. "We found the car. It's parked in the Belleview apartment complex. I'm looking at it right now."

"That sounds familiar." I reached in my pocket and pulled out the letter from Steve's wife I had found on the counter at Steve's house. She wrote her address as 1703 Belleview. "Let me guess, it's in front of building seventeen?" I asked.

"Yeah, how'd you know?"

"I have to make a stop by my house to get Cearbhall and then we will be on the way. Just hang tight and keep an eye on things," I said. "We'll handle it together when we get there."

CHAPTER · 17

"Looks like someone's here," I said to myself, spotting a Subaru in the driveway beside Holt's Honda. I pulled the truck in line and got out. Halfway up the steps, I noticed the door was cracked. I stopped before going inside and listened. I could hear a motor running somewhere inside but nothing else. No movement or footsteps. If Cearbhall was inside he was staying perfectly still. Then again, maybe there were still some demons hanging around. Petra seemed to have a lot of friends from what Hob said.

I made the change to krasis and pushed the door open with my foot. Stepping inside, I found the living room trashed. The couch was the only thing in the right place. Everything else had been tipped over, tossed, or lost. That's when I smelled it, demon stink. Not fresh stink either, the kind of stink after they have been dead for a couple days, like the snakes outside in the truck. No doubt if any live demons were still around they already knew I was here, so there was no point in being quiet.

"Cearbhall, you here?" I called.

There was no response, no movement, no sounds at all except the strained hum of the motor coming from the kitchen. I followed it to find the kitchen in the same state of disrepair as the living room. The refrigerator had been tipped and was leaning against the counter with the door open. Luckily there wasn't anything in it but some ketchup and a bottle of pickles, both of which had been dumped out on the floor. Its motor strained impotently, trying to maintain the proper temperature. Broken dishes crunched and cut my feet as I crossed to the fridge. I leaned forward over the busted condiments grabbing the shelf in the fridge door. I pulled it up to close it and revealed a hell hound on the floor behind it. Startled, I let go of the door and fell back into the rubble. The door swung open, hitting the beast in the head. From my new vantage point on the floor I could see that the hound hadn't moved. I got up and stepped forward gingerly, peering under the door.

The demon was clearly dead. Its body had claw marks but Holt had finished it off by ripping its throat out. I reoriented the fridge and closed the door, muffling the noise. Stepping over the hound, I continued my search of the kitchen. The only thing intact I could see was the sink of dirty dishes Holt had still not bothered to clean. I wondered if Petra knew they were a sore spot from Naylet's memories and left them on purpose, or just missed them somehow. I did my best to step around the chairs and broken flatware littering the kitchen floor as I moved to the hallway leading back to Holt's room. It was relatively clear, as there had been nothing in it to begin with. I moved slowly, on guard, listening for anything.

I could smell the sweet copper of Keeper blood from the hallway. I took a breath to prepare and moved into the room. I half expected to find him in his chair facing the TV like I had seen him many times before. A couple steps in and I could see the writing on the wall. Scrawled in Holt's blood was written: RETURN HER. I touched the H and pressed it between my finger and thumb. It was dry.

I was about to head to my room when I heard footsteps coming up the front steps and inside. I moved as quickly and quietly as I could around the random debris, stopping at the corner just out of sight of my mystery guest. I popped out, intending to use the element of surprise, but instead found a fist speeding toward my face. Too late to block, my only recourse was to move with the fist to reduce its impact. As it contacted, I used the momentum of the spin to whip my tail toward the intruder and felt it impact. A second later a stabbing pain shot through my tail. I looked back to see Cearbhall with my tail in his mouth. He was in krasis, his large wolf jaws easily wrapped around my tail.

"How did you beat me here?" I asked.

He spit my tail out. "I guess you still drive like an old lady. Besides, I know some shortcuts."

Bound to the gray wolf, he was as imposing as I remember. I had forgotten how intense his stare was in krasis, missing an eye seemed to amplify its intensity more than two-fold. He'd sustained that injury long before me and had always refused to talk about it. I couldn't help but wonder, why couldn't I have been joined to an animal with a little more street cred? Otters just don't demand respect the same way some other predators do. Even Holt, bound with the Doberman, while not traditional, demanded a certain respect.

Cearbhall stretched and rubbed his jaw. I couldn't help but feel a little proud that the strike had bothered him that much—he wasn't one to acknowledge pain openly. "I followed a demon trail into the woods and turned around when I heard someone pull up. This is definitely where your apprentice was taken from. He killed at least one before they got him," he said. "He was your responsibility. You were supposed to be looking after him."

"I guess I'm still a disappointment. Good to know some things never change. They found the detective's car, so if you don't mind I'm going to go help him," I said.

I didn't wait to see if he minded and went into my room for a change of clothes and a new pair of shoes. I changed back to human form, picked something to wear that I didn't care if it got ripped up, and grabbed a change of clothes just in case. I found Cearbhall, also in human form, waiting by the door. I heaved the hound from the kitchen over my shoulder and went outside, leaving him alone in the house.

"Hold on, I'm coming with you. In fact, why don't you let me drive? We'll have more room than in your Honda," he said.

"You know that's not my Honda," I said without turning around. "You really want these demons in your car?"

"It's not mine, it belonged to those hunters from last night."

"I'll take the truck. You can do whatever you want," I said.

I wasn't thrilled about driving around in what was essentially a stolen car, especially with a demon in the back. I put the hound in the back with the bag of snakes and covered it all up with a tarp. Cearbhall joined me in the truck and we headed to the apartment complex.

"So what's with the message on the wall of your house?" he asked.

"As far as I can tell, Petra feels some kind of connection with Naylet. She tried to get her from me the other night when we fought. She doesn't know where I've hidden her. I guess she wants to get her back," I said.

"That's good," he said. "It gives us something we can use against her."

I didn't like the idea of using Naylet as bait or some kind of bargaining chip, but he was right, if leverage was needed, she could provide it. I would save that for a last resort.

"I just need a little time to figure out how to get her back to normal. There has to be some way to do it," I said.

"What did Hob say?" he asked.

I paused before I answered. "Nothing promising."

"You need to remember the bigger picture. Petra is going to be hunting, and since she knows everything Naylet knew, anyone close to you could be in danger, not to mention the humans. There's potential for a lot of people to get hurt here, and that's without Thera nuking the region. You might want to come to terms with the idea that she's gone and focus on what you can do to stop Petra," he said.

"I'll stop Petra and get Naylet back. Wait and see," I said. "Was Livy okay?"

"She was fine. I moved her to DeSoto Falls. It's a safe place," he said. "I hope you're right about Naylet, I just don't see it. Try not to worry, Obie, we'll get it straightened out."

I looked out the window. "Who said I was worried? I know you find it hard to believe but I have the situation under control."

"If that were true then I wouldn't be here."

What could I say to that? He's right. I didn't have to tell him though. Better to say nothing than swell his ego any further. With any luck Petra would be at the apartment and we could put an end to this, but then again, if I killed Petra today, would that mean Naylet would be lost? I might need to find a way to pull her out of Petra before I killed her. I needed more time, time I might not have.

CHAPTER • 18

"You don't really notice how clean the air is up here until you've been away," Cearbhall said, breaking the silence.

"Yeah, must be nice to be back," I said.

"So, what do we know?"

"Not much, really. Petra took a baby in Alpharetta a few weeks ago and attacked Naylet yesterday. I found a stuffed bunny at the kid's house with some weird perfume on it." I pointed absently toward his feet. "It's rolling around in the floorboard there."

He retrieved it, stuck a finger on the discolored spot and gave it a whiff. "People used to do this in the old days. They made perfume out of oil and spices. I haven't seen this for a long time. This demon has been around for a while if she knows how to do this."

"We don't know about her whereabouts except that she was meeting with a pastor, Steve Heck, who wouldn't give her up and died in a house fire. She has a grimoire that she was copying pages out of to give to him. He was being trained to summon. I found a note in his office that said P.V.T. Moca, GA. Steve referenced P.V.T. in his blog as well. I'm guessing the 'P' stands for Petra so that should be the initials of the name she is going by, at least for now. The only clue as to her location is 'Moca', have you heard of it before?"

"Never. If neither one of us has heard of it it's probably not a city. Could be a code for Starbucks for all we know," he said.

"Steve's widow probably knew but I found this note at his house," I said, fishing the letter and scrap of calendar out of my pocket to hand it to him. "I think she is the one who wrote it on the calendar judging by the handwriting. See? Same handwriting. The kicker is, the Tortured Occult found Farwell's car in front of her building. That's the apartment complex we are headed to right now."

We followed what seemed to be an unnecessarily winding road leading to the apartment complex, only to be stopped short by a gate.

"Humans love their false sense of security," Cearbhall said. "Park and walk in?"

I spotted a car coming up behind us in the mirror. "We'll scoot in behind this car." I pulled into the guest entrance and started hitting the buttons like I was looking for someone.

The car pulled up and the young woman driving scanned a card. When the gate opened I pulled up quickly behind her and we drove in before the gate could close. The complex was made up of two-story buildings set in large rectangles, with parking and green space in the center. We found building seventeen on the lower level, tucked away to the side. Hank, Fisheye, and Razor had their motorcycles parked on the opposite side of the parking lot. They lounged on the bikes watching the building. Hornet, wearing a vest with *Prospect* on the back, leaned against the club's black van. I pulled into an open space, biker adjacent, and killed the engine.

"What's the word?" I asked through the open window.

"It's been quiet," Hank said. "No movement, the car is right there in front of the building. Haven't gotten close enough to check it out, but it looks empty and undamaged from here."

"Wait here, I'm going to get a closer look," I said, getting out of the truck.

I crossed the parking lot to Farwell's car and looked in through the windows. Nothing looked out of place and there was no visible damage to the interior. I tried the door, it was unlocked. I found a few spots of dried demon blood on the headrest, and the entire thing smelled like Petra's perfume. The keys were in the ignition. I grabbed them and went back to where everyone was waiting.

"She's here, or at least she was. First priority, let's get Farwell his car. Hank, can you have someone detail it and return it to him as quick as they can, please?" I asked. "I'll cover the cost."

"Prospect," Hank shouted.

Hornet held out a hand for the keys. "I got it."

I tossed her the keys with a nod. She walked over to the Explorer, got in, and drove away.

"It's your territory. What's our play?" Cearbhall asked.

"We don't know what we're dealing with. We'll keep someone in the front and send one to watch the back, the rest of us will go in. If anyone wants out now is the time," I said.

"Fisheye, head around back, Razor will stay up front. We're ready when you are," Hank said.

"All right," I said. "Then let's go."

Cearbhall, Hank, and I crossed the parking lot as the two bikers took position. Approaching the door to apartment 1703 I put a finger over my mouth, signaling to my companions, and put my ear to the door.

Inside a rhythmic *tick-tick* repeated over and over. I couldn't place what it was coming from; if it was a clock it would have to be the loudest in existence. The knob turned freely and I opened the door slowly, the ticking becoming much clearer. The smell of blood and the spices of Petra's perfume filled the air. I moved in quietly, not wanting to announce our presence, just in case. The door opened to a kitchen on the right, with a dining area to the left that spilled over to the living room. The ceiling fan was broken, and hanging lopsided from the ceiling, throwing it out of alignment, making it tick with every rotation. Cearbhall and Hank came in, closing the door behind them. We gave each other a nod and made the transformation to krasis.

I couldn't have picked two finer people for backup; Cearbhall with centuries of experience and Hank, huge, fearless, and strong as, well, the bear that he was. I couldn't say if we were heard coming in or if it was the sound of the Velcro on my pants I pulled apart before the change that alerted them, but no sooner had I finished my change than two large hounds burst into the kitchen and attacked. Being the first in, I was knocked down with one on top of me, sinking its teeth deep into my arm and shaking violently like a dog with a toy. Pain shot up my arm as I tried to position myself to gain the advantage.

A loud clap rang out. The hound let go of my arm and was lifted off of me. Hank had sunk his claws into its sides and lifted it effortlessly over his head. It screeched and squirmed, scratching the ceiling and sending drywall and blood cascading down around me.

"You okay?" he asked.

"Yep," I said, rolling out of the way and getting to my feet.

When I was clear, he slammed the beast down onto the linoleum. The building shook from the impact but the hound was still. Cearbhall had dealt the other hound a mortal wound and had it pinned to keep it from biting anyone as it bled out.

"Go ahead, I'm right behind you," he said.

I rounded the corner into the living room to see Petra exiting through a back door onto a patio. She clutched a book to her chest and had the imp with a gimpy leg on her shoulder. She slammed the door behind her when she saw me.

"Find Holt," I shouted as I chased after her.

I pulled the door open and ran out into a small screened-in porch just as Petra jumped through the screen and over the railing. The apartment backed up to the woods with a two-story drop. She flew off, weaving around the trees, carrying the book and imp away. Below, Fisheye had taken off after her. Not content to be left out, I leapt off the balcony through the hole in the screen, landing hard on the ground below.

When I caught up to Fisheye he was busy stomping out a fire on the forest floor under a large oak tree. Petra had landed on one of the upper branches out of reach. The imp had busied himself throwing little fireballs. They weren't large enough to do any real damage beyond starting a small brushfire. Petra stood with her wings stretched out, the significant wingspan making her look much larger than she was. The bald head was replaced with bulbous scabs where the snakes had been the day before. One of her wings looked to be a little crooked.

"Where is she, Obie?" she asked.

"Who, Candice Heck? How should I know, we just got here," I said, looking up at her.

She scowled. "Not that incessant do-gooder. Naylet."

"Somewhere safe," I said.

"I will find her," she said, looking down her nose at me. "It's just a question of how many of our friends get hurt before I do."

Calling people she's about to kill "our friends", and the way she spoke to me last time, told me she thinks of people the same way Naylet did. Maybe she even considers me her cupitus. The difference is this demon clearly lacks Naylet's compassionate nature. Petra will hurt anyone that gets in her way. The imp tossed down another fireball that landed a couple feet to my left, and Fisheye went to work on it right away.

"You want Naylet back. I want your grimoire, and there's no reason for anyone else to get in the middle of it. Let's make a deal," I said.

"Are you proposing a trade? I don't have any reason to bargain. I will get what I want either way," she said.

"Maybe, but how long will it take? You've lost the advantage. I didn't fully understand this situation before, but I do now. As soon as I leave here, Naylet will be gone. You won't be looking for her anymore, you'll be looking for someone that knows where she is hidden, and I'm not even going to know myself," I said. "I'll arrange someone to make arrangements with others I don't know to make other arrangements. It will take decades, even centuries, for you to track her through a labyrinth of acquaintances—if you can do it at all. To be sure, you'll have to absorb them all. Are you up for that?"

"I won't trade the book for her," she said. "And I can live forever. It will be an inconvenience, yes, but I will have her if I choose."

"If not a trade, then how about a duel. We fight to the death, winner takes all," I said.

She glared at me through slanted eyes. "How do I know I can trust you?"

"Have I ever lied to you before?" I asked.

She paused to think about this which is exactly what I was hoping for. I never needed to lie to Naylet, she knew who and what I was and our relationship wasn't the sort where secrets needed to be kept.

"An intriguing offer . . . The two of us together, like old times," she said.

I held up three fingers. "The three of us. I want Cearbhall in on this."

"I will need a day or two to prepare."

"What do you need to prepare? I could tell you where Naylet is and just finish it now."

"I have to fix my hair," she said. "Two on one isn't a fair fight without my snakes."

"Two days then, I'll come up with a private location for our meeting. In the meantime, don't mess with my friends, don't look for Naylet, you lay low," I said. "No more trouble."

"That's fine, Obie, but you haven't seen the preacher's wife, so please don't be mad at me about that." She grinned in a way that made me think she wasn't looking for absolution.

"We have an agreement then?"

"It's a date," she said leaping into the air.

"Wait, how do I find you?" I shouted after her.

She hovered overhead for a moment before saying, "I'll be at the Museum of Contemporary Art of Georgia. No surprises."

She didn't stick around for anymore conversation before she flew away.

"You're really taking that 'love thy enemy' thing seriously, huh," Fisheye said.

CHAPTER · 19

I walked in silence with Fisheye back to the porch of the apartment. Keeping an eye out for nosey neighbors, I jumped up, grabbed the porch, and pulled myself up. Fisheye followed behind me. The apartment was quiet when we came back in, minus the ticking of the broken fan. I had missed a large blood stain on the carpet below the fan, with a drag mark flowing down the hallway like some kind of twisted brush stroke. I flipped a few light switches before I found the one to turn it off. A small sofa sat on one side of the room with the TV mounted above a fireplace. Candice hadn't made herself at home yet. Maybe she was hoping Steve would come to his senses and she would be back home soon. That wasn't going to happen now, assuming she was still alive to worry about it.

"Come take a look at this," I heard Cearbhall say from the other room.

We followed his voice, and the blood trail, into a spare bedroom. I rounded the corner to find the stolen dust crates and Holt laying on his back in the middle of a large circle drawn in dust. It looked similar to the sum moning circles I was familiar with, but not the same. I didn't recognize all the demonic runes and the ones I knew weren't in the correct places. Cearbhall, Hank, and Razor had changed back to human form. Fisheye and I followed suit.

"What is it?" Hank asked.

"It's a binding circle. I haven't seen one of these in a long time," Cearbhall said, kneeling for a closer look. "It's used to hold someone inside it. Until the circle is broken the person trapped is held in a kind of stasis."

I looked at Holt lying unconscious in the circle. The dust that made the circle was rising a grain at a time, evaporating on the way up to fuel the binding. There looked to be enough dust in the lines to keep it going for days at the rate it was being consumed.

"So, is there a process here or do we just scoop it up?" I asked.

"Nothing special to it," he answered. "Grab that open crate and we'll shovel what we can back in."

I picked up the crate and placed it on the floor beside the circle. Cearbhall scooped up a handful of dust and dropped it in the crate. A piercing shriek that I didn't recognize as a scream at first assaulted my ears. Clasping a hand over each ear, I collapsed to my knees, involuntarily squeezing my eyes and mouth shut as if they could help block out the sound. It was over as abruptly as it started. I took a breath and opened my eyes to see Cearbhall in a similar position and the T.O. looking like they were practicing surfing. That's when I realized the ground was shaking. Thera appeared in front of me looking generally pissed off.

"Tomorrow at midnight or I finish it myself," she said before disappearing.

Cearbhall and I got to our feet as the rumble of the earth died down. He had seen and heard her just like I had but the bikers lacked the necessary gift.

"What was that?" Hank said after the rumbling had subsided.

"Thera's not happy," I answered, moving over to check out Holt.

He didn't appear to be hurt but had a pale complexion with sweat dotting his forehead. His shirt was soaked in blood around his stomach and running down from his clearly swollen shoulder that was. I pulled his shirt back for a closer look. It was shredded around his stomach but there was no sign of injuries underneath. I spread his shirt above his shoulder and found four uniform holes in it—fang marks. Petra, sans snakes, appears to have bitten him. She must have the same poison that the snakes did. She had done a number on him for sure. The injuries to his belly had probably been sustained during the original attack. Instead of dying he had healed, but looked to be losing the fight with the poison. Regardless, there wasn't much I could do for him, but with the snakes I found, Livy could help him. I had to get him back to her fast.

"Mrs. Heck I presume," Razor said, from behind me. "Come take a look at this. That demon did a number on her."

I turned to see a woman hanging in the closet. She wore a white sundress with a blue floral pattern. The poker from the fireplace had been used to suspend her from the shelf in the closet. It had been bent into a hook shape and shoved into her head. The pointy end wedged close enough to her left eye to make it bulge in its socket. While she wasn't a large woman by any standards, the shelf bent, barely holding onto the wall under the load. Her body hung limp with her legs touching the floor and bent awkwardly at the knees, reminding me of a marionette. She was covered in blood that had run down her neck, soaked her dress, and pooled on the floor around her feet. A cross on a chain was tangled in the fingers of her right hand.

"What do you think? Take her down?" I asked, not taking my eyes off the woman dangling in the closet.

"We have to clean up a lot of stuff here the cops shouldn't see," Cearbhall said. "She's not one of them."

I thought about it but I didn't want to leave her hanging. "Let's take her down and I'll call it in. Doesn't seem right to leave her like this. Hell, the cops are probably already on the way from all that racket we made. Can you all get the dust and demons loaded and I'll take care of this?"

I reached out to take her down. When I touched her, she let out a gurgling sob that bubbled blood out of her nose. I recoiled a step from the surprise. My heart dropped in my chest followed by an uneasiness in my stomach. It had never occurred to me that she could still be alive.

"Fuck, hold her up," Cearbhall said.

I stepped forward and wrapped one arm around her waist and put my other hand on her neck for support. I lifted as Cearbhall unhooked her as carefully as he could from the shelf. Muffled sobs escaped her pinned jaw and tears rolled out of her one good eye. As a Keeper I was used to death, I was baptized in it and forged by it. I had become an efficient killer early on, of both man and beast. I won't apologize for it. If Candice had been killed and strung up for whatever reason, I would chalk it up to normal demon shit and move on. This was something else. The infliction of pain and suffering for its own sake is a sickness with no place in the world. It highlighted why we needed to put an end to Petra and I couldn't help think that Thera was right; I should have finished her there in the yard, even if it meant I died doing it. This was my fault. We laid her on the floor as gently as we could.

"End her suffering," Cearbhall said, the disgust in his voice revealing he shared my view.

"You're going to kill her? Can't you do that healing voodoo on her?" Razor protested.

"With a fire poker jammed in her skull? We would have to take it out and that would kill her anyway," I said.

"It just don't seem right," he said. "There has to be something we can do."

"There is. You can get the dust and demons loaded. I'll take care of this," I said.

The bikers and Cearbhall grabbed the crates and made their way out of the room. I raised a hand to her throat and she grabbed it with both hands. She clutched it against her chest as she sobbed. Maybe Razor was right, there was another way.

"Candice, I'm here to help you. If you hear me squeeze my hand," I said, trying to sound as soothing as I could.

I felt a squeeze.

"I can end this for you or I can call an ambulance. Give me one squeeze if you want to be finished or two for the ambulance," I said.

There was no response at first. I can imagine what she must have been going through. In the course of my work I have experienced extreme pain. The difference is that it's temporary for me. I heal so fast, the worst is over in minutes. When pain is so short-lived, it's an easy thing to look past. I could feel the hesitation in her answer when I received it, two squeezes.

"Hold on," I said, "Help is on the way."

I went to look for a landline but there wasn't one. I found her purse on the kitchen table and dumped it. Her phone toppled onto the floor in a pile of gum, tissues, and tampons.

"What are you doing?" Cearbhall asked when he came back in and found me rummaging through the purse's contents.

"She wants to live," I said.

He put his hands on his hips. "Since when did we start giving anyone a choice?"

"Since now."

Hank came in a second later. "Fisheye is pulling the van around. Doesn't appear to be anyone around so we should be able to get everything loaded," he said. "What's he doing?"

"Calling for help," Cearbhall said. "The lady wants to live."

"Good for her," Hank said. "That means we have to move."

I went back into the room with Candice, knelt beside her, and dialed the number.

"911, what is your emergency?" the woman on the other end said.

"Candice Heck has been attacked in her apartment at 1703 Belleview Way. She needs an ambulance," I said.

"Did you attack her, sir?" the woman said as I put the phone down on the floor beside Candice.

"Help is on the way. Be well, Candice," I said.

I picked up Holt in a fireman's carry and headed for the door. I stopped short before going outside, waiting for Hank to give me the all-clear. He did a scan of the area and waved me out, opening the truck door for a quick entry. I sat Holt into the passenger seat and closed the door.

"Livy should be able to work with the snakes in the back to help Holt. I have to get Naylet and I'll meet you up there," I said. Cearbhall nodded and pulled out as I turned to Hank. "I'll drive the van."

CHAPTER • 20

DeSoto Falls wasn't much more than a campground, a hiking trail, and a trickle of water pouring over a rock. What it lacked in extravagance it made up for with seclusion. Located inside the Elvin Nation, right off of GA 19, it wasn't much to look at. Parking in a small gravel lot by the road was mandatory. Access to the falls and campground was by foot only. I didn't know why Cearbhall brought Livy here. It meant nothing to me, I hadn't spent any real time here, and maybe that was the point. There would be no reason for Petra to think it's where we would be hiding out. If everything went according to plan, she would lay low and stick to our agreement, which would make this precaution a moot point. Fingers crossed.

After we dropped the demons off at Hob's and picked up Naylet from the clubhouse, Hank drove me up. I tried to talk him out of it, as he wasn't exactly welcome this far into the Elvin Nation unannounced. But a quick trip in and out would most likely go unnoticed. We found the truck parked on the edge of the gravel parking lot. The truck was empty and I figured Cearbhall had Livy set up at one of the campsites. I gave Hank my thanks and he left Naylet and me alone by the truck, not wanting to spend any more time here than he had to. I knelt and found their scent leading down a gravel path in the direction of the camping area. Heaving Naylet onto my shoulders, I started after them. It was hard going with the extra weight she had put on; hopefully Livy wasn't too far away. I followed Cearbhall's scent down the path, past some picnic tables, but instead of leading right to the camping area, it went left to the hiking trail.

"Where are they going?" I asked myself absently.

I followed his scent up the trail, stopping every few minutes to squat and make sure I was still on track. Cearbhall's scent led off the trail to the north, through the woods. I knelt, wondering if he was playing some kind of joke on me. Lead me on some roundabout way through the woods, hauling Naylet's now cumbersome form. Normally I'm on board for a nice nature hike, but not today. While I pondered, some hikers had come up on me from the trail to my right. I would have slipped into the woods if I had been aware of them a minute sooner. Better to stay out of sight than have to explain why I was carrying a statue into the woods. I stood up, already smiling and ready for the cordial hellos that strangers around here exchange for casual meetings. The hikers, a man and a woman looking mostly miserable, kept their eyes on the ground and walked by without acknowledging my presence.

Deciding to follow Cearbhall's scent, I ducked into the woods as soon as they were out of sight. After about ten minutes of walking I could smell a campfire, and found Livy's camp set up in a holler, shielded by mountains on all sides. I set Naylet beside the tent and stretched my back, glad we had made it. Cearbhall was sitting by the fire, poking at it with a stick. Livy and Holt must be in the tent.

"What took you so long?" Cearbhall said as soon as I finished my stretching.

"Nothing. Just dropped the demons off and got Naylet. How's Holt?" I asked.

"Don't know yet." He tossed his stick into the flames. "Livy's working on him in the tent. There's someone I want you to meet."

I looked around but didn't notice anyone with us. "Are they in the tent, too?" I asked.

"No, he's right here," he said. "Quiet your mind and listen. You will hear him."

I stood still and listened. I heard the birds, the rustle and pop of the fire, the wind moving through the trees. That was all at first, and then it wasn't.

<More company. Alone for so long and now five, but two are not well.> The voice, deep and groaning, seemed to come from inside my head rather than outside.

"What was that?" I asked. "Did you hear it, too?"

"Yeah, he's talking to both of us. That's Walasi, an Old One," he said.

I had heard stories about Old Ones throughout the years. Thera's original Keepers. Forces of nature stronger than anything I had ever come across. I always thought the Old Ones were long gone and the stories were embellished. I guess I was about to find out.

"Where is he?" I asked, my excitement evident. I looked all around but still didn't see anything unusual or particularly old looking. "The stories say Walasi was a frog the size of a house. So either they are wrong or I'm just not looking at the right place."

"He's right here," Cearbhall said throwing a thumb over his shoulder. "Why don't you show him?"

A tremor ran through the earth as the trees on the hillside directly behind him began to shake. It seemed to be an earthquake or landslide at first, until the earth itself began to rise. I didn't put together what was happening until two round eyes the size of large tractor tires opened about fifteen feet apart on the hill. Two large legs lifted the body from the ground, revealing an enormous toad protruding from the hillside. Its head cocked to one side, putting an eye in position to give me a thorough inspection. The eye itself had a horizontal, oval pupil with a light green iris. Black streaks ran through the iris and I could see they moved like the electricity in a plasma globe. Just a hint of the power this Old One contained, I deduced.

"Bigger than a house," I said, staring up at the megatoad.

<You fought a snake head. It did not go well.> Walasi eyeballed the statue of Naylet behind me.

"It's still not going well," I said. "It's still out there."

"Hey, Walasi, see that poplar over there," Cearbhall said, pointing to a tree on the opposite hillside. "Pretend that was a snake head and show Obie how you would handle it."

Walasi's head shifted toward the tree and Cearbhall lay flat on the ground. I opened my mouth to ask him if I should take cover as well but before I could get a word out Walasi sent his tongue shooting across the holler. It slammed into the tree, shearing it from its roots and, having a solid hold on the tree, brought it back with terrifying intensity. I dove to the ground to avoid the arboreal missile. Walasi caught the tree in his mouth, spit it out on the ground in front of him, and raised a giant foot, sending it crashing down, splintering the tree to pieces and forming a toad-print crater at the same time. The ground shook from the impact, toppling Naylet. I looked at Cearbhall in shock.

"And now we have firewood," he said, grinning.

Livy's head popped out of the tent. "It's bad enough you bring me rotten snake heads and Holt on death's door but now you're making all that racket and shaking the whole world. Keep it down. I'm trying to work!" she yelled before disappearing back inside. "I swanie!"

Walasi sank back down into the hillside while Cearbhall and I said at the same time, "Sorry, Livy."

It was probably best to leave Livy alone for a bit, so I helped Cearbhall gather the wood. Cearbhall jumped into the crater, standing waist deep and tossed the splintered wood out for me to stack by the fire. I thought about trying to lure Petra up here to have Walasi deal with her. After all, it looked like he would have no trouble handling her. That would be taking the easy way out. This was all happening because I didn't finish Petra off that night in the yard. I could use Walasi as a backup plan, but I needed to see this through myself. Plus, if there was any hope for getting Naylet back, I had to get Petra's blood and figure out how to separate the two of them. Walasi smashing Petra into dust wouldn't leave me much to work with.

Walasi's voice popped in my head. *<I sense uncertainty.>*

I looked over at Cearbhall who didn't seem to get the same message. Walasi must just be speaking to me now. I walked closer in a futile attempt for a little privacy. "I fought the demon once and didn't kill it. I am trying to figure out how to kill the demon and undo the damage she caused," I said, motioning toward Naylet. "You are so powerful and I'm struggling. It would be easy if I had the kind of power you do."

The giant toad lowered his head, putting one of his electrically charged eyes in front of me. *<Focus on the gifts you have, not the gifts you don't. My gifts are my prison. I stay hidden here.>*

That was a good point. He couldn't exactly go anywhere or even move around that much without risking busting the veil wide open. It must be a miserable existence. "Any other tips for me?"

<Trust Thera, she is life.>

The blind faith in Thera didn't surprise me but I wasn't sure putting trust in someone who was prepared to kill all of us to suit her own needs was wise. I started to compile a list of the things I was good at. I was a great swimmer but demons avoid water like the plague so I probably wouldn't talk Petra into an eight hundred meter freestyle to settle this. My claws had already proved to be useless. With Otis's help I'd managed to arrange some form of cooperation between almost everyone in the region but I couldn't cooperate Petra to death, or could I?

"I'm going to go fight the demon again. If I lose, she will come for Naylet," I said. "Will you protect her for me?"

<She is safe here.>

"Thanks, Walasi. I need to check on Holt. I will talk to you again soon," I said.

I stuck my head in the tent to test the waters before diving in. Holt lay on the cot from Livy's house and she sat on a stool beside him, putting a reddish liquid into his mouth one drop at a time.

"In or out," she said, still annoyed. "You're going to let the bugs in."

It seemed safe enough so I stepped into the tent and closed the flap behind me. "How's he doing?"

"Too early to tell. He's a tough one, that's for sure, but those snakes you brought me had started to turn," she said, motioning with her head to the bag in the corner. "They're stinking up the place good and I don't think the antivenom is quite as strong as it could be."

"I'll get rid of those," I said, picking up the bag to dispose of later.

"I've got a couple vials sitting on top of my kit there in the corner. Two doses of antivenom. It's better to take it right before you get bit, but we won't know how well it will work until we see how Holt responds, so it's probably best to not get bit at all if you can help it."

"That is the idea," I said. "Do you need anything before I head out?"

"You just got here. Where are you running off to so soon?"

"I got to get back to work," I said. "No rest for the wicked, right?"

"Be careful out there," she said, methodically administering the antivenom.

"I will, I promise," I said.

When I made it back outside Walasi had disappeared into the mountainside. He blended in completely, his rock skin the perfect camouflage.

Cearbhall looked up from the fire when I came out of the tent. "Ready to go?"

"I was planning to go alone. Did you want to come?" I asked.

"There's nothing for me to do here and you might need my help. When was the last time we visited a museum anyway?" he asked, getting up from his seat.

"First time for everything."

CHAPTER • 21

"I'm not interested in meeting on her terms," Cearbhall said, eyeballing the area. "We need to find out where she's staying now and catch her off guard. Put an end to this before it gets any more out of hand. I don't like this."

The Museum of Contemporary Art of Georgia was tucked down a side street on the north side of Atlanta behind a collection of shops and an electrical substation. It wasn't a high traffic area and it was easy to see why Cearbhall was concerned. For a city, it was about as secluded as a place could get. The empty parking lot gave away that they must not get a lot of business in the middle of the day, heightening the sense of seclusion.

"It will be okay," I said, turning off the engine. "I don't think she will try anything."

"What makes you so sure?" he asked.

"I'm not sure at all," I said. "Petra is unpredictable at best. There's no telling how many people she has rattling around in her head. The thing is, one of those people is Naylet. I don't know if she is actively conscious in there or if it's more that they merged, but either way she's in there and I have to believe that counts for something. I don't think Petra will try anything here."

He shot me a look from the passenger seat. "Am I talking to myself here? It's a bad idea."

"I hear you. I have no intention of meeting on her terms, but I gave my word and I intend to honor it," I said. "Besides, our best chance of finding her is to play along for now."

He chuckled to himself at my statement. "You gave your word to a demon, and you intend to honor it?"

"Doesn't matter who I gave it to, my word is good," I said, getting out of the truck.

"That's very principled. What idiot taught you that?" he asked.

I leaned against the door and spoke to him through the window. "You did," I said.

He cocked his head to the side in fake contemplation. "Hmm, doesn't sound like me."

"It was a long time ago," I said. "You coming?"

"No, art isn't my thing."

The building was unremarkable from the outside, it looked like an industrial building, except for the large triangular awning over the steps leading up to the front door. Well-kept bushes planted on either side of the steps, combined with the awning, went a long way to give it a classy feel otherwise absent in the surrounding area.

Part of me was glad Cearbhall decided to wait in the car. If he went inside there's a good chance things would devolve quickly—he's not always good with tact. I had spent a lot of time thinking on the way down on how to handle this. I thought about both of us going in and taking our chances. Maybe we could kill her right here and be done with it. Then again, she could have a building full of demons waiting to eat us alive. Petra seemed to be sincere in her invitation, so maybe it would turn out all right.

Going through the glass doors at the top of the steps, I followed the signs in the hallway around to the entrance to the museum. I found the entrance to my left and went in. A young lady behind a counter, seeming bored, stopped typing to greet me. I paid the admission fee and listened to the spiel about the different exhibits. The last one she described caught my attention.

"In the back is our most recent addition, a selection of sculptures by Petra Von Thelan," she said. "The artist is on site today."

"That's what I came to see," I said. "Tell me the truth, what do you think about it?"

She looked past me to make sure the coast was clear. She whispered, "Honestly, it gives me the creeps. It's a little too real for my taste, but it's very well done."

I thanked her and headed to the back. It was an open floorplan; most of the building was empty space. The floors were concrete painted in a splotchy brown. The walls were beige with pieces hanging every few feet with little tags describing the work. The ceiling was unfinished with pipes and beams visible but everything painted white, giving it a sophisticated industrial vibe. I heard the clicking of heels echoing from the other room. As I rounded the corner I found its source: Petra walking in my direction. She looked human again, no doubt an illusion. She smiled as she walked over to me, her head wrapped in the scarf like a cancer patient, and looking genuinely happy to see me.

"I thought I heard you, I'm so glad you could make it. I'm excited to show you my work. I think you'll like it," she said, opening her arms as if she was going to hug me.

I held my hand out to stop her and said, "I found Candice."

"You knew she wasn't going to get out of this alive. Don't be mad at me about that, Obie, it will make me think you aren't happy to see me. Besides, I have kept my end, haven't I? That Candice business was before our agreement."

I would have to play along. If I didn't I couldn't get her where I wanted her. "Actually, she survived. Definitely worse for the wear, but still with us."

"You didn't kill her? Wouldn't that have been the humane thing to do? I mean, the way her eye popped out I doubt she will ever look right again." She laughed. "She's tougher than she looks, I'll give her that."

Bitch.

"Are you going to show me around?" I asked, extending my arm and smiling through the disgust.

She beamed and wrapped her arm around mine. We walked to her exhibit arm in arm, which made my stomach turn. The exhibit consisted of four adults with six babies in front of them. The layout reminded me of an apocalyptic nativity scene, with five too many baby Jesuses. A closer look of the horror on their faces and I understood why the receptionist didn't care for the exhibit. I wondered how she would feel if she knew these used to be living people, locked forever in their last moment of agony.

"They are all wonderful, Obie, but this is the one I really want you to meet. His name is Titus Ovidius Malleolus. He was a sculptor outside of Rome many years ago. So skilled and so passionate, and very attractive, don't you think?" she said. She paused for my input.

His face was frozen in a scream, with his hands gripping at his chest as if he were still alive in the stone and was trying to tear himself out of it. I cocked my head to one side, inspecting his tormented features. "He's all right, I guess."

"Yes, quite all right indeed. I couldn't resist having him. He is one of my favorite companions. I've used his passion ever since, all the way to my current masterpieces like baby Stephanie here," she said, running a hand over the baby on the far right. "I used that passion in creating my most recent work, Naylet, who I hold as important to me as Titus. She is just as remarkable and has shown me so much. Having her away from me has forced me to use my passion in other ways, like the message I made out of sweet Candice Heck." Her voice took on a decidedly darker tone. "I hope that you are receiving that message, Obie, because the truth is, all this is to say that you shouldn't fuck with me."

This was becoming more confrontational than I was hoping for. I thought for a moment, what would I say to Naylet in this situation? I couldn't quite come up with it so I went for sarcasm instead. "Ladies and their drama. Is all that necessary? We were getting along so well."

She glared at me through squinted eyes. Her gaze softened and she smiled before saying, "Obie, I wish things had worked out differently between us. I just hate that I have to kill you."

"And I hate to have to die," I said. Looked like the honeymoon was over already. "Are you ready to talk business?'

"I'm listening," she said.

"It simple really, you fight Cearbhall and I, to the death. Winner take all. You win, and you get Naylet, we win, and we get your grimoire," I said.

She considered it for a moment. "And where would this fight take place?"

"Browns Bridge outside of Gainesville. Meet us on the bridge at ten PM sharp," I said.

"Why a bridge?" she said suspiciously.

"I know some people that can shut down the road. It will give us a nice private place to resolve our problem."

She smiled. "And no weapons?"

"No weapons. Just the three of us fighting until someone wins," I replied.

As she pondered my offer, she walked back to her statues. She moved among them, putting her hand on the shoulder of one, touching the face of another. I guessed that she was drawing on their experiences. Again I wondered if the people she absorbed were trapped in her, still conscious but disembodied. Was she actually speaking to them in there, or just running through lifetimes of memories to come to the best conclusion?

"How do I know I can trust you, Obie? What assurance do I have that this isn't a trick?" she asked, turning to face me.

"I give you my word as a gentleman," I replied using the same words I used with Naylet in hopes that it jogged some sentiment inside her. "If you agree and can beat Cearbhall and I, you will get what you're looking for."

"If that's the best you can do . . ." She trailed off with a distant look as if she was trying to remember something, before coming back to the present and saying, "Agreed."

"All right, then I will see you tomorrow at ten," I said, turning for the door.

"Obie," she called after me.

I turned around to see what she wanted. "Yeah?"

"It's a date," she said with a smile and a wink.

Back at the truck, Cearbhall was sitting on the tailgate. "Well," he said when I came outside.

"It's on, tomorrow night at ten," I said.

We got in the truck. Before I could start it he said, "What's the plan?"

"First we need some help. I'll drop you off at the clubhouse. I need you to get Hank and have him meet me at ground zero, bottom level. I will explain everything when I get there," I said.

"Where are you going?" he asked.

"I have some other friends to talk to," I said.

CHAPTER · 22

It's not hard to find elves, if elves are all you're looking for. All you have to do is take a drive into the Elvin Nation, the area covering northernmost Georgia and part of Tennessee sharing a border almost exactly with the Chattahoochee National Forest. The royal court, on the other hand, can be hard to track down. I'm not sure if it's paranoia from the strained relations with the T.O., or if the Queen just prefers a more mobile lifestyle. Whatever the cause, the court was never in the same place for more than a few days and there was no way to tell where it would be at any given time. The only way to find her highness was to go through an elf with connections. Luckily for me, there are outposts set up on the edges of their territory to accommodate these kinds of requests. The southernmost outpost sat in the mountains just north of Dahlonega.

I pulled up a winding mountain road, barely more than a horse trail, that snaked around the mountain to the outpost on top. I drove slowly, the truck lurching into the potholes and over the occasional root. I think they kept the road in such poor shape to deter visitors, as if their general dispositions didn't do an adequate job already. A little over halfway up I came to a small security building that looked wholly out of place in the middle of the woods. A barricade with a stop sign blocked the road. It was undoubtedly excessive, one of those things I thought the Queen did more for show than anything else. The elves didn't get many visitors as far as I knew, and someone would have to be plumb crazy to attack them outright.

An elf stepped out of the building, taking a tactical position as I rolled to a stop in front of the barricade. Her sleeves rolled up, hands resting on the rifle attached to the harness on her vest. Her golden hair pulled back, proudly showing her pointed ears. She stood sleek and muscular, form filling the camouflage uniform exquisitely. I could see the silhouette of another elf behind the tinted glass of the security building, probably watching the feed from the camera focused on me from the roof. A window slid open, revealing the second elf, looking very much like the first except for her hair hanging lazily about her face.

She addressed me without looking up from whatever had her attention. "What's your business?"

"I am Obie, Keeper of Thera. I need to speak with the Queen regarding a threat to the Elvin Nation," I said.

The elf looked up, brushing her hair aside to see me clearly. Her eyes went wide, and she slammed the glass closed. The first elf stared at me as I sat there with the truck idling, not moving a muscle. I gave her a friendly nod and smile; she didn't return the gesture. I was just starting to think I should have brought a book or some Sudoku when the elf stepped out of the building and up to my window.

"We need to search the car. Please step out," she said.

"Do we really have to go through all that?" I asked.

She gave me a grin. "Only if you want to get in."

I did in fact want to get in, so I got out. I was frisked, and a pretty thorough job was done searching the car, even going so far as to take a mirror and looked underneath for explosives. They confiscated my kit from behind the seat but otherwise I made it through unscathed.

"We will keep this at the checkpoint. You'll get it back when you leave," she said, walking my bag into the building.

I nodded and got back in the truck. They slid the barricade open allowing me to continue to the compound. The road corkscrewed around the mountain, ending at a huge octagon shaped house. Three stories tall with the entire top story being mostly windows. Three large wraparound porches encircled each story, giving quick access to any side of the house. There were a few vehicles in a paved parking area in front. I put my car in line with the rest and got out to see Harlan coming down the stairs to meet me. He wore black fatigues instead of the camo like the ladies at the checkpoint, with a loose fitting beanie covering his head. His blond hair, also as long as the ladies, stuck out in places making him look like a military hipster. He was the Queen's son but, being male, was forbidden from serving in the Nations Army. Being that the Elvin males were smaller and weaker in stature, the Queen deemed them insufficient. Many were put to work as servants. Harlan, due to his birthright, achieved as much as an Elvin male could hope for.

"Obie, it's good to see you. What have you been up to?" he said, extending a hand.

I shook it. "Oh, you know, life of a Keeper, it's all glamour and women. What are you doing here?"

"I run the outpost now. It's nothing to be excited about, just something to keep me away from my mother's ears. Wouldn't want my presence to remind her of what a constant embarrassment I am," he said.

"She must think highly of you to put you in charge here, protecting the border with the T.O.? That's a big job," I said.

"I wouldn't call protecting a border from a conflict that only lives in the minds of the elders a big job. Nothing ever happens here and even if it did, the guard could handle it without me. Hell, they already do it without me. I'm just here to greet guests and make them feel special to be greeted by the Queen's son. So I hope you feel important or I've failed in my duties."

"I'm just tickled," I said.

He held an arm out to direct me toward the stairs. "Come on up and get comfortable. The Queen will be here soon to talk to you."

I started walking and stopped abruptly as I passed him when a scent caught my nose. I knew it immediately, sweet and delicate with a slight metallic undertone, not unlike an Elf in general. It was blood—Elvin blood specifically.

I stopped walking and looked at him. "Are you injured?"

"No, it's nothing," he said, clearly not wanting to engage in the subject.

"Hello? Keeper here, mystical healer with the nose of a basset hound. I can smell the blood on you. Let me take a look, it will just take a second," I said.

He looked worried at this and glanced around to see who was watching. A sentry on the middle level was making her rounds. She was out of earshot and didn't take any interest in us or our conversation.

"Come over here," Harlan said, pulling me under the porch in a corner. "I . . . uh . . . Well, I'm leaving." He lifted the side of his beanie to show me his ear. It was bandaged on the top and I could see red soaking through.

I took a step closer to whisper, "Harlan, what did you do?"

"Just something to make fitting in easier where I am going," he said.

"But no elf kingdom will accept you with trimmed ears. You'll be an outcast," I said. "Where are you going to go?"

"You can't be an outcast from something you're not a part of, Obie. I don't fit in here, I'm not happy. I'm going to go somewhere and start fresh. Just find a place for myself with the humans," he said.

"Hold still," I said, raising a hand up on either side of his head. The blue light emanating from my hands was largely drowned out in the daylight, only illuminating his cheeks and reflecting in his eyes. The wounds on his ears closed quickly. A slight ache worked its way into my arms and was gone a moment later.

If he was willing to trim his ears there would be nothing I could do to change his mind. "You know when the Queen finds out about this—"

He didn't let me finish my sentence. "She doesn't have to find out. Just don't say anything, okay? I will be gone tomorrow night."

If the Queen finds out I knew she would probably refuse to help me, not to mention what she would do to him. On the other hand, it's none of my business and I did have plausible deniability. "Okay, I won't say anything. I hope you know what you're doing."

He thanked me and escorted me into the top floor of the compound. It held a kitchen on one side with the rest of the floor a single open room. It had a few couches, tables and chairs, a pool table, and a large fireplace opposite the kitchen. A couple of sentries patrolled outside on the second and third floor with rifles. I doubt there was much to see but the Queen was ever vigilant with the security of the Elvin Nation.

"I can have the kitchen boy make you something," Harlan said. "Something to eat or drink, tea maybe?"

"No thanks, I'm fine," I said.

I changed to krasis in preparation for my meeting with the Queen. After a short wait, two vehicles pulled up to the compound. The first was a truck with two people in the cab and an elf in the back. From above I could see what looked to be an empty bracket welded to the center of the bed with a pole rising up from it. The elf sat on a large lockbox mounted against the cab. No doubt the heavy firepower. The second vehicle was an SUV with blacked out windows. The vehicles didn't bother parking neatly, instead they just stopped caddy-corner in front of the compound. The Queen was followed by the royal guard, a seven elf strong, well-armed, and very well trained security force made up entirely of women. Her personal attendant, a thin male in plain clothes who looked unimpressive by comparison to the rest of the entourage, brought up the rear. Not a group I would want to tangle with, personally, although the attendant wouldn't be so bad. As the Queen ascended to the third level, the security force broke off, taking positions to secure the area. By the time they reached the top it was just the Queen, her attendant and two guards. The guards took position on opposite sides of the room while the Queen came to greet me, ignoring Harlan completely as she passed him.

She was tall and slender, standing almost six feet, a full seven inches taller than Harlan and her attendant. Her long blonde hair was pulled back showing her pointed ears like a badge. She wore combat boots, jeans, and a black spaghetti strap top. The most noticeable part of her outfit was the Old West style six-shooters hanging from a belt that sat lopsided off of her hips, which accentuated their sway as she walked.

"Obie, I hear you have a warning for me. Are you here to deliver the warning or is this a courtesy?" she asked.

Say what you want about the Queen, but she was sharp. She understood my position on a level that few did and knew I could be here as a friend or as Thera's representative. "It's a courtesy, Your Highness," I replied. She wasn't my Queen and I really had no obligation to address her that way but I have found stroking egos tends to make things go easier.

"Then please have a seat and give me your message," she said.

I sat down at the closest table. She took a seat opposite me. "I am hunting a demon on Thera's orders. I have a plan in the works but if I fail, Thera is prepared to destroy the region to eliminate it. If this happens, you and your people will most likely be killed along with everybody else. I wanted to warn you and ask for your help to ensure my success. It would be minimal risk to your people but there are a few things we would need to discuss."

"I appreciate the information, Obie. You are again showing your intention to be a friend of the elves. What are you asking of me?"

"This creature can fly. To make sure she can't escape I need to keep it on the ground. I was hoping you could provide some air support."

"That's simple enough," she said. "What's the catch?"

"Well . . ." I pulled out my most charming smile. "This demon is a gorgon and, like the old legends say, can turn people to stone. I don't know the specifics of how it works but your elves could be in serious danger. I have a plan to prevent this but I am afraid you won't like it."

"Let's have it then," she said.

"The Tortured Occult have a natural resistance to her magic. If you can keep her grounded, they can shield you from her magic. That way your elves will be safe and I can focus on killing her, instead of worrying about if your people are in danger."

She leaned back in her chair in thought. I was hoping she was considering my proposal rather than deciding how to tactfully banish me from the kingdom.

"I would like to help you, Obie, but they are not trustworthy. They would pose as much of a threat to us as this demon, if not more. We will help you, but not with the Tortured Occult," she replied.

"I know you have a strained relationship with the T.O., but this threat affects both of you, and you know what they say about the enemy of my enemy. This could be an opportunity to start mending fences with them. Surely you could both benefit from a better relationship," I said.

"It's true that there could be benefit," she agreed, "but it doesn't change the fact that they can't be trusted."

"What if I take responsibility for them?" I said.

She squinted at this turn. "Meaning if they turn on us, you will make it right?"

"Yes, whatever it takes," I said. "Will you at least meet with them to see if we can work something out?"

"If you take responsibility for them, then yes," she said. "We will meet, but I promise nothing else."

I couldn't help but let out a sigh of relief. Just getting her to agree to show up was a giant step. We might actually be able to pull this off. "Thank you. The meeting is set for tonight at ground zero. I can escort you there whenever you are ready."

The Queen turned to the member of her security force closest to us. "Stock up on silver bullets. Harlan, you will attend our meeting as well."

"Do you need me there? Wouldn't it be better if I stayed behind?" Harlan answered.

Her response had an air of disdain. "I don't need you but you are in charge of the southern border. Any agreements reached will impact your responsibilities. So do us a favor, quit whining and go get in the truck."

CHAPTER · 23

Dawson Forest, a ten-thousand-acre nuclear test site turned wildlife management area, was known as the Dead Forest to ultras. It still housed several concrete structures that had been too expensive to tear down when they were abandoned. The largest of these buildings was three stories tall and fenced off to the public with No Trespassing signs. We referred to it as ground zero and used it as a meeting place when the more public venue of the clubhouse wouldn't work. The general public was largely unaware of the place and the only people that might be around were high schoolers looking for a private place to get into trouble. We parked our three-car caravan off one of the side roads close by and walked over to ground zero.

The building was completely obscured by the trees and undergrowth. It didn't become visible until we were almost to the fence. Cotton and Razor were standing by the hole that had been cut as an entrance. Razor held the fence open for us as we approached. We ducked under it one by one and proceeded inside. One of the security force followed the Queen, her attendant, Harlan, and me into the building. Inside it was dilapidated and dark. We made our way through the skeleton of a building, consisting of a steel reinforced concrete frame and garbage. No doors or windows, only empty spaces where they used to be. Pipes coming out of the floor and walls had been cut off, leaving hints as to what had been there. The ground was covered with debris: pieces of concrete that had broken free from the walls and ceilings, and garbage that had been brought in and left. Graffiti lined the walls, partially covered by vines growing in through the empty window slits. The free flowing air combined with the concrete gave the area an old smell, stone and nature combining into something that I think buildings of long abandoned civilizations would smell like.

I led the Queen's procession down the stairs to the lowest level; The attendant stepped aside and waited at the top of the stairs. He would be able to hear everything from there but it was far enough away to not be considered a part of the meeting. The large room below ground level was nothing but trash and rubble. Hank waited with Cearbhall and Otis on the far side of the room. A lantern was placed in the center of the room, providing enough light for our meeting but casting long shadows across the floor and walls. I could feel the tension in the air as soon as we stepped into the room.

"What the hell's this?" Otis said.

"An opportunity. If you all will just bear with me for a few minutes," I said. "Pun intended." One day Otis is going to find the humor in bear puns, until then I'll just have to keep trying.

It's customary to conduct business unveiled, the idea being that pacts made behind disguises can't be trusted. I kicked off my shoes and changed into krasis. Cearbhall, Otis, and Hank did the same. The Queen had come with her ears showing; her guard took off her cap and pulled her hair back revealing her ears. Harlan stood against the wall behind the Queen in the dark and kept his hat on. It hadn't occurred to me until now, but if he took his hat off there's no keeping his secret. No wonder he didn't want to come. The Queen and her guard had her back turned to him. I decided to ignore him and with any luck Otis wouldn't make a big deal about it.

"Let's get started," I said. "First, thank you all for showing up. As you have heard already we face a threat that is putting not just your families in jeopardy but the entire region. I believe that by meeting and speaking we can come to an under—"

"Hold on, Obie," Otis said, stepping forward. "That one in the back is still veiled."

The room turned to look at Harlan, who had deer-in-headlights down pat.

"I'm sorry, sir, no disrespect intended. I'll just go wait outside. Please don't let my mistake affect your negotiations," he said, moving for the stairs.

"Stop," the Queen said. "This is my son, Harlan. He runs the Southern Outpost and if something were going to come from this, you would be his responsibility. Take off your hat and step forward."

He looked at me over her shoulder. I would have loved to help him out but there was nothing I could do. I shrugged.

"Now," she commanded when he didn't respond immediately.

He met his mother's eyes and pulled the beanie from his head with one hand. He pulled his hair back showing his cropped ears. No one said anything at first—there was a fair amount of shock to go around—but the Queen never looked away from her son or showed any emotion.

"Take him to the truck," she said and turned her back to him. She stood quietly facing Otis until the guard had escorted him out leaving her without any backup. If she was upset, she wasn't showing it.

"Please excuse my son, he is . . . Let's just get this over with," she said.

"Right," I said, glad to get back to business, "So, I believe that the two of you would benefit from a better relationship. We are in a bad situation with this demon, but we can turn it into something positive by using it as an opportunity to mend fences."

"As I have said, Obie, if the Tortured Occult shows itself to be trustworthy, you will have Elvin support," the Queen said.

"Tom C's word is good. The organization is run by honor above all," Otis said.

"Yes, I am well aware of the honor among your kind," she said.

"You are the one that brought silver to a peaceful negotiation. I can smell it on you." Otis took a step forward.

"I leave the silver when you pull your fangs," she said stepping forward to meet him.

"I'll pull my fangs when you cut your ears," Otis snarled back.

Admittedly, that was a low blow considering what she had just seen with Harlan. They stood face to face, or as close as face to face as they could get with Otis in krasis looming a good two feet over the Queen. Otis's breath hit the Queen in strong bursts, pushing her hair back with each breath. Her hand drifted lazily down to her pistol. If she was intimidated, she didn't show it. Even with the difference in size and strength between the two, it would be foolish to underestimate her, and Otis was no fool. Bullets hurt and even without silver the Queen's reflexes, speed, and skill made her a dangerous adversary.

"Friends, let's step back and focus on what's important. We don't have much time to pull this off and I really need your help. Please," I said, motioning for a tactful retreat.

Otis was the first to step back but their gazes didn't unlock until they both moved back a few feet. The mood in the room lightened somewhat.

"Excellent, thank you. The plan is simple. This demon can fly. The elves keep her pinned down so Cearbhall and I can deal with her. The T.O. keeps her off the elves. Neither one of your groups should be in any real danger. You are not there to get involved. You're there to make sure the demon doesn't get away when things start going bad for her," I said.

"So we are only there to keep elves safe," Otis asked.

"Yes, exactly," I replied.

"The T.O. will help. In return for protecting the elves, I want access to ride and run inside Elvin lands. There's not a lot of forest secluded enough in our territory for a full pack run," Otis answered. "Additionally, if we are going to be friends again, then the elves need to come to the meetings."

The Queen didn't have to think about her answer, "There will be no shifter packs running freely on Elvin lands. You may schedule a preapproved quarterly run, so long as you stay within a designated area. At the first sign of aggression, the agreement is void, and you and your kind will be expelled from our lands—the ones that survive anyway."

"Agreed," he said.

"I will send a representative to attend the council meetings, but I want the meetings moved to the Southern Outpost. Additionally, there will be no restrictions on the materials, silver included, that the Elvin Nation can import," she said.

"Those are decisions the council would have to vote on," Otis said.

"Yes, but there are five seats and three of them are in this room. We can pass the resolution without the support of the rats or that fat Tailypo Wilix. That is, if we all agree," she said, looking at me.

This is exactly the kind of back door dealings that I try to avoid but I needed her help. Besides, moving the meeting place was not a big deal and she could get any materials she wanted as it was. She was probably just testing us. If Thera floods the region, we will have bigger problems than where we have social hour.

"Actually, Wilix lost a lot of weight and was replaced a few years ago by a fat Kobold, Hambone. Regardless, I will vote yes if it gets this done," I said.

"You'll have my vote, too," Otis said. The Queen smiled at getting her way, until he followed up with, "On the condition that your son, the one that was here earlier, holds the seat for the elves."

"It's my right to appoint whomever I choose to the position," she said.

"I'm not challenging your authority. Politics is about give and take, I'm just asking for a little consideration. You said he is already running the outpost, so he'll already be there. You don't have to change anything."

She wasn't smiling now. "Fine. When is it taking place, Obie?"

"Tomorrow night, Browns Bridge on 53, just outside Gainesville at ten sharp. You should get there early to have everything set up and concealed," I said.

"We will be there," she said and turned to head back up the stairs.

"We are also calling a meeting tonight to update everyone on the situation," I said. "We can take your votes tonight and make everything official, but you will need your representative for it to pass."

"You may take Harlan and bring him back tonight. If he doesn't return, the deal's off," she said.

"Highness," Otis said after her.

She stopped but didn't look back.

"My youngest is six and has watched nearly every Disney movie made, about five hundred times. Drives me crazy. She is now telling me she doesn't want to hunt. She doesn't want to hurt the innocent animals. A bear that won't hunt, it's terrifying," Otis said.

"And what did you do?" she asked without turning around.

"I remember that she is going to grow into her own person and hope she comes back to reality. Forcing a hunt on her would only make her hate it that much more. I also remind myself that even if she never hunts, she can still be a valuable member of the pack and do great things. Being different isn't a bad thing, unless we make it that way," he said.

The Queen turned around to meet his gaze, "If I wanted two-bit advice from a flea bitten mongrel, I would find a stray bitch in the woods to ask council of." With that, she turned and headed up the stairs.

I looked at Otis, ready to jump in the way if he lunged after her but he was smiling. Not a happy smile but a smile nonetheless.

"I'm starting to think she doesn't like me," he said.

"I'm sorry, guys. I didn't expect that level of vitriol. She always seemed more reasonable to me," I said.

"She is stuck in the past. We will keep our word, but I'm afraid we won't have peace as long as people sacrifice the future for old grudges," he said.

"I have one more favor," I said. "Tomorrow night I need the bridge closed. We don't need any traffic happening by. What will it cost me to have you make some calls and make sure the bridge is under construction?"

"I am tired of bargaining. We will do it for friendship and mutual benefit. Just remember who your friends are, Obie," Otis replied.

"Thank you. If I'm still alive in two days I will never forget it," I said.

I changed back into human form and headed up the stairs. The Queen's reaction surprised me. I had never seen her lash out like that. I'd seen her lash out with her pistols, but she was still calm while doing it. She lost her cool down there. Harlan must have really gotten to her. I caught up to her just outside the fence.

"Highness, there was one more thing I wanted to talk to you about. I heard about a magical device called a soul stone. It supposed to contain a person in it. Kind of pulling a person out of their body and keeping them in storage, so to speak. Do you know of it?"

She gave me a sideways glance. "I am familiar with it. Why do you ask?"

"This demon has taken someone very dear to me. I believe I can restore her but to do it I will need a soul stone. I was hoping you could get me one. I know it's a lot to ask," I said.

She spun to face me, obviously still upset. "Have I not been imposed on enough with those curs? You know I banned magic in my kingdom. Why do you think I would be willing or able to supply magical artifacts?"

She didn't worry about the bikers standing within earshot by the fence. They took note of the disrespect and took a few steps in our direction. The Queen didn't appear concerned, but her guards made ready with their guns. We continued toward the cars as we talked, the guards following behind keeping an eye on Tom C.

"Rumor has it that when you banned magic, you collected everything in the kingdom and locked it up. If that's true you might have what I need. Look, I'm desperate here," I said.

"I apologize, Obie, these negotiations have brought up some old feelings I thought had dissipated, and that's on top of what my idiot son did. You have always been a friend to us, but soul stones are hard to come by. I'm not saying it's impossible, but if I can, what are you willing to give for it?" she asked.

"I've got money, name your price" I said.

She gave me a dismissive smile. "I don't need money, Obie."

"What do you need then?" I asked.

"Security. I'm afraid this bargain will be short-lived. When it falls through, there's a good chance it's going to be bad. If that happens the Elvin Nation will need friends, and a Keeper is a good friend to have. I'll get you a soul stone and as payment, some point in the future, I'll call on you for a favor. You come when I call and do what you are asked. No questions," she said. "Also, if hostilities break out you will side with me."

This kind of offer was something I was obligated to pass on. My loyalties had to be to Thera first, but what are the chances the Queen would call in a favor that would interfere with my obligations to Thera? I knew Otis wasn't going to do anything to break the peace so having either one of them to side with shouldn't be an issue. It had to be slim to none, besides, with only a day to spare, I didn't have any other options. Without a soul stone, there was no other way to get Naylet back. We made it to the cars and the attendant opened the door to the SUV for the Queen to get in. I was out of time to think about it.

"Agreed," I said, extending my hand.

She shook it and got into the car. Harlan sat in the back, looking at the floor. I didn't envy him.

"Give us a minute, Obie," she said, closing the door.

I could hear the Queens muffled voice from inside the car—she was clearly not pleased. While I waited, I thought about my plan and all the moving pieces that had to come together to make it work. The best I could do was show up and hope everyone came through. If they do then we just might pull it off. If just one thing fell through, then the plan for killing Petra probably wouldn't work and getting Naylet back would be impossible. The sound of an opening door brought me back to the present. Harlan got out of the SUV while the Queen rolled down the window.

"I will be expecting you tonight," she said.

CHAPTER ∘ 24

"It's not at all like I pictured it," Harlan said when he spotted the clubhouse on top of the hill surrounded by the junkyard.

Otis had it built in the Forties, around the time Harlan was born. They made the transition from the local werebear pack to what would become the modern Tortured Occult. By that time, the Shifter and Elvin cold war was well under way, so Harlan would have never had the chance to see the headquarters of the Elvin Nation's most hated enemy.

"Not as nice as what you're used to?" I asked.

"I've never seen anything like it. It's magnificent," he said. "The stories I've heard make it sound—"

I knew why he stopped talking; he was about to say something he shouldn't. "How could you hear stories about it if the elves stay within the Nation? The Queen wouldn't have spies running around would she?"

"Would it surprise you to hear that she did?" he asked.

"I would be disappointed if she didn't," I said.

I parked in my usual spot beside the clubhouse. We went in through the front, stepped into the changing room and closed the door behind us.

"You should probably leave the hat. You can stick it on any of those pegs," I said, pointing to a row of open pegs behind him as I slid my shoes off.

Harlan was reluctant but removed the beanie from his head. Completely understandable considering what he had just been through. "How does this work?"

"It's very informal. The only people here will be the five council members and Cearbhall. The meetings are closed to the public but we do have others attend if they have a reason to be here. All you have to do is make the proposals the Queen instructed and vote on anything that comes up."

An overweight coyote squeezed its way into the changing room through the dog door. It sat down and looked at us with its tongue out panting.

"Does he bite?" Harlan said, eyeballing the creature.

"Not unless you're made of nougat," I said. "This is Hambone. He represents the masses. This is Harlan, prince of the Elvin Nation."

The coyote shifted into a panting kobold. "A pleasure."

"Nice to meet you." Harlan extended his hand.

Hambone shook it with all the enthusiasm he could muster. "Wow, an elf, here and royalty no less. I can see why you called a meeting. It's very nice to meet you," he said. "I'll see you back there, okay?"

Hambone exited into the bar. Chatter flooded into the changing room when he opened the door.

"What's this?" Harlan asked, showing me one of Hambone's buttons.

"Oh, it's close to election time. He loves passing out those buttons," I said. "Just throw it out."

"This should be interesting," Harlan said, taking a breath.

"Nothing to it," I said, shifting to krasis. "Let's get back there."

The chatter died off almost completely in the packed clubhouse when we stepped through the door. Most people here hadn't seen an elf in a century or more and some never had, much less part of the royal family, even if it was just one of the males. I spotted Cearbhall, Otis, and Adan in the corner and gave them a nod. Hambone was busy buttering up some constituents at a nearby table. Harlan followed me to the back room for our meeting. Inside was a large pentagonal table with five chairs. We each took our normal seats, with Cearbhall leaning against the wall by the door. Harlan hesitated before moving to the only vacant chair, between Hambone and me.

He pulled the chair out, picked up a doughnut box off of it, and peeked inside. "What about the moldy doughnuts?"

"Oh, sorry about that. Your seat has been vacant so long, I was using it," Hambone said.

"Should I throw these out?" Harlan asked.

Hambone fell back in his seat like he had been struck. "Throw them out? There's nothing wrong with them!"

Harlan gave the doughnuts a second look. "Ugh, they're fuzzy."

Hambone patted the table in front of him. "Doughnuts are like wine, they get better with age. Just set them here."

Harlan complied, brushed some crumbs off the chair, and took his seat.

"Let's get this meeting started. Harlan, you have met Otis, and Hambone. The last member of the council is Adan, the emissary for the wererats in Atlanta."

They nodded a greeting to each other.

"Thanks, everyone, for showing up on such short notice. I called the meeting because we have a serious situation that I wanted to make you aware of. There is a demon on the loose that's caught Thera's attention. I won't go into the specifics, but Thera is prepared to bring down floods, tornadoes, the whole nine if we can't kill this demon quick. The result would be death and devastation on a massive scale of both humans and ultras. I have a plan in place to deal with the demon. The elves and the T.O. are both helping, so if everything goes according to plan, tomorrow night we will kill the demon and things will be back to normal."

"And if it doesn't go according to plan?" Adan asked.

"Then I feel sorry for anyone living in North Georgia," I said.

"Maybe we should evacuate," Hambone said.

"What about the humans?" Otis asked.

Hambone rifled through the doughnuts and began chewing one, his canid jaws sending crumbs falling all over himself and the floor and muffling his words. "The humans aren't our responsibility, besides, how would we warn them? Call in a bomb threat for the state?"

"I think it might be wise not to tell anyone," I said. "Any kind of mass exodus could scare the demon off, ensuring what we're trying to avoid. We need everything to look normal."

"And if you fail, we let everyone die," Hambone said.

I leaned forward to accentuate my point. "We won't fail."

Adan stroked his muzzle. "What about the elves?"

Everyone looked at Harlan. "The Queen is moving all nonessential personnel to the northern border."

"Why do the elves get to evacuate but no one else can?" Hambone said. "That's not right."

"I went to the Queen to get her help, so she was aware of the threat ahead of time. Elves move around all the time, and with the way relations have been, no one is even looking at them. It won't change anything," I said.

"That's not the point. We are talking about keeping a secret that could cost the lives of our friends and neighbors, unless it's the elves, which aren't really our friends. No offense, Harlan, you're wonderful," Hambone said. "You know Adan is going to report back to Atlanta and they will do something, too. If the T.O. is helping in this fight then they are already aware. The only people left out are the ones that are going to die ugly."

"I don't like it any more than you do but it is what it is. We can't risk a panic messing things up," I said.

"Vote then," Otis said. "All in favor of keeping it secret."

Everyone except Hambone raised their hand.

"Opposed."

Hambone held the opposition alone with a scowl.

"It passes. We don't make an announcement. Do we have any other business?"

Harlan took the cue and opened his mouth to speak. Before he could get a word out Hambone cut in. "I want to talk about the dust. While a lot of the dust was recovered from the recent theft, we lost four crates. That's a big problem both in potential threat, and the hit we are going to take to our supply. Assuming we're all still alive in a few days, we need to address the issue. Word has already gotten out that Hob was attacked. People are worried."

"I agree. It will take months to recover and with the supply down, prices will rise. Trouble is inevitable if the dust runs out or people can't afford it. Some people will stop practicing magic but some will go to the black market to get dust and that's bad for all of us," Adan said.

"I've been looking at the numbers and there's another problem. Base supply is down about twenty-five percent," Hambone said.

"Sorry, what's base supply?" Harlan asked.

"It's materials taken from the ultras that are produced in daily life, fingernail clippings, shed scales, lost teeth, and hair from haircuts for example. Things that can be dusted without harming the donor. When someone dies they have the option to donate their body as well," I said.

Harlan nodded and Hambone continued. "That by itself is within the normal ranges but it's just going to exacerbate the problem if it doesn't turn around."

"There's nothing we can do about base supply. It is what it is," Otis said.

"We have to do something," Hambone said, starting on his second doughnut.

"Could we recover the missing dust?" Adan asked.

"I think it was used. Hank and Cearbhall saw it as well. This demon had a magic like I had never seen before. It looked like it was burning the dust pretty quick. The good news is it's not out there to cause trouble," I said.

"Yeah, but we can't get it back either," Adan said.

"A couple of days isn't going to make a difference. Why don't we table this until we settle the bigger problem of this demon?" I said.

"Anyone opposed?" Otis asked.

The table was silent.

"Any more business?" Otis said, looking directly at Harlan.

"Yeah, I have a couple things. The Queen is willing to participate in the council again. I have been appointed as her representative. There are changes she would like. First, she would like to move the meetings from the club-house to the Southern Outpost," Harlan said.

"That's pretty far away," Adan said.

Hambone wasted no time in voicing his disapproval. "That's not going to work! I don't want to move into the Elvin Nation. There's no way I can run that far for a meeting."

"I can give everyone a ride to the meetings, it's not that big of a deal. Less than an hour away," Otis said. "My only concern is that we have our privacy. We need a place to talk freely."

"That's not a problem, there's a room on the second floor we can use. It's private and can be designated as our meeting room," Harlan said.

"A snack table," Hambone said.

"What?" Harlan asked.

"If I'm going all that way there's going to be a snack table, since I don't have an empty chair anymore, and you provide the doughnuts."

"Sure, no problem," Harlan said.

"And candy bars."

"Candy bars too," Harlan conceded.

"Maybe some chocolate covered slugs?" Hambone's eyes widened in anticipation.

"Don't push your luck," Harlan said.

"Vote," Otis said. "In favor of moving the meetings to the outpost?" Everyone but Adan raised their hand. "It passes, we will have the table moved and starting with our next meeting will be at the Southern Outpost. What's next?"

Harlan continued, "The Nation is used to a certain level of freedom. The Queen is looking for a promise that there won't be any restrictions placed on the Nation."

"So that would mean nothing would change really," Otis said.

"Do we need to discuss it or can we vote?" I said.

"Vote," Adan said. "In favor."

Everyone raised their hands.

"Excellent. Well, if you will excuse me, I have a lot to prepare for," I said, standing up from the table.

"One second, Obie, I have one more thing," Harlan said. "The Queen would like the use of magic to be banned from the region, both its use and the production and distribution of dust."

"Outrageous!" Hambone said, his mouth falling open, spilling half chewed doughnut on the table.

I sat back down and shot a look to Otis. He didn't appear to have any more answers than I did. This wasn't agreed to. Did she expect that we would back this? She couldn't think that we would.

"You can't be serious," Adan said. "The rats will never agree."

"Oh, I don't expect it to pass. I was told to bring it to vote and that's what I'm doing," Harlan said.

"Ok, vote then," I said. "In favor."

Harlan raised his hand.

"Opposed?"

The rest of the table voted as expected.

"Motion denied," I said. "Anything else?"

Harlan smiled and shook his head.

"Let's get out of here," I said, getting up from the table.

We all stood up and made our way to the door, except for Hambone who remained in his seat.

"Well, wasn't that an exciting meeting," he said. "It sure is nice to have the elves cooperating again. I'm just so happy that I got to meet you, Harlan, it was a pleasure. Obie, could I bother you for just a minute, please?"

The others left and I sat back down. This better not be about dust again. "What's up?"

"Snack table aside, I'm really not happy about this," he said.

I listened to Hambone complain for a good fifteen minutes before I could make it out. When I finally did, I found Harlan sitting at the bar alone. Hank and Cearbhall were at a table close by.

I walked up to the table. "I need to get Harlan back to the Queen. You coming?" I asked.

"I'm going to hang out here tonight. I'll catch up with you tomorrow," Cearbhall said.

"Suit yourself. I'll see you on the bridge," I said.

I turned to see Harlan walking over from the bar. I motioned toward the door with my head and we crossed into the changing room. Harlan grabbed his hat and I assumed a more suitable appearance for the outside world before leaving. We got back into the truck.

"Where to?" I said, cranking it up.

"Any chance you'll let me go?" he asked. "I'll just disappear. You can say I got away from you."

"If you want to disappear in two days, then great. I need the Queen's help tomorrow and the only way I get it is if I take you back. I know you're in a bad spot but there's nothing I can do. If I let you go, she will blame me. She's not the most forgiving person," I said.

"I understand. Let's get it over with," he said.

I followed his directions to a place deep inside the Elvin Nation. Turn after turn of backroads, winding through dense woods. Finally, we pulled up to a couple RVs with the Queen's SUV and escort truck parked beside them. The Queen was sitting at a picnic table with a grill set up beside it. Her guard patrolled the area, on the lookout for any threat. The scene looked like a normal campsite except with armed guards around the perimeter. I parked beside the Queen's SUV. Harlan and I got out and went to the table where the Queen was sitting.

"Delivered, as promised," I said.

"Have a seat," she said. "We have one more order of business."

"Okay, what's going on?" I asked, sitting at the table beside her, hoping she was going to say she found a soul stone.

"Harlan told me you healed his ears earlier today. It wasn't your place to intervene in my affairs," she said.

"I'm sorry if I overstepped, Your Highness. I only saw someone in pain that I could help. There wasn't anything malicious in it. Is this going to cause a problem for our plans tomorrow night?" I asked.

"I'll honor our agreement but I need you to know where the lines are. If you are aware of a situation with my family, especially one that would disgrace my house, I expect that you will bring it to my attention. I also expect that you would consider my wishes before getting involved," she said.

"I understand," I said.

"Good, then there's just one more thing. Take him," she said to the guards. Two of them stepped forward and grabbed Harlan by the arms. "Would you like a snack or some refreshment? I can have my boy make you something."

"What are you doing?" I asked as they dragged him over to the back of the RV.

His arms were tied to a ladder on the back. The head of her security force, Harlan's sister Patsy, looked back at their mother for confirmation. The Queen nodded. Patsy pulled out a pair of scissors and cut Harlan's hair. When he was as close to bald as she could get, she cut off his shirt.

"Harlan is being punished for his transgression," the Queen replied.

Patsy retrieved a coiled leather whip from the truck and took position behind him. Harlan kept his eyes straight ahead and his body still, as if he knew what was coming. Patsy again looked over at us.

"Ten," the Queen said.

Patsy released the whip and gave it a wiggle, unfurling it out onto the ground behind her. From the way she took a ready stance and gave her arm a few shakes to loosen it up, it was clear she had no intention of going easy on him. I wonder if that was ordered from the Queen or if she decided to do as much damage as she could—neither would surprise me. She drove the whip forward into his back. It made a ripping sound that reminded me of a zipper as it came into contact, tearing his skin with a splash of blood. Harlan was silent other than a sharp gasp. I wasn't as composed. Having lived through the tail end of slavery and the following years of Jim Crow, I've seen a few lashings and lynchings. I've never cared for either. Something was different about this from the other lashings I had seen, there was too much blood. That when I spotted the glimmer of metal on the end of the whip. Small pieces, barely sticking out at all but enough to add a bite that did some real damage. I put my hands on the table and pushed up to stand, not really sure what I was going to do, just knowing something had to be done. Before I was halfway out of my seat, the guards had guns drawn and pointed in my direction. I froze in place.

"Obie, you aren't planning on interfering with my family business, are you? I thought we had an understanding," the Queen said.

"We do, I still have some things to do tonight and I've seen floggings before. Thought I would head out," I said.

"I would prefer you stay," she said. "We have more business to discuss once this is done."

For the first time I thought maybe my plan wasn't such a good idea. The only thing keeping me from stopping this was that I was sticking to an idea that I needed the elves. There had to be another option. The Tortured Occult had guns, just not as big, but they aren't nearly as good with them.

"Obie?" the Queen questioned.

I lowered myself slowly back to my seat. Patsy struck him again and again. By the fourth, his legs were giving out and he could no longer stifle the sounds of his pain. By ten, he hung limply from his wrists, quiet and bloody, his back shredded. Patsy wound the whip and placed it on the table in front of me, the lamp light reflected in the blood covering its end.

I wasn't going to give the Queen the pleasure of knowing how much this bothered me. "What's the other business you mentioned?" I said.

The Queen motioned to one of her guards, who placed a plain wooden box in the center of the whip.

"If you take this then I will hold you to our agreement. You come when I call and do what you're asked," she said. "And if hostilities should erupt you will help us."

I opened the box to see what looked to be a baseball-sized diamond. It was perfectly clear but had no sparkle. It felt empty, as if it had its own gravity trying to pull me in. I closed the box and considered my options. I didn't want to be indebted to the Queen, especially considering the demonstration I just witnessed, but this was my only option if I wanted to get Naylet back. If there was a chance, I had to try it.

"It's a deal. What's going to happen to him?" I said, nodding to Harlan's limp form suspended from the RV.

"He will represent the Elvin Nation at your meetings as promised. We can discuss any final details later. I know you have a lot to do to get ready for tomorrow night, and I would hate to keep you," she said.

I smiled and nodded. I wasn't going to ask about healing Harlan. She wouldn't go for it and might actually make things worse for him. I took the box, getting a little blood on my hand as I did, and headed for the truck. I wiped it on my shirt as I got in. I couldn't wait to get out of there. As I pulled out, the headlights illuminated Harlan, his blood and pain. He was still hanging there when I pulled away and they didn't seem to be in any hurry to help him.

CHAPTER · 25

If I was being honest with myself, Petra could probably kill Cearbhall and me at the same time on an even playing field. The poison tipped the scales in her favor and she knew it. I promised no weapons, but that didn't mean I had to fight fair. Walasi was right; I could get the advantage back by fighting her my way, on my terms, and taking advantage of Livy's alchemical skills. If everything went according to plan, the demon would be dead and Naylet would be back to normal in a few days.

I pulled into Northside Cherokee Hospital, found a parking spot, and picked up a passing shuttle to the front entrance. Inside I found the receptionist playing with her cell phone behind the desk.

When she saw me approaching she put it down and smiled. "Can I help you sir?"

"Hi, could you tell me if Rebecca Lin is working tonight," I said.

She typed away on the keys of an undisclosed keyboard behind the counter. "Is she expecting you?"

"No, I'm an old friend, just stopping by. It's really important," I said.

"What's your name?" she asked, picking up the phone.

"Obie."

"Have a seat," she said, stabbing the keypad with a pin. "I'll page her."

I found a large cushy couch by an enormous window in the corner to wait. Putting my feet up on the table, I leaned back and rubbed my eyes.

I was suddenly aware of a presence to my left. I knew it was Thera before she spoke. "Holt is awake."

"I guess Livy's antivenom works then. That's good news."

She sat beside me on the white upholstery, grass and wildflowers cascading down to the floor.

"Have you decided if you can work with him?"

"Haven't really had time to think about it. I've been too busy trying to keep you from killing everyone," I said. "What happens if I can't? Can you make him human again?"

"Once the link is established it can't be undone, but it can be broken," she said.

"And breaking it would kill him wouldn't it?" I asked.

"Yes."

I didn't like the sound of that. "I don't want him to die but I don't want things to be the same either."

"Things never stay the same for long. Tell me and I will cut the link. Then you will pick someone new to take his place," she said.

"I pick? I thought you did the picking," I said.

"No, Obie, you choose who you want to work with, just like Cearbhall chose you and Cedric chose Holt," she said.

"Wait, Cearbhall chose me?" How have I gone this long without knowing Thera didn't choose new Keepers? "I thought he resented me."

"He always had positive things to say," she said.

I had spent my roughly two hundred years working with Cearbhall thinking I was a burden. It put all the times he tortured me in a new light. He wasn't trying to make me fail but pushing me to be my best. It changed everything I thought I knew. I searched myself, trying to make sense of our relationship. The times he was hard on me and what seemed to me now to be my childish responses.

"I can work with him," I said. "If Cedric chose him then there must be more to him than I am seeing."

...

"As opposed to if I chose him?" she questioned.

"Let's be honest, you don't really get people," I said.

She changed the subject instead of arguing. "I know why you're here. You're wasting time."

"No, I'm waiting. There's a difference," I said. "Besides, this is important."

She leaned back in the couch in feigned relaxation. "You've made progress then?"

"It ends tonight," I said.

"And the grimoire?"

"Will be recovered," I said. "The situation is under control. Even if Cearbhall and I die tonight, the demon wants Naylet. Walasi is watching her. If the demon shows up there, she will be killed for sure. It's a solid plan. I've seen how important the demon's victims are to it."

"You sound confident," she said.

"I am, this will work. By this time tomorrow things are going to be back to normal. I hope this means you have changed your mind about the whole mass destruction thing?"

"Do you talk to yourself a lot?" Rebecca had walked up without me seeing her.

Rebecca Lin was a surgeon I helped a couple of years ago. She was short, even by Chinese standards, and couldn't have weighed more than a buck ten soaking wet. She wore her white coat over jeans and a nice blouse rather than her usual blue scrubs. Bright white shoes that looked brand new finished the ensemble.

I stood up and gave her a hug. "I am an excellent conversationalist." Spotting the new title on her name tag, I said, "Administrator . . . you got a promotion?"

I looked back to the couch to find Thera had vanished.

"Obie, what are you doing here?" she asked, obviously not feeling like small talk.

Right to the point then. "I need a favor. A woman was brought in yesterday, she was attacked in her apartment. Candice Heck."

"Yes, she's upstairs, that poor woman. You wouldn't believe what some sick bastard did to her," she said.

"I'd believe it. I'm the one that found her," I said.

"So what do you want with her then?" she asked.

I smiled. "Just to help. You know me, always lending a helping hand."

She looked over her shoulder as if she was afraid someone was watching. "Help her the way you helped me?"

I nodded. "I just need a couple minutes."

"You could have done that at her apartment. Why wait until she's here?"

"She had a fire poker shoved in her head," I said, making a jabbing motion with my finger under my jaw. "I'm good at a lot of things, but removing giant hooks from someone's face isn't one of them."

She crossed her arms and put a hand over her mouth. "I don't know, she just got out of surgery an hour ago, they wired her jaw shut and have experts coming in in the morning. How would I explain it?"

"You don't have to, miracles happen every day. Two minutes, please."

She groaned with frustration. "Come on. We'll go the back way, but this better not come back on me."

She took me up a stairwell and through a few hallways before we came to the room. Inside Candice was lying with her head bandaged—everything except her right eye, which was closed.

"I don't think she's woken up yet," Rebecca said.

I gave the machines she was connected to a once over. I didn't know what anything on the screens meant except for the steady beep of the heart rate monitor. "Do you want to wait outside?"

She closed the door. "I think I'll stay. I'm curious how you do it."

I placed a hand over Candice's head and concentrated. The room took on a blue hue from my eyes and hands as the energy began to flow.

"Jesus, your eyes. I didn't see that last time. Do they always glow like that?"

"Only when I'm working," I said without looking up.

Rebecca stepped up to the bed. "That's it? I thought there would be more chanting and arm waving."

"You watch too much TV."

Candice began to moan and shift around in her bed as the healing took hold. The beeping of her heartrate monitor sped up with the little line on the screen bouncing around like a game of Pong on steroids.

Rebecca reached out a hand to intervene but stopped just before she touched me. "Obie, her heart, you need to stop."

I could feel the energy pouring into her, swirling and pulsing. I could feel some resistance coming from her stomach, maybe some kind of cancer, couldn't be sure. Might as well take care of that since I was already warmed up. I focused on the obstruction and it melted away in a matter of a few seconds. I could tell when she was healed because instead of going in, the energy flowed over her like water spilling out of a cup—she was full. I took my hand back and her heart went from racing to normal in an instant. Rebecca looked at the monitor, giving it a tap to figure out if it was malfunctioning. Candice opened her unbandaged eye and looked around.

"Candice, you're in the hospital. Don't try to speak, your jaw was wired shut," Rebecca said, leaning over her bed.

"You're safe now. Try to take it easy. It will take them a few days to figure out you've been healed, remove the wires, and let you go," I said, resting a hand on the side if the bed. "Oh, and I took care of that stomach issue, too."

Candice nodded, tears welling up in her eye. When Rebecca stepped back Candice saw me and reached out to hold the hand I had on the railing of the bed. She raised the other hand and made a scribbling gesture in the air. Rebecca got a pad and pen and handed it to her. She wrote one word and turned the pad over for me to see. *Angel?* it said. I took the letter she had written Steve with her rings in it and placed it her hand. Rebecca was still busy when I left. I wanted to get out discreetly. I was barely out of the room when I heard Rebecca calling after me. She caught up to me just as I opened the door to the stairwell.

"Obie, wait. Listen, I was thinking maybe you could take a look at a couple other people while you're here," she said.

I was afraid of this. "I can't, sorry."

She crossed her arms. "You can't or you won't?"

"I won't."

"You could help so many people with your gift and you just won't? I thought you were better than that," she said.

"We all make mistakes," I said, starting down the stairs.

"At least tell me why," she said.

"One is a miracle. Any more than that and people dig for an explanation, and they won't let it go until they find one. They will find the surveillance video of us and they will come asking questions we can't answer. Maybe they give up eventually or maybe word gets out that I'm some kind of faith healer. People will come from far and wide looking for their own miracle and then I won't be able to do my job. See, healing people isn't why I'm here, it's just a bonus I get to help some people sometimes. I wish I could do more but it's not possible," I said. "If you know someone that needs help and they aren't admitted in a hospital or have extensive medical records give me a call."

She didn't say anything but stood there processing. After a few seconds without a response, I headed for the truck.

CHAPTER · 26

It was a little after nine in the morning when I left the hospital, giving me about half a day before my battle with Petra. With nothing to do but wait, I headed to the clubhouse. It was mostly empty inside. Besides the goblin at the bar looking like he already had a few too many, the only other person was Adan, sitting at his normal table in the corner by the pool table. He had a plate of bacon and eggs with a beer, looking over papers spread all over the table. The rats in Atlanta handled not only the broad distribution network for the dust but also the necessities for modern life like driver's licenses and bank accounts. As the representative of Atlanta, he handled all those things for the ultras in the area. I joined him at his table.

"What are you doing here? Don't you have a demon to get ready for," he asked.

"I'm as ready as I am going to be. Just wasting time," I said. "I do have some business I wanted to talk to you about."

"Oh yeah, what's that?" he asked, taking off his reading glasses to give the full attention that business requires.

"Holt told me he hadn't set up his accounts yet. I wanted to get that in order for him," I said.

"He was in bad shape last I heard. Rumor has it he isn't going to make it," he said.

"Well, I know he's awake. He's strong, he'll be okay," I said. "I just need the usual, bank account, debit card, he already has a license but it's for Tennessee, so we need to have that updated to Georgia. Go ahead and transfer ten thousand from my account to get him started, and fifty percent of the take from the dust going forward."

"Are you sure? That's pretty generous," he said.

"Yeah, just make it happen," I answered.

"It's your money," he mumbled jotting down notes on a scrap piece of paper. "You must be feeling pretty confident about tonight if you're making plans for the future."

"Of course he's confident. Keepers always win," Otis said from behind me, putting his hands on my shoulders.

"While I appreciate the vote of confidence we both know that's not true," I said.

He sat down in a chair to my right. "It's true enough. Listen, Obie, we have about ten hours until we have to be at the bridge, and I know you don't drink, but we're going to have a few today."

"What's the occasion?" I asked.

"The world as we know it could be ending," he said, getting up and heading to the bar.

"How is that different from any other day?" I shouted after him.

Otis returned a few minutes later carrying six large mugs and having to step around a knocker that scurried across the floor in front of him. He put them down on the table, getting beer rings on Adan's papers, who didn't seem to mind in the least.

"Any luck finding a home for the knockers?" I asked when he sat down.

"Not in the least. They won't go back to the mine and no one wants to take them in. Imagine that," he said.

Tico called over from the bar. "Travis is snooping around the shop."

"Travis? What's that about," Otis said. "I got to check this out."

"I'll come with you," I said, getting up from the table. "Adan?"

Adan reached for a beer. "I'm good here. You fellas go ahead."

We changed back into human form and walked over to Morrison

Salvage and Repair, the more legitimate business of the Tortured Occult. We walked into the shop through one of the open garage doors. The mechanics always kept the doors open with giant fans running in the middle of summer, not that it did much to stifle the heat. The building had a small waiting room with a window to the shop where people could watch their cars being repaired. Travis stood by the window with a magazine, trying to discreetly watch one of the mechanics. He fancied himself as a hunter, and he did in fact hunt, he just never caught anything, which made him mostly harmless. Otis and I joined him in the waiting room.

"Something wrong with the car?" Otis asked when he opened the door.

"Just getting an oil change," he said.

"Weren't you in here a couple weeks ago for an oil change? Unless I'm mistaken," Otis said. "There has to be something other than that. You're holding your magazine upside down."

He wasn't, but since he wasn't paying any attention to it he did a double take before he figured out Otis was testing him.

"All right, you got me," Travis said. "You know how I look into strange things sometimes. Well . . . I've got a story for you."

He put the magazine on the table and took a seat on the couch. Otis and I took chairs across from him.

"First, tell me about that feller working on the Buick," he said. "How long's he been 'round here?"

Now that Travis mentioned it, I hadn't seen the guy around before. He looked Japanese, wore navy coveralls, and was focused on his work.

Otis turned to verify who Travis was talking about before responding. "Five or six weeks. He was passing through, looking for work. I don't know if he's planning on staying or not. We call him Panda," he said, giving me a look to let me know the name was more literal than he was letting on. "Is there a problem?"

"Well, now that's what I'm trying to figure out," Travis said. "Have you noticed any funny looking scars on him? Maybe something looking like a penny-gram?"

"A pentagram?" Otis asked. "No, he stays covered up most of the time. What's this about?"

"Couple days ago I was checking out an old house in Dahlonega, behind the Dairy Queen. It's been abandoned for a while and all overgrown. It just looks like a place you could find a ghost or spook or something. Well, I was there poking around and I run across this light coming out from under the door in one of the rooms upstairs. It was kinda shimmering and I didn't know what to make of it. So I pop the door open, ready for anything, and there's a tiny little person with wings flying around, like Tinkerbell or something. It's got this little rock that's giving off all the light. I didn't waste any time grabbing it up. So then I'm thinking what do I do with it now?"

"What did you do with it?" I asked.

"This is the good part," Travis said leaning forwarded in the couch. "So this little thing starts talking. Stuff like 'please let me go' and all that. I'm thinking no way I'm letting it go! Then it says how it's harmless and never hurt nobody and if I let it go it can tell me where a real, honest to God, werewolf is. I says, 'baloney, you're just trying to get away'. Then it says it will tell me where there's a werewolf and these little things called tommy knockers, both. I didn't know what they were until it told me. It told me where there's this mine close by with these little yellow-eyed critters in it. I checked it out and sure enough there was. I didn't catch any but they were there. That checked out so I thought there might be something to the werewolf. It says there's one working right here. I know if you had some kinda maneater working in yer shop you want to know, so I come a looking. Now I've seen y'all around and I know you good people, the only feller I don't know is that one. It has to be him," he said pointing discreetly in Panda's direction.

"So let me get this straight. You're telling me that you caught some kind of fairy that told you there was a monster working in my shop? Do you hear what you're saying?" Otis asked.

Travis looked a little hurt by the lack of confidence. "I know how it sounds but as sure as the day's long there's some funny stuff going on around here. I just want to make sure folks are safe, that's all."

"Why did you ask about a scar?" I asked.

"I don't reckon I know anything about werewolves other than that what ya see in movies and whatnot, so I looked in the Google. I found all kinds of stuff I never heard of. One of them was that werewolves have a scar in the shape of a penny-gram."

"I see," Otis said. "While I appreciate you looking out for us I can say with one hundred percent certainty that he is not a werewolf, okay? I like you, Travis. You're a good guy but please don't come around here snooping around for some kind of monster or something. It's bad for business and people are going to think you're nuttier than a squirrel turd."

"Well, I don't mean to cause you no trouble, that's for sure," Travis said, looking a little hurt.

Otis stood up and shook hands with Travis. "Don't worry about it. It's always good to see you, and that oil change is on the house, okay?"

We said our goodbyes and went back to the clubhouse. It was a strange story, one I felt we needed to figure out. We made it back to the table where Adan had finished off four of the six beers.

"Really?" Otis questioned, when he saw the work Adan had done on the beer. "We were gone for five minutes."

Adan was just putting down his fourth empty mug. "What's that saying? A fool and his beer are soon parted?"

"You're getting the next round," Otis said, sitting down and claiming the remaining two beers. He put one in front of me and kept the other for himself. "Drink."

"What do you think about Travis? It sounded like he was talking about a pixie to me, and we both know a real pixie would have evaded or killed him rather than be captured," I said.

"I think someone's playing games. Maybe sending a message," he said, taking a drink.

"What message is that?" Adan asked, holding up three fingers to Tico for another round.

"That they aren't afraid to cause problems," he said.

I picked up the beer. "Who do you think is responsible?"

"There's only one person that has any kind of beef with Tom C: the Queen," he said.

"Assuming we make it through the night, what are you going to do about her?" I asked.

"What can I do? Sometimes you just have to wait for the old to die and take their ideas with them," he said taking another swig. "Maybe whoever replaces her will be more interested in getting along."

Adan took a long swig from the beer. "You know how long elves live, especially paranoid ones with armed guards?"

"We can address that at the next meeting. Let's not let it spoil our good time," he said. "Obie, drink up, we have another on the way."

The first gulp gave me a strange sensation in my throat. It was the first thing I had to drink in a long time, and I had forgotten what carbonation felt like in my throat. There was a good chance this was going to be my last day, even if I wouldn't admit it to anyone else. Sharing a few cold ones with friends was a good way to spend it.

CHAPTER • 27

Traffic backed up about a mile away from the bridge, to be expected with the detours in place. I waited in the line of cars approaching the bridge, where a cop parked in the road was waving traffic onto a side street. Behind him, some assorted machinery, I had no idea what any of it was, was sitting in the road. I recognized Razor and Cotton dressed up as construction workers, milling around the machines, not really doing anything—they were pulling off the disguise of your average road worker to a tee. When the officer saw me, he waved me into the construction site. I pulled slowly around the police car, giving him a nod as I went by. I arrived at the bridge a few minutes behind schedule, but still with time to spare for the final arrangements. I found the elves and T.O. parked on opposite sides of the road, like boys and girls at a middle school dance. I pulled up close to where Cearbhall and Otis were sitting on a tailgate, and got out.

"You smell like beer," Cearbhall said when I had walked over to them.

"I'm fine," I said. "I was wasting some time with Otis today."

"He needed to loosen up a bit," Otis said.

"You do look a little more relaxed," Cearbhall said with a smile. "I'm sorry I missed it."

"Let's get ready, we don't have long," I said, stepping out toward the center of the road and waving everyone in. "Thanks for coming, folks. Let's get everyone together and go over the plan one more time to make sure we're all on the same page."

Looking over the crowd I saw the Queen hadn't attended our little soiree, but I spotted Harlan with a weird looking hat in one of the trucks. She had held up her end of the bargain and sent him to handle business with Tom C as promised. A small group of eight elves represented the Elvin Nation with what looked to be ten from the T.O. in attendance, on top of what I already saw manning the construction equipment. Harlan still sat in the truck by himself and didn't seem to notice we were getting underway, so I walked over to see if he was okay.

When I got close he got out of the truck, slowly and deliberately, clearly in pain. That's when I noticed he wasn't wearing a hat, he had bandages on his ears again. This time, they were covered completely with the cloth wrapped all the way around his head, so only his face and the back of his head were uncovered. His head had been shaven clean, and blood was soaking through on each side of the bandages where his ears were.

"What happened, Harlan?"

"My dear mother has punished me for embarrassing her. I couldn't be banished because of the agreement with the Tortured Occult, but I don't really think she would have banished me anyway. I imagine I would have just disappeared and been forgotten like so many others. Since that wasn't an option, she said if I wasn't proud of my ears then I shouldn't have them. So she had Patsy cut them off," he said. "I'm not allowed to hide my shame, with a hat or hair."

"She cut off your ears?" I said, not really believing what I was hearing. "Let me help."

"Just stay the hell away from me. She wants me to suffer, you're just going to make it worse," he said, shooting me a look that actually gave me pause.

"We aren't in the Elvin Nation and she isn't my Queen. Show me," I said.

His expression softened. "If you wanted to help you would have let me go. If you heal me she'll just hurt me again. There's nothing you can do. The best thing you can do now is leave me alone."

"I'm sorry, Harlan. I hope you believe that," I said.

"Let's get down to business. Why don't I show you what your loyalty bought?" he said.

He walked slowly, almost shambling, but with his head up. He was in pain, a lot of it, but he didn't let it show or make apologies. He ignored the sneers of the elves and the concerned looks from the T.O. as he approached the trucks. Each had a large bulge covered by a heavy tarp in the back. He waved a hand and a couple of elves pulled the tarp back, revealing the largest gun I had ever seen.

"We have two trucks mounted with M134D Gatling guns. These will take down anything we run into tonight, flying or not. We would normally have tracers, but since we are trying to stay low profile we aren't using them. The upside is there won't be streaks of light to attract unwanted attention, the downside is it will take an extra second or two to acquire the target once we open up. Each truck has a crew of four with additional small arms if needed."

I stepped forward to get a closer look at the machine. "I am going to be honest, I don't know what that means, but it sounds good. Like I said, I am hoping they won't be needed. It's just insurance. If you do shoot them, I am guessing it's going to attract a lot of attention, right? Even without the tracers? Are we going to be on the clock to wrap this up and get out of here before the National Guard shows up?"

"I think we will be okay. Yes, they are loud but you have to understand that these fire three thousand rounds a minute. Shooting that fast the gun doesn't go bang-bang, it hums. If anyone around is familiar with it they might be able to tell what it is, but we are working under the pretense that there is construction going on tonight. It would be easy for the layperson to confuse it for machinery and not give it a second thought. As long as we position the trucks where the muzzle flash can't be seen from passing boats, then it should largely blend in. We're going to have two or three feet of fire coming out of the barrels when we let go, so placement is important."

The members of the T.O. standing around began to mumble among themselves. They hadn't had any real dealings with the Elvin Nation in over a hundred years. Weapons had come a long way in that time and I don't think they realized the resources that their historical adversaries had access to. A bit of a wakeup call, to say the least.

Harlan waved again and the tarp was placed back over the gun. "We should be able to find a good position in the tree line that will serve our purpose."

"Okay, great, that sounds good. Otis, can we have the machines making as much noise as possible to conceal any sounds from the fight or gunfire?"

"Sure, not a problem," he said.

"Ok, don't open fire unless she tries to fly away. Just hang back and let Cearbhall and I finish her off. The T.O. will keep her away from the elves in case she gets away from us. That's it," I said.

"What if she kills the both of you?" Harlan asked.

"Then you all can do whatever you like. It won't matter to me," I said. "All we have to do now is get into position and wait. Please don't kill each other in the next hour or so. I'll catch up to you when it's done."

Cearbhall and I got in the truck while the T.O. and elves split into two groups. One group went into the trees on the close side of the bridge; the second group took position on the opposite side. We drove to the center and parked. The machinery started up a few minutes later, flooding the area with the rumbling and clanging of construction. With an hour to wait, we got out of the car and made the change to krasis. I put the box with the soul stone and the two vials of antivenom on the hood and we took a seat on either side.

"Thera told me something interesting today. She said that you chose me to be a Keeper. Since our fight, I spent all this time under the impression that you resented me," I said.

"What fight?" he asked.

"You know, the one where we had it out and started working separately."

He scratched his neck, his face wrinkled in contemplation. "I really don't remember any fight. We split up because you were ready to get out on your own. Don't get me wrong, you still do stupid stuff, like making that lit-tle club, but you're a good Keeper. I wouldn't have left if you weren't ready."

All that time, I had been carrying around hostility and hurt over some-thing that he didn't remember. What a waste.

"Livy said the antivenom might not be at full strength, so let's take it right before and try to avoid the snakes as much as we can," I said, handing him one of the vials.

"What's in the box?" Cearbhall asked.

I opened it to show him the stone. I held it up to the moon, expecting to see right through it but while the stone looked clear, no light passed through it.

"It's a soul stone. Once we have Petra beaten down, I am going to use it to take her soul to hold until I find a way to extract Naylet from her. I know how to restore her body but this is the last piece of the puzzle. It should buy me the time I need," I said.

"Can I see?" he said, holding out his hand.

I passed the stone to him without thinking about it. He held it up to inspect it while I looked at the paper to decipher the procedures to trap a soul; it looked pretty straightforward.

"Yeah, this is the real thing," he said. "Do you think it's a good idea to keep a demon soul, especially one like Petra's, locked up for later use?"

"I don't like it any more than you do but it's my only option to get Nay-let back. It's what I have to do," I said.

"You know Thera isn't going to let that stand," he said, bouncing the stone in his hand, feeling its heft. "If you trap it, the demon wouldn't be completely dead. You're not thinking this through. Where'd you get it from anyway?"

"I got it from the Queen, we made a deal," I said absently.

"Must have been pricy," he said. "Why don't you send it back with Har-lan and call the deal off. It's not too late. She may not like it, but I doubt she would refuse."

"I know it's stupid, but I love Naylet. If there's any chance, I have to take it, regardless of the consequences," I said.

He looked over at me and said, "Then I'm sorry about this," and threw the stone down into the pavement.

I couldn't see where it hit, the truck was blocking my view. The shattering sound made the bottom immediately fall out of my stomach and nausea set in. I jumped off the hood and moved around, half in shock, to get a look at the damage. Maybe it wasn't so bad. What had been a solid object just seconds before had disintegrated into a small pile of powder on the asphalt. I couldn't stop staring at it, trying to make sense out of what had just happened. My body started trembling and my eyes began to water. I had been through so much getting to this point and the one person I was supposed to be able to count on had sabotaged my plan. Without the soul stone there was no hope to restore Naylet. It was too late to come up with another plan. At that moment I might have actually been crazy.

Cearbhall didn't look happy about what he had done. He started to say, "I'm sorry," but I cut him off with a fist to the throat, reducing his apology to a rasping gurgle. He didn't fight back or try to stop me and I didn't stop hitting him until he collapsed off the side of the hood. He landed motionless beside what had been the soul stone. Looking up I could tell that had caused some commotion with the elves and the T.O., no doubt they were wondering what was going on. A stiff breeze ran across my face, tingling my whiskers and bringing the smell of rain. I noticed the stars were gone, a storm was moving in. We still had a few hours before the deadline Thera set, she was being impatient. I looked down at Cearbhall as the trembling in my body subsided and I came back to my senses.

"Shit," I said, realizing what I had done.

I needed him one hundred percent before Petra arrived. He would come to soon, I just hoped it would be soon enough. If we made it through this, we were going to have to settle up, and I wasn't sure what that would look like. I sat down on the bridge beside him and the hopelessness of it all came crashing in. I had been a fool. All the effort I had put in trying to hold onto something that I never really had a chance to get back. Cearbhall was right. Thera wouldn't stand for the demon to live in any form, even trapped in a stone. I had lost Naylet when she was turned and I was never going to get her back. I had been clinging onto a fantasy and things kept getting worse because of it. No more fairy tales, there is no happily ever after for my kind. I've had it drilled into me since the day I became a Keeper.

I heard flapping overhead and looked up to see Petra landing on the bridge twenty feet in front of the truck. She wore no disguise, or clothes. The curves of her unmistakably feminine form were only covered by her black scales. She had a leather bag slung across her back, secured by a strap running over each shoulder. She looked different than she had at Naylet's house. Before, her scales had looked scuffed and dull, now they were smooth and shiny all over. The snakes that had lay flat during flight were now rising up over her. They were much smaller now and looked to be just over a foot long. That should be much more manageable, at least I had that going for me. I looked back to check on Cearbhall, he was still unconscious. I needed him to wake up soon. I would have to stall her if I could.

"Why is it every time the two of you get together you fight," she said. "I mean, I know about that business with the siren, and I still agree he was out of line, but you two should really leave your problems in the past."

I just smiled. "I love what you've done with your hair, it suits you."

"Why do you show me such animosity?" she asked. "There's no reason to be so hostile."

"I have to admit, I am going to miss our back and forth after I have killed you," I said.

"Is there a line I should wait in? You seem to be killing everyone around you tonight," she said, looking at Cearbhall, still lying on the ground. "Perhaps you want to do me a favor and take care of those men on the trucks? That wasn't part of the agreement, Obie. You weren't supposed to bring help."

"They are just here to make sure you live up to your part of the deal," I said.

She laughed. "And you thought a few men with rifles would do the job? You underestimate me."

"Those are soldiers from the Elvin Nation. That makes them women with rifles but they brought a little more than that," I said, sticking a thumb out at the truck behind me. "That's not to mention the T.O. backing them up. As long as you stay on the bridge until the fight is over, then they stay out of it."

"This isn't what we agreed to," she said. Her disposition was growing increasingly sour by the second. At this rate we would be fighting before Cearbhall woke up.

"This is exactly what we agreed to," I countered.

"We agreed that if I win I would get Naylet, you don't appear to have brought her. Where is she?" she asked stretching her arms wide.

"Naylet is at DeSoto Park, just north of the campground in the woods. Livy is camped there, keeping an eye on her. You won't have any trouble finding the place," I said.

She gave her wings a couple of agitated flaps. "How do I know you're telling the truth?"

I shrugged. "I've never lied to you before, besides, it's not like you have a choice. What about the grimoire? Did you bring it?"

She took the bag off her back and opened the top, revealing a plain leather-bound book. She placed it, still in the bag, on the bridge behind her. "Are you ready then?"

"Answer one question for me first," I said. "Why Naylet? You were living off babies under the radar for who knows how long. Why go out of your way to kill the woman I love?"

"I didn't kill her, Obie. I told you, she lives in me now. But to answer your question, I have been here since these humans were beating each other with rocks and cowering in caves. I have always been on the run, hiding from the mighty Keepers. I'm not doing it anymore. I came to Georgia for a start fresh and I decided instead of waiting for one of you to find me, I would strike first. Of course that meant finding you, but that was easy enough. That idiot Steve was easy to manipulate into getting your attention. After you showed up at the church, I followed you until I found someone that could tell me everything I needed to know about you. I didn't realize you were a couple at the time, or I wouldn't have done it. Feelings can be such sticky things. Your kindness and generosity, it's sickeningly endearing."

"I led you to her." The realization that I was the one that was responsible for Naylet really stung. Petra seemed to take my statement as a question.

"I had an imp at the church and Steve's house. Once he told me you paid Steve a visit I went to his house and waited. I followed you from there," she said. "So yes, you made our bonding possible."

"And Thera?" I asked. "Was the plan to kill her, too?"

"Even if I could, I wouldn't want to. That would ruin this rich buffet of a world," she said. "No, I needed her trapped, not killed. Her Keepers are her weakness as well as her strength. I was trying to bind her to Holt. Then she would be trapped in a vessel that doesn't have to eat and can't die. I could keep her in that prison for centuries before Holt's inevitable death freed her, and with his arms and legs removed it would be no trouble keeping him under control. The rest of you would have been easy enough to handle without her. You ruined that for me though."

I heard Cearbhall moving behind me. I turned to see him pulling himself to his feet.

"We're going to have a long talk when this is over with," he said.

"Fair enough. You ready to do this?" I said, walking back to the truck to get my vial of antivenom.

"Let's get it over with," he said, downing the other one.

I drank my vial. "Well, Petra, I wish I could say it's been a pleasure, but I'm afraid your time is up."

"I feel there is one more thing I should tell you," she said. A grin spread across her face, exposing her fangs and giving me a general feeling of uneasiness. "I didn't come alone either." She spread her wings and gave three flaps. Almost immediately commotion broke out at the truck on the bank behind her. Dark figures moved all around, with muzzle flashes accentuating the scene like a strobe light. I turned to see the same thing happening at the truck behind us. There was nothing I could do to help them, not until after Petra was dead. They should be able to hold their own, as long as they worked together.

"We can't help them. Let's handle what's in front of us and then see what we can do for them," Cearbhall said.

I nodded in agreement as rain began to fall.

CHAPTER · 28

He went right while I went left, positioning ourselves at opposite sides of Petra. We circled for a few seconds, looking for an opening but none presented itself. The snakes on her head shifted around, monitoring our positions—she had too many eyes. I lunged forward, dodging and swatting snakes. She turned to face me, bringing the full fury of her rage. Putting most of my attention into dealing with the snakes left me vulnerable to her claws, which dug in repeatedly on my arms and chest. This gave Cearbhall the opening he needed to close in from behind. I could see his arms popping up and down behind her as he landed multiple blows to her back. Even though her scales were shiny and new, they were still tough. If his strikes had any affect I couldn't tell, but I was too busy trying not to get bit to know what was going on.

Suddenly, she yelped and jumped to the side, retreating a few steps to put some distance between us. Cearbhall stood with a snake in one hand and black demon blood covering the claws of his other.

"Strike upwards under the scales," he said, gesturing upwards with his bloodied claws. "They aren't so tough if you can get under them."

I nodded. "Are you bit?"

"Yep, you?"

"Not sure, scratched up pretty good," I said.

The shirt I was wearing was in tatters and blood soaked. Couldn't tell the extent of my injuries, but my shoulders and chest were on fire.

"Got an idea, see if you can knock her down," he said.

We split up again for our second attack. She didn't appear much worse for wear so far, besides a little blood trickling down where Cearbhall had removed the snake and a couple of bloody footprints on the pavement. Her face contorted in anger as she gingerly touched the place on her head where the snake had been. Cearbhall threw his prize on the pavement between them.

"You're losing your cool, Petra. Feeling a little outmatched?" I asked.

"This is the end for you, Obie. I have tried to be reasonable and you have given me nothing but contempt. You don't worry about the snakes. My venom isn't going to kill you. I am going to eat you alive."

"Then I will have to kill you with indigestion," I said.

Again I closed in, pressing the attack. This time giving two high strikes before dropping suddenly and spinning, sending my tail out to sweep her legs. She collapsed to the ground, landing hard but recovering almost instantly, or would have if Cearbhall gave her the chance. He was on her in an instant, grabbing one of her wings and using it as a shield to protect him from the snakes. Throwing the full weight of his body on her head, he had her pinned for the moment.

"Now!" he yelled.

I jumped forward, being careful to avoid the couple of snakes that had worked their way free from under her wing. She squirmed, unable to escape, her exposed belly prime real estate where I wasted no time moving in. Strike after strike sent my claws digging under her scales into the soft flesh underneath. She shrieked and writhed under Cearbhall's weight. The more blows I landed, the more enraged she became. She thrashed wildly and rolled Cearbhall off onto the bridge beside her. She spun and jumped on top of him, digging her claws deep into his shoulder. He bared his teeth and snarled in defiance as he grabbed her hand and pulled it out. I tried to get her off but her snakes turned, hissing and striking, keeping me just out of reach.

Petra's position made it nearly impossible for Cearbhall to get the angle needed to get under her scales. He wouldn't stand a chance if I couldn't get her off him. I moved around behind her as she drove her fist into his head. He deflected a few strikes at first, with the amount of blows Petra was able to land cascading into a wave of punishment. After a few seconds his defense was shot. She landed a few blows with his head trapped between her fist and the concrete; he lost consciousness. Her wings stuck back far enough to be out of reach of the snakes. I grabbed them and spun, slamming her into the side of the bridge. She collapsed to the concrete, lying still. I knelt for a moment to take a look at Cearbhall. I needed to know about how long he would be out for. His head was intact with blood running out of his mouth, nose, and ears, so maybe a couple minutes.

The sprinkling rain turned into a light shower pattering on the bridge. Lightning flashed and thunder rolled, rumbling the bridge under my feet. The storm was making enough noise to keep me from hearing Petra get up. I wasn't aware she was moving again until she was almost on top of me. I tried to jump clear but slipped in the water. She leapt on my back, sending me face first onto the water.

"A promise is a promise, love," she said, and drove her teeth into my shoulder.

I kicked and screamed my way out of her bite, not entirely sure I was still in one piece. My shoulder revolted and stung; blood poured down my back. I managed to crawl a few feet before she grabbed me from behind, lifted me above her head, and threw me into the front of the truck. The collision, along with all the other injuries I had sustained, had taken their toll. I hurt all over and was glad to have at least a few seconds to rest. I slowly lifted my-self into a seated position and waited for her to come to me. Petra composed herself and walked slowly in my direction, my blood running down either side of her mouth. I saw her jaw moving but couldn't hear what she was saying. It took me a second to realize she wasn't speaking, she was chewing.

She swallowed and said, "I have to hand it to you, Obie, you are a tasty dish. I bet you will go right to my hips, but what the hell. We'll call it a cheat day."

I reached back to where she had bit me to find a gaping wound, it stung when my fingers touched the exposed flesh. There's no way I was going to win this one on one in my current condition. I needed to buy time for Cearbhall to recover. I tried to think of something to say but it was too hard to concentrate with the burning in my shoulder. I looked around, desperate for anything I could use against her. The truck would be no use. The glass vial that had held the antivenom had found its way onto the ground beside me, probably knocked off when I collided with the truck. I grabbed it without having in mind what good it could be. Something was better than nothing. I threw it at her and then got the other vial out of my pocket and threw that one too. The first one missed and she didn't bother dodging the second. It bounced harmlessly off her chest and shattered when it contacted the concrete. I shuffled backward around the side of the truck as she closed in on me. My hand landed in something that made it tingle on contact. I looked back to see the powder of the soul stone Cearbhall had smashed. The rain had turned it into a kind of soul paste. I stopped backing away and waited, taking as much of the goop in my hand as I could. The tingling changed into a burning sensation as I scooped it up. I wish I had taken a few minutes to finish reading the instructions that came with the stone. Regardless, this had to work.

She straddled my legs, grabbed my ripped shirt in one hand, and pulled me close to her. "You're going to have to do better than that," she whispered almost seductively.

"How's this?" I said, smearing the paste into her eyes and face.

She fell back off of me, screaming and clutching her eyes. Liquid goo ran down from underneath her hands as she clawed at her eyes. Using the truck for support, I got to my feet. As Petra suffered and thrashed, I took a minute to catch my breath. I felt my shoulder and the crater in it again. That would take a while to heal. I looked up to where the elves and T.O. should be. The commotion had died down, no more muzzle flashes, but the rain kept me from seeing how they were doing. With her hands over her eyes, Petra spread her wings and crouched as if she was about to take off. Hopefully there were still some elves alive to work the guns.

"You sure that's a good idea? You can't see it but the elves are back on the guns. What do you think the odds are you can outfly bullets?" I said.

She paused and stood erect again. She didn't make a sound, standing as still as one of her statues. I was starting to feel a little better. My back felt like it had stopped bleeding. I took a step forward. "I believe the agreement was to the death. What do you say we finish this?"

The snakes turned toward me. "You've taken my eyes but I'm not blind." The calmness of her voice bothered me more than any anger I had seen from her so far. "Yes, we will finish it and I won't underestimate you again." She spread her wings, not to fly but to make herself as large and imposing as possible.

Cearbhall lifted his head off the concrete behind Petra. He rose slowly and quietly off the ground and crouched. Before she knew what happened he was on top of her. He wrapped his arms under her wings, pinning her arms to her body. He winced as the snakes bit him repeatedly, he didn't try to defend. This was my chance.

"Jump!" I yelled, and rushed in.

He did, lifting them both off the ground. I charged into them, grabbing them around the waist, pushing with everything I had to drive us into the side of the bridge. Their higher center of gravity was enough to send us toppling over toward the water. Petra spread her wings, flapping as hard as she could. She was able to slow, but not stop, our descent. Cearbhall shifted his grip and grabbed a wing. The result sent us spiraling out of control as the other wing flapped helplessly. Pushing off, I turned head first into a dive and glided smoothly into the water. The cool water was refreshing on my fur and my shoulder. With only a second to enjoy myself, my moment was interrupted by Cearbhall and Petra's collision with the water. I picked up the vibrations in my whiskers telling me the direction and distance of their impact. In contrast to the gentle pattering of the rain on the surface, the initial shock felt like a violent wave, immediately followed by smaller but frequent tremors running through the water from their movement. Glad to be in my own element, I rose to the surface.

It was hard to see anything. The storm had made the lake choppy and the rain didn't help. I caught glimpses of a dark figure I thought to be Petra splashing on the surface about ten feet away. There was no sign of Cearbhall. Two spotlights came on from the trucks, flooding the area with blinding light. I squinted as my eyes adjusted and considered diving just to get away from it when Petra surprised me. I wouldn't have thought it possible, but she started to lift out of the water. She floated face down, her large wings sticking out of the water and catching just enough air to take flight. By the time I realized it, it was too late to catch her. She was going to get away.

The water's already tumultuous surface exploded in a large circle off to my left like the rain had intensified tenfold in a finite circle. I had never seen anything like this before. It wasn't until I noticed the humming a split second later that I realized the elves had let loose with the big guns. I looked to the top of the hill to see a line of fire coming out of the end of the gun, illuminating the truck as well as the elves and shifters watching. The bullets slamming into the water were redirected onto the fleeing demon. Some ricocheted into the water off her scales, while others tore her leathery wings to pieces and hammered her back into the water.

The fire ceased when she had disappeared back into the lake. Now it was my turn. Taking a breath, I disappeared under the water. I could feel the vibrations of her movement in my whiskers, indicating her direction before I spotted her. The spotlight penetrated the water revealed her, or what was left, I should say. The light surrounded her, casting a long shadow into the darkness below, looking almost like the darkness was reaching up to claim her. Her wings looked to be intact structurally, but the leathery skin that ran between them had been shredded.

I came up underneath, grabbed her foot, and pulled her under. At first she struggled to return to the surface but when that didn't work, she turned down to try and attack me. I let her go and swam out of reach before she could get me. She again tried to get to the surface but the extra drag created by her ripped wings combined with the inability to swim made it impossible for her make any progress before I pulled her even deeper. We repeated this dance a few more times until she was still. I stayed under with her a few minutes extra, just to be sure.

CHAPTER · 29

The spotlights were still on, scanning the water in lazy circles, when I pulled Petra's now lifeless body to the surface. It didn't take long for them to find me when I appeared, but the lights only stayed on me for a moment before being redirected into the sky. I looked up to see an athol with what looked like Petra's leather satchel dangling from one of its feet, circling toward the bridge. The elves on the bank closest to me opened fire. The creature lacked the protective scales Petra had, and after a violent jarring that seemed to suspend it midflight, it fell lifelessly into the water twenty feet to my right. I made a quick detour to retrieve it and pulled the two demons to shore.

Cearbhall was waiting on the bank when I finally made it to shore with Petra. He sat on a large rock under the bridge with his head between his knees.

"It's done," I said. "You going to make it?"

"Aye, feeling dizzy. The antivenom works but not all the way," he said. "I got bit a lot."

"Hang out here until you feel better," I said. "I better check on everyone."

I hauled Petra's body up the steep incline, opting to retrieve the athol later, stepping over large rocks and using trees to pull myself to the top. Coming over the crest of the hill, I found multiple demons lying dead, strewn around the truck. Two elves sat wounded but conscious against the truck while a third tended to them. Harlan stood by himself but was in one piece, as far as I could tell. Otis laid lay in the road with Hank and a werewolf named Chisel crouched over him.

Hank stood and turned to the elves with a fire in his eyes I knew from past experience to be wary of. "You killed him."

If Otis was dead Hank was next in line for leadership. Chisel followed Hank's lead and took a threatening posture but waited for Hank to start the attack. They both bared their teeth and emitted low rumbling growls as they started to stalk forward.

The elf tending to her comrades rose and spun, raising a pistol in their direction. I threw Petra's body on a collision course that made impact just as she was in position to fire, sending her sprawling defenseless onto the ground. The pack charged, but I was already on my way to intercept. I leapt in front of the snarling group before they could tear the elves to pieces. I wasn't sure they would stop, they could plow right over me and there wouldn't be anything I could do about it. Hank put the brakes on with only inches to spare. The T.O. jumped to the side but didn't attack—they wouldn't go against him. If Otis was in fact dead, Hank was in line to be the new club leader.

"Let me take a look, maybe I can help," I said.

"Can you raise the dead?" he asked, spittle flying out of his mouth onto my face.

I wiped his anger from my nose and whiskers. "No, just let me take a look." I moved around him, holding palms out. Otis lay on his back. His stomach had some large gashes, probably from the claws of the demon that lay a few feet away. That shouldn't be life-threatening but he didn't appear to be healing. I knelt beside him and found a bloody spot on the side of his head. Moving his hair back I found an entry wound. I turned his head and found the much larger exit wound, still something he should be able to heal through, unless . . . I held my hand out and concentrated. The energy didn't flow, there was nowhere for it to go. Otis was, in fact, dead.

"Who shot him?" I said, turning back to Hank.

He pointed a finger at the elf that had just made it out from under Petra. Again, she raised the pistol, this time as much in my direction as Hank's.

I walked past him directly into her firing line, moving up to where her gun was three inches from my face. "What happened?"

Her voice was stern but I could see the uncertainty in her eyes. "He had a demon on him. I tried to help, it was an accident."

"Elves don't miss," Hank yelled from behind me.

He was right about that. I reached up and put my hand on the pistol. She let me take it without a fight. I released the clip and looked at the cartridges. As I suspected, silver bullets. Otis didn't stand a chance after a head-shot with these.

I slid the clip back in and handed the gun back to her. "Let me see your AK."

She slid it off her shoulder and handed it to me. Again I released the magazine, no silver here, but there were rounds left. She wouldn't have need-ed to draw the pistol as long as the rifle still had rounds. I looked up at her and she knew she was busted. I replaced the magazine and put the gun in the back of the truck.

"Load your wounded and get out of here," I said.

"Now just hold on a damn minute!" Hank screamed.

I turned, holding my hands out again to put myself between them. "She's empty, Hank. She must have pulled the pistol trying to help and a shot got away from her."

"They don't miss, those guns are their lives. No way it was a mistake," he said.

"Maybe she's just not that good of a shot." I turned to see if I had hit my mark.

She was helping the second wounded elf into the back of the truck and paused from my comment. Elves are too proud. I could see her contemplat-ing her next move. She could admit she killed Otis on purpose and start a war, or take the shame of one of the worst insults you can give to an elf. She clenched her jaw and loaded her comrades into the truck before quietly get-ting in herself and starting the engine.

Harlan had gotten in his truck and pulled up, followed closely by the elves and T.O. from the other side of the bridge. "What happened?"

I moved over to the truck so I could speak a little more privately. "Otis is dead. Y'all should get out of here. Tell the Queen I will be by to see her soon."

He pulled out without another word. I waved the other two trucks of elves off and they followed Harlan out. The first stopped just long enough to let the shifters jump out of the back. We had at least avoided a war tonight. Maybe Hank could cool off for a couple days and things could calm down. The Tortured Occult surrounded Otis's body, beginning to come to grips with their pack leader being dead. There was a lot of anger, but more uncertainty. It was going to be a hard few weeks for the T. O. to move forward from this. I found Hank standing off by himself by Petra's body, while the pack stood vigil over Otis.

"Have you given any thought to joining the T.O.?" he said. "With Otis dead we're going to need new leadership. They would follow you."

"You know I can't. My loyalty has to stay with Thera first. That's something I haven't been as good about as I should have, but I'm going to do better. You don't want to lead?"

"I always figured I would lead one day, somewhere off in the distant future," he said. "I'm not ready. I don't know what I'm doing."

"I think you're more ready than you realize. Otis already relied on you for a lot of the management of the T.O. You're a strong and competent leader. I know you are going to get through this just fine," I said.

"What about them?" He looked over at the club.

"They'll be fine, they have you," I said.

He looked uncertain. "Maybe you're right, but I don't feel ready."

"If everyone waited until they were ready to do things, then nothing would get done," I said. "I'll load the truck and take the demons to Hob. The pack should stay together tonight."

"That's a good idea. Thanks, Obie. One more thing, her eyes are gone. Looks like they melted out. What did you do to her?"

There were black charred holes where Petra's eyes used to be. "Old Keeper trick," I said. "Cearbhall is down by the water, he should be up soon. He got a lot of poison in his system. I need to get some things done. Can he stay at the clubhouse tonight?"

"No problem," he said.

I helped Cearbhall get back up to the bridge and in a car, and put the athol in the back of the truck with the rest of the demons. After fifteen minutes of searching, I found the remains of the leather satchel. It was little more than a strap and a few scraps of leather. The book had either been shredded by the guns or was somewhere in the lake. Otis was put into the back of a truck and we all pulled out together.

CHAPTER · 30

I split off from the T.O. and headed to Hob's to drop off the demons. It was the largest haul that I ever remembered delivering at one time, maybe the largest we had ever had. It might even have been large enough to keep Hambone from complaining, but I doubt it.

"Is it finished?" Thera asked, from what had been an empty passenger seat a moment before.

"Yes, the demon that was causing you problems is dead. I am taking her to the duster right now," I said.

"And the grimoire?"

I was hoping she would have forgotten about it, not that that was a real possibility. "Well, it's either destroyed or somewhere in Lake Lanier."

"Which is it, destroyed or in the lake?" she asked.

"Same thing. I got a look at it, it's an old book. Even an hour floating will severely damage it, if not completely destroy it. Just because I don't have it in hand doesn't mean it's going to cause any more trouble," I said. "Even if it is still out there somewhere, which it isn't, then whoever finds it won't know what to do with it. They will think it's worth something and try to sell it and get it translated and then I will find out about it. There's no scenario where that book shows up again without me finding out about it."

"I would rather you have found it," she said.

"Well, me, too," I replied.

I didn't get the impression that she was happy about the grimoire being unaccounted for, but she must have accepted it because she vanished from the truck and the rain seemed to lighten just a bit. By the time I got to Hob's farm it had stopped completely. I pulled in slowly, not so worried about alerting my presence since they had seen me in this truck the day before. The lights were still on in the house so I parked there instead of going around to the barn. Hob was sitting out on the porch, enjoying the night air. I got out of the truck and joined him in a vacant rocking chair.

"I have always enjoyed the rain," he said when I took a seat. "Does this mean the battle is over then?"

"Yes, it's finished," I said.

"I'm glad to see you have lived," he said.

We sat quietly for a few minutes, listening to the katydids. My mind wandered to the Queen and Otis's assassination.

"What are elves like in other places?" I asked.

Hob looked a little confused by the question. "Elves are people like all other people. What do you mean?"

"I'm pretty sure the Queen had Otis killed tonight," I said. "I'm just trying to wrap my head around why. As you know I've never lived anywhere else so the Queen's rule is all I've ever known. It seems normal to me. Are there places where elves aren't so . . . you know, authoritarian and murdery?"

"In my homeland we had a Queen *and* a King. They worked together for the good of their people. Magic wasn't shunned like it is here. It was seen as a valuable tool to be used for the good. When I came here I was surprised to see how the Queen behaved. I knew right away I wouldn't be living with my kind anymore, and that was okay. I worry if she has done this then she might be making plans for a larger attack. If I am lucky, she has forgotten about me."

I shook my head. "She doesn't forget anything. I'm going to pay her a visit and see what I can find out. I should probably get going before she moves her camp again. Is Wilix in the barn for me to unload?" I asked, getting up from the rocking chair.

"Ja, he is there. What about Naylet? Have you made up your mind about the blood?"

"I wanted to talk to you about that. Have you actually seen someone that was restored that way?"

"I knew of a human child in the Fatherland many years ago, I think in his sixth year. His family had a small farm close to where I lived. He was a good boy. One day, he was made to stone from a gorgon. There were rumors going around that I was a witch and his father came to me to ask for help. To make the long story shorter, I help him. I got the blood and the boy was restored. His father was so happy but the boy wasn't the same. Where he had been so full of life before he had become quiet, like he was empty. There was no more playing for him and he would just stare off blankly into nothing. A few months after, I went to check in on him. I was curious, you see because I had heard stories, but it was the first time to see it in person. The boy had killed his family with the sickle. When I found him he had cut his sister open and was eating the insides." He leaned back in his rocking chair and put his feet up on the railing. "I left my homeland for America a few weeks after."

There was no way I would bring her back to have her change like that. She wouldn't have wanted it, and neither did I. "No, I won't be needing the blood," I said. "If I had some way to bring back her memories then maybe, but I've come up empty on that."

"It is for the best," he said. "Come. It is not good to dwell on the past. Let us get your truck cleaned out."

We had the truck empty in twenty minutes flat and I was on my way. It was a long drive to the Queen's camp, made longer by a couple of wrong turns on the unfamiliar backroads. By the time I arrived, the Queen's RV was just pulling out, with a guard truck on either side. I pulled up in front of the convoy, blocking the road, got out, and waited. They rolled to a stop in front of me, headlights illuminating my truck and hurting my eyes. They didn't try to drive around but no one came out to talk to me either. I leaned against the truck and waited for a good two minutes before the door to the RV opened and the elf that had shot Otis stepped out. She held the door open and stood to the side so I could enter.

"Took you long enough," I said, stepping past her into the RV.

Two of her guards sat up front, driver and shotgun, literally. The other elf followed me in, and went to stand by the back of the RV. I found the Queen at the table and sat down. We stared at each other for a few seconds, both waiting for the other to start.

"I wanted to give you the opportunity to explain yourself," I said, tired of the game.

"Obie, we have done some business and you have shown yourself to be a friend to the Nation," she said, leaning forward and pointing one of her revolvers at me. "Don't make the mistake of thinking that that grants you the right to question or detain me. We are not equals."

"Is that supposed to scare me? You think I haven't been shot more times than I can count already," I asked.

"You don't think I know how to kill a Keeper?" she replied.

I leaned forward into the gun. "Then do it, but if you do, my kind will take everything from you."

That wasn't an empty threat and she knew it. The response to murdering a Keeper is both immediate and absolute. She sat still for a few seconds before returning the six-shooter to its holster.

"Why are you here?" she asked.

"Did you have Otis killed? I want the truth," I said.

She relaxed back in her seat. "Do you know what the most admirable thing about a dog is? It doesn't know it's going to die. It lives in the moment because the moment is all it knows. It can't contemplate the future. Occasionally, it can be beneficial to remind a dog of its mortality."

"Why don't you cut the crap and just give it to me straight," I asked.

"Yes, I had him killed. Are you happy?" she said.

"Not even a little bit," I said. "Why would you do that? We were finally, after years of tension and hostilities, starting to work together. Is peace not important to you at all?" I asked.

"Peace." She laughed. "What kind of peace could we ever have with those beasts? They aren't capable of it."

"You don't think Otis was serious about the agreement?"

"I have no doubt he meant it when he said it, but he would break his word eventually. He couldn't help it, his nature would get the better of him."

"What nature is that exactly?" I asked.

"Shifters have violent tendencies, I don't need to tell you that. It's not their fault, they just can't control themselves. Combine their violent nature with the primitive male mind and throw in an entire pack that blindly follows, the threat was just too great. It had to be eliminated for the good of the Nation."

"I see," I said. I knew she felt some hostility toward males and shifters but I didn't realize the extent of her prejudice until then. I didn't think I was going to change her mind, at least not right then, and with everything that had happened, I wasn't up for trying. "One more thing and I'll go. I can't owe you a favor. It could conflict with my obligations to Thera and I can't be indebted to someone like that. It was wrong of me to make that agreement. I will be happy to pay for the soul stone, just let me know what you want."

"See, you're proving my point, not twenty-four hours into our agreement and you're already backing out. It's not your fault, males are dishonest by nature. Just return the stone and we will pretend it never happened. I would rather not have something that powerful unaccounted for anyway," she said.

"Well, that's a problem," I said. "It was destroyed."

"In that case I will hold you accountable to our original agreement."

"I can't do that," I said.

"Maybe you should spend some time thinking about it. You're smart for what you are, you could make the right decision. I will come to you to fulfill our agreement and if you refuse you will have to face the consequences. Either way, you are going to pay for that stone," she said.

"I'm trying to pay for it," I said.

"You've held us up too long already," she said. "You're dismissed."

There was no point trying to reason with her. We would have to settle it later. I slid out of the seat and went back to the truck without another word.

CHAPTER · 31

I pulled into DeSoto Falls a little after three in the morning. Besides the fact that the park was supposed to be closed, it was an excellent time for discretion. I found an open spot to park the truck and made my way down the trail beside the campground. Most of the campers were asleep, a few adding gentle snores to the ambience of the forest. The few that were awake huddled beside dying fires. Most of the time people built fires for novelty, and not just the tourists. The easiest way to spot a tourist wasn't by the campfire on a sweltering night; it was that they wouldn't look at or speak to you. Afraid to make eye contact, no friendly greeting in passing. I just have to remind myself that they don't mean to be rude, they just aren't from around here. A moot point when they're all unconscious.

I followed the trail to where I cut into the woods toward Livy's camp. When I arrived, I found a few glowing embers of what was a campfire. That, combined with the gentle breathing I heard coming from the tent, lead me to believe Livy had gone to sleep hours ago. Thera had said Holt was awake but that didn't mean he's mobile yet. Deciding to let them rest, I got a couple of the tree shards and rekindled the fire.

Walasi's voice entered my mind. *<Is it finished?>*

"Yes, the demon is dead. Everything is back to normal, sort of," I said, looking at Naylet's figure in the moonlight.

A crack opened in the hillside as Walasi peeked out, the electric green of his eye illuminated the campsite. <*Will you be leaving soon?*>

"We will pack up in the morning and get Livy and Holt home. It's time to get on with things," I said.

<*No need to hurry. You could stay and rest.*>

He wasn't wrong. A few days in the woods might be a nice break. I would miss Otis's funeral if I stayed and I needed to be there. "I would like to but there are some things I have to take care of."

He settled, sending a shudder through the ground and little bits of dirt and rock cascading down the hill. I got the feeling he was disappointed.

"You okay?" I asked.

<*Always alone.*>

It hadn't occurred to me until now, but there was no telling how old Walasi was, and he had to be in hiding here for three or four hundred years at least for me to have not known about him. It would be a horribly lonely existence. Could there be a time when I wouldn't be able to blend in anymore and would be in a similar boat? I wouldn't want to be out in the woods on my own like that.

"I'm sorry. I'll try to get back up here soon," I said.

"I thought I heard someone out here," Holt said with his head sticking out of the tent.

"Good to see you're awake. How are you feeling?" I asked.

He came over to join me by the fire. He moved deliberately, obviously still recovering from the venom. "Like I was hit by a train. I'm sore but I'll be okay. Did you take care of the demon?"

"She is on a date with Hob as we speak," I said, poking the fire with a branch from the tree. "We need to talk. Since you showed up we haven't been much of a team. We need to fix that if we are going to work together. I don't want to keep doing things the way we have been."

"It hasn't seemed like you want to work together. You've just been on my case about everything," he said.

I nodded in agreement. "You're right. I wish I had a good excuse but the truth is I just don't know what I'm doing. You're my first apprentice and I have been treating you the way Cearbhall treated me. I learned some things recently that changed things for me. I'll just say, I don't want the same kind of relationship with you that Cearbhall and I have."

"I was excited when I found out we were going to be working together. One of Cedric's favorite stories was when the two of you shut down those hunters in Chattanooga. Then I got here and things weren't what I expected. If I'm being honest, I don't know what I'm doing anymore," he said. "With Cedric it was easy. Then he died and ever since I've been lost. I don't feel like I belong here, or anywhere for that matter."

"I've heard losing a mentor can be really tough. It can be disorienting to have such an important figure disappear overnight. Let's start over together. Everyone should have the right to reinvent themselves. We will take it a day at a time and it will get better," I said.

"It sounds good, but I don't know how to do it," he said.

"You haven't met most of the people here so there's still time to make those first impressions. The people you have met don't know you well so they will come to know the person you become instead of the person you were. In the spirit of our new partnership, I spoke to Adan and set up a split for our dusting profits. You should have enough for your TV and anything else you want in a few weeks."

He stretched his back, cringing at the stiffness. "Right now, all I want is to not feel like death."

"As soon as Livy is awake we can get packed up, and get you somewhere comfortable to recover," I said.

"Oh, she's not asleep. She was meditating or something, sitting there staring off into nothing for hours. It's kinda creeping me out," he said. "What is she doing?"

"She's a shaman, it's called journeying. She sends her consciousness to the spirit world looking for answers or help. I don't really understand it that well myself."

"Aren't they supposed to beat on drums and stuff?" he asked.

"She quit using the drum a long time ago. I don't think she needs it anymore," I said. "I'll go wait on her to come back in the tent. We will get packed up and go as soon as she does."

I got up and moved to the tent where I found Livy sitting cross-legged on the ground, eyes open, staring off into the infinite. If she saw me come in, she didn't show it. I took a seat on the cot and waited.

After a few minutes of silence, she turned to me and said, "Obie, I am glad to see you safe."

I smiled. "You ready to go home?"

"I'm sorry, Obie. I have been searching for Naylet, asking the spirits for guidance but I couldn't find her. I tried my best." Tears started to well up in her eyes and she covered her mouth with a hand.

"Oh, hey, don't do that," I said moving down to give her a hug. "It's really okay. I'm coming to terms with . . . everything. You know what, let's get both of you back home before we start worrying about anything else," I said. "I'll get the camp packed up."

"What about Naylet?" Livy asked.

"I'm going to leave her here with Walasi for a bit. I'm not ready to deal with that yet," I said.

In an hour we had the truck loaded. Everyone piled in and we headed to Livy's. I unloaded the truck and got her settled before we left. Holt waited in the car. It wasn't long before we said our goodbyes and I was on my way, glad for things to start to resemble normal again. We couldn't go home. It would take some work before it would be livable again after what Petra had done to it. It was no place for Holt to recover. I had him up to speed on what the Queen had done by the time we got to the clubhouse. The junkyard was busier than normal. All the space not taken up by junked cars, waiting to be stripped and crushed, was being used for parking. A few of the T.O. were outside greeting people as they came in. I pulled up to Fisheye and rolled down the window.

"What's going on?" I asked.

"Service for Otis. There's still a little parking left on the south side," he said, pointing to the far side of the property.

I gave him a nod and drove slowly, maneuvering around the cars and people making their way into the clubhouse, to an open patch of dirt large enough to park the truck on.

"The Queen really had Otis killed," Holt said more to himself than me, still trying to wrap his head around it.

"Listen, before we go in there, I need to make sure we're on the same page. I lied about it to Hank and said it was an accident. I would appreciate it if you keep that between us. I don't want a war to break out over this. It would destabilize the region and cost a lot of lives. I'm going to tell him when things calm down and we will figure out how to handle it then."

"I get it, but what about the Queen? She just gets away with it?" he asked.

It's a fair question, there should be some consequences for her. "I'd like to think it will come back around."

"Maybe we should make sure it does," he said.

"Justice isn't really our mission," I said. "Come on, let's go inside."

"Kind of fast to hold services isn't it?" he asked, getting out of the truck.

"They don't embalm, so things have to move quickly before the body decays," I said. "It's an abomination to preserve a body and prevent it from rejoining the earth. We did the same thing with Cedric, remember?"

Hank was halfway to the truck by the time we got out. Deciding to wait on him so we could speak without a crowd around, I lowered the tailgate to sit on. I was hesitant, knowing that only a few hours ago it was filled with demon bodies, but Hob had sprayed it out before I left and there wasn't a trace of what had been there hours before. I hopped on the tailgate and waited. Holt eased his way from the passenger seat to join me at the back of the truck.

"Holt, good to see you up and about," Hank said.

"Thanks, I hope to be one hundred percent in a few days," he said.

"We're having a little get together to honor Otis. We're taking him to

Hob tonight so if you want to pay your respects sooner would be better than later."

"He's not getting buried?" I asked.

He shook his head. "He wanted to be dusted. I guess he really believed in what the two of you put together here."

That stung a little considering I was keeping a secret about his death.

"I'll go in and pay my respects, but after that, I have a couple things to take care of, not least of which is finding a place for us to stay."

"What do you mean?" Hank asked.

"Petra trashed the house. It's pretty much destroyed." I said. "It's going to take a while to get everything cleaned up and fixed."

"You'll stay at the clubhouse and the T.O. will help you fix it up," Hank said.

"I appreciate the offer but I can't. I will figure something out," I replied, probably out of guilt more than anything.

"You can and you will. You saved a lot people on both sides of the veil tonight. It's only fair that your life be put back as close to normal as we can get it. Luckily the Tortured Occult specializes in helping ultra-naturals down on their luck," he said.

"All right, I appreciate it."

"I haven't had a chance until now to say it, but I'm sorry about Naylet. Any chance of getting her back to normal?" Hank asked.

"I've been giving it a lot of thought," I said. "Do you still have that moving truck?"

"Yeah, it's parked around back," he said.

"I need to borrow it for a while," I said. "Let's go pay our respects first though."

I went back to the truck and picked up the pink bunny that had rolled under the seat and stuffed it into the pocket of my cargo shorts.

CHAPTER · 32

I watched Carolina wrens chasing each other through the trees. Diving and banking, the aerial maneuvers were enough to make a Blue Angel jealous. Their rusty brown wings fluttered as they jumped from branch to branch, only stopping their games to sing their songs. They blended in well with the trees beside the little path leading back to where I had everything set up. I had arranged this little rendezvous on some private land where I knew we wouldn't be disturbed. With everything in place, I just had to wait. I was feeling anxious and was glad to have the distraction the birds offered.

Farwell pulled his black SUV up beside the moving truck and rolled down the window. "Could you have picked a spot that's harder to find? I got turned around twice already. You want to tell me what we're doing here?"

"I'm about to make you famous," I said, getting out of the truck.

"Make somebody else famous and leave me alone," he said, looking generally sour.

"I'm afraid you're my only option," I said. "I don't have a lot of contacts in the police department. If you want to introduce me to someone else, I'll be happy to bother them—if you want to explain all this to them that is."

"So what do you want?" he questioned.

"You know all those missing babies over the past year? I think we found them. If everything goes according to plan, they will be here for you to return to their families soon," I said. "I'm just waiting on a few more people to show up and we can see."

"Let me get this straight, you don't know if you found them, but you think you might have, and I'm here just in case it turns out that you did, in fact, find them?" he asked.

I gave him a smile. "Exactly."

"How can you not know if you found them or not? That doesn't make any sense," he said.

"Do you really want to know?"

"Not really," he said. "So, how am I supposed to explain finding a bunch of missing kids? Assuming you did find them, that is."

I pulled a piece of paper from my pocket and handed it to him. It was a note giving directions to where we were and explaining that the missing children could be found here. I had cut the letters out of magazines and pasted them to a sheet of paper; it looked like fun on TV, turns out it's a lot of work. "Now you have an anonymous tip."

"Goodie," he said, looking at the note.

The rumble of motorcycles down the road foretold the T.O.'s arrival. Hank pulled off the road a minute later, followed by eight motorcycles and a van. The bikes parked in a line facing the road with the van to the side. Hank was the first off his bike and came over to where I was standing beside Farwell's car.

He leaned with an arm against the roof. "Hey, Farwell, good to see you again."

Farwell looked Hank in the eye and rolled the window up without breaking his stare.

"He definitely doesn't like us," Hank said.

"I don't know what you're talking about. He was chatting my ear off before you showed up," I said. "Did you bring everything?"

"In the van, come on." Hank led me to the back of the van and opened it. Inside were stacks of blankets, some clothes, and bottles of water. "Want me to help you out?"

"Nah, I need to go alone. We will know if it works soon enough," I said. "Before I forget, are you still having problems with those knockers?"

Hank put his hands on his hips and shook his head. "Yeah, they burrowed passageways to just about every room in the clubhouse. I have to get them out of there soon."

"I have a friend that could use some company. I think they would be a perfect fit," I said. "I can swing by and pick them up tomorrow, if you don't have any objections."

"By all means," he said. "I'll have them ready to go."

I grabbed a stack of blankets and headed down the trail about thirty feet to a clearing where I had arranged Petra's statues in a semi-circle. After Petra disappeared the museum was glad to be rid of the statues. I think they freaked out more than the receptionist. Naylet was on the left, with the babies in the front, not unlike Petra had set it up at the museum. I put each baby in a blanket and draped one over every adult, except for Naylet, who still had her clothes from when she was turned. I pulled the pink bunny out of my pocket and put it in the blanket with Stephanie. Stepping back to survey the scene, I decided it looked as good as it was going to get.

"Thera," I said to the open air, "I need to talk to you."

I waited. The birds chirped, a gentle breeze rustled the leaves, but no Thera. Calling her was a little unorthodox for sure. Normally she just popped in when she wanted something and that was that.

I had decided she wasn't going to show, and opened my mouth to try again, when she spoke from behind me. "Why are you calling me, Obie?"

"I need your help," I said.

She looked a little confused at my statement. "You aren't injured."

"I need your help with something," I clarified. "I was talking to Walasi and he told me that you were life. I thought he was saying I should focus on my duties to you and he was right, but the more I thought about it, I realized that he was also speaking literally. You are the essence of life. These statues used to be living people. The demon that was attacking you attacked them as well. I called you here to ask you to put them back to normal, return them to life."

"I can do this," she said. "But why would I? We are surrounded by life already and it would take more to restore them than I would get from them."

Thera was too removed to feel any kind of attachment or responsibility for a single life, or a small group of them for that matter. She was more of a big picture kind of gal. I knew a heartfelt plea about humanity and how everyone was special wouldn't mean anything.

I said the only thing I could think of that might have a chance of working: "Because I'm asking you to."

"What right do you have to ask me for anything, especially considering how we came to know each other?" she said.

She was referring to how I had gotten Cearbhall's attention by summoning that demon when I was a boy.

"That was a long time ago. I've done a good job for you for well over three hundred years," I said.

She scoffed. "Do you know how long three hundred years is for me? Imagine three hundred breaths and then convince me that I owe you something."

"It's not about you owing me something. You don't owe me anything, I know that. They didn't deserve this," I said, waving a hand at the statues. "They are victims of that demon, the same as you. I'm asking you, not out of expectation or entitlement, but simply a desire to help them."

"It won't bring her back. Her mind is gone," she said.

"I know."

"And you would still want her restored, even if it means you could never be together again?"

I shrugged. "It's not about me,"

"I'll ask Cearbhall. If he agrees then I will restore them."

She vanished from in front of me. Cearbhall was resting at the clubhouse. His wounds weren't as serious as Holt's. I didn't expect Thera to get a second opinion. After smashing the soul stone on the bridge, could I really count on him to back me up on this? I waited, trying to figure out what the chances were that Cearbhall would support me. After a few minutes, Thera returned.

She looked past me to the statues. "I'll need your help. I told you I have trouble with precision on this level."

"What do you need me to do?" I asked, relieved.

"Put your hand on each one," she said. "I can use that to focus on them."

I went to Naylet and touched her face. It felt cold and gritty, no longer smooth and warm like I remembered. Thera raised her hands, making vines and brush grow rapidly to cover Naylet's stone form. We repeated the process for each person. The vegetation engulfed the statues, forming cocoon like shapes that closed in tight around them. A light, pure and white, shone through the cracks as Thera's magic went to work. When we finished with the last statue, I could start to hear muffled cries coming from inside some of the cocoons. I turned to see Naylet pulling her way free, looking confused and scared. I wanted to run over and help her, but when she saw me she ducked back behind the brush in fear. I knew I wouldn't be the one to help her.

"Thank you," I said to Thera, who had already vanished, before going back up the trail to where Farwell and the T.O. were waiting.

Hank met me on the trail when he saw me coming. "Well?"

"It worked. They are ready for you," I said.

He waved to the rest of Tom C. that was standing around and they went down the trail to help everyone. Hank arranged for all of the adults to get the help they would need to have some kind of normal life again. The babies were returned to their families, since the lack of a memory wasn't an issue for them.

"Thanks, Hank. I'll be by tomorrow to get the knockers out of your hair," I said.

"You're not going to stay? You don't want to talk to her?" he asked.

I shook my head. "I've thought about it a lot and the thing is, she doesn't know me. That's not the Naylet I knew. She's going to need some time to figure out who she is. I'm not going to drop a bomb on her like that. It wouldn't be fair for me to be hanging around with these expectations."

"Anything she needs, have Adan put it on my account."

"I will," he said. "We're going to take real good care of her."

I gave Farwell a thumbs up. He was still in the car with the windows up with no sign of coming out. I got back in the truck and drove away. Maybe one day Naylet and I would end up back together. She would need time to figure herself out. It would happen if it was meant to, but in the meantime, I had work to do. I was going to be busy training Holt, dealing with the mess the Queen started, and that imp was still out there somewhere. He would show up again, and when he did, I would be ready.

Scan this QR Code for a message from the author.

Acknowledgements

First, I would like to thank all of my family, especially Ashley and Lily. They kept me going when I thought I would quit, and put up with the times when I was preoccupied with an idea, problem, or just trying to finish that chapter. Their encouragement and support made this possible.

Jaye Manus and Sam Hoy, my editors, whose attention to detail gave me confidence I needed in the finished book. I also need to thank a group of close friends who served as beta readers, were there to flesh out ideas with, and offer a helping hand. Thank you, Tucker, Andrea, Claire, and Sean. Also, my artist, Lauren, one of the most talented people I know.

Special thanks to Maria (Mab) Morris. I'm lucky to have made such a good contact and friend in the writing community.

Last, I would like to thank you, the reader. This book has been a labor of love and I hope you found as much enjoyment reading it as I did writing it.

Message from the Author

Becoming an author has been a dream of mine for as long as I can remember. I tried to write my first novel in middle school. It didn't work. I made some assumptions about my writing ability and put the dream away. In 2013 I attended Dragoncon for the first time and checked out some of the writing panels. I had the opportunity to hear authors talk about all aspects of the craft. It was an epiphany moment for me. I realized that I could do it! I spent the next three years learning everything I could before I started writing *Petrified*. It took me another two years to complete it. There's been a lot of ups and downs on the path to becoming an author but I wouldn't change a second of it.

I wanted to take a moment to thank you for checking out my work. Every time someone reads it I am one step closer to achieving my dream. If you enjoyed it please consider signing up for my newsletter on my website at **www.authorbenmeeks.com** and follow me on Instagram and Facebook, user **authorbenmeeks**. It's the best way to stay up to date on new releases. If you would like to help me on this path please consider leaving a review on Amazon and Goodreads, and referring *Petrified* to a friend.

Made in the USA
Columbia, SC
27 November 2021

49861162R00140